a geography of secrets

a geography of secrets

FREDERICK REUSS

Grateful acknowledgment to:

Kapuściński, Ryszard, *The Emperor: Downfall of an Autocrat*; translated from the Polish by William R. Brand and Katarzyna Mroczkowska-Brand. New York: Vintage Books, 1984.

Okara, Gabriel, *The Voice*. Introduction by Arthur Ravenscroft. New York: Africana Pub. Corp., 1970.

Robinson, Tim, *Setting Foot on the Shores of Connemara & Other Writings*. Dublin: Lilliput Press, 1996.

Unbridled Books

Library of Congress Cataloging-in-Publication Data

Reuss, Frederick, 1960–
A geography of secrets / Frederick Reuss.
p. cm.
ISBN 978-1-60953-000-6
1. United States. Defense Intelligence Agency—Officials and employees—Fiction.
2. Cartographers—Fiction. 3. War victims—Fiction. 4. Secrets—Fiction. 5. Psychological fiction. I. Title.
PS3568.E7818G46 2010
813'.54—dc22
2010023434

ISBN 978-1-60953-000-6

1 3 5 7 9 10 8 6 4 2

Book Design by SH • CV

First Printing

FOR SOPHIE AND AVA

part one

A map is a sustained
attempt upon an
unattainable goal, the
complete comprehension
by an individual of a
tract of space that will be
individualized into a place
by that attempt.

—TIM ROBINSON, "INTERIM
REPORTS FROM FOLDING
LANDSCAPES"

Breitenrainplatz

46°57'30.25"N

7°27'14.74"E

Driving into work one day, I found myself in a different city. Geographically, it coincided with Washington, D.C., yet it was a completely new place. It happened as I was crossing the Fourteenth Street bridge. The sky, which was overcast, suddenly became brighter. Everything stood out crisply and distinctly, the way things look after a heavy thunderstorm, but the monuments and landmarks all seemed diminished, mere objects laid down on the landscape. Traffic on the bridge flowed like the surface of the river, emptying onto the flat estuary of the Mall and downtown. I got off at the next exit, parked on Ohio Drive, and sat in the car staring out at the unfamiliar landscape. I didn't know what to make of it.

After a while, I got out and walked to the water's edge. A cement walkway, littered with debris washed up from the river, runs the entire perimeter of East Potomac Park. An elderly black man wearing a desert camouflage cap was fishing over the railing. A veteran, I figured. It was hard not to think he'd always been there. Just beyond him a group of teenagers was listening to hip-hop on a boom box. Farther down, a man in a suit stood smoking a cigarette. A Park Police cruiser pulled up, idled briefly at the curb, then slowly drove on.

I sat down on a bench and watched the old man work his reel. A large schooner was moored in the middle of Boundary Channel. Behind it were the Maine Avenue waterfront, the Southeast/Southwest Freeway, and the drab brown federal buildings of L'Enfant Plaza. I felt as if I knew exactly what was happening behind every louvered window and ciphered door in every one of those buildings as well as downriver in the generals' houses at Fort McNair, at the War College, the Anacostia Naval Air Station, Bolling Air Force Base—even in the heart of the old veteran, who didn't seem bored or frustrated by his poor catch, just tired and lonely. I knew all this, and yet where I was had become unfamiliar.

It felt good. Not euphoria—that's not in my nature. Just it's-all-there-and-I'm-all-here-and-it's-all-okay good. For the first time, I was looking at the place as it really existed on the landscape, not as a complex of fixed coordinates and bundled meanings. I felt unburdened. A trio of blue air force Hueys came choppering up the channel and passed overhead, rotor wake trembling on the surface of the water. The man glanced up indifferently and began to reel in his line. I wondered if choppers roaring overhead could be felt by the fish, if they scared them away or caused them to bite.

It's easy to feel like a stranger in Washington, D.C. Even with a house inside the Beltway, a family and a career, it's hard not to feel that you're merely holding down a place until someone else steps in to take over. The White House is the symbol of this permanent flux at the top, but it's no less so in the middle and at the bottom rungs of government—from General's Row to highway planning, education programming, nutrition guidelines, or the three–bedroom, two-bath brick colonial up the street that came on the market yesterday. When I was growing up, change came in the form of Allied Van Lines and huge wooden crates stenciled with an APO address. The mystery of where we were going was never made clear until the last minute, when my father's travel orders were finalized. Until then, there was only guessing. Delhi? Athens? Perhaps. Cairo? Not sure. Ouagadougou? Then came the thrill of arriving in a new place and being a stranger all over again. American? Yes. From Washington. It was added only by way of explanation, not as one would invoke a hometown. People understood right away. As a Foreign Service brat, I grew up with vagueness and a fluidity of identity that made fitting in anywhere easy. I became a real pro. As an adult, separating where I am and where I'm from, what I do from who I am comes naturally, even if the distance between them is never greater than my own self-delusion. I suppose I have my father's example to thank for that. It's a gift I plan not to pass on.

Actually, I wasn't going to work that day. I wasn't going anywhere, in fact, but was just driving around aimlessly, looking for distraction. My father had died a few weeks earlier. Long retired, he'd been living in Switzerland with his second wife. We were close but not really intimate. I hadn't seen him for several years and declined to view the body when I arrived in Bern for the funeral. I didn't want the sight of his corpse to become the coda of his memory. Waxy skin, blue lips. I've never understood why people insist on viewing the dead. I wasn't even tempted.

The women had no such qualms. They all went to the morgue for a last look. They left the apartment together, and I couldn't help seeing some element of sexual revenge in it, a settling of accounts on some high archetypal plane. It was cozy inside the apartment. Outside, it had started to snow. I watched from the window as they waited at the tram stop, bundled against the cold. They returned an hour later, shook their overcoats and stamped their feet in that levity of mood that comes with new-fallen snow. A pot was put on for coffee. A bottle of kirsch appeared on the kitchen table. The doorbell rang, and people began arriving with things to eat.

The apartment soon filled with friends and neighbors. It was impossible not to feel warmly enveloped. There was little talk of him. I don't think there was much talk at all beyond who was arriving when from where. Jan, a saxophone player, was ferrying people from the airport and the train station. He had picked me up in Zürich early that morning. We'd never met before, but somehow the fact that he was driving my father's car made it seem we were old friends. On the autobahn I broke down and cried. Everything seemed so familiar, even the highway signs. It was those drives to and from the Zürich airport that concretized what having an expat father meant. Zipping along a Swiss highway in a thrilling easiness of place. To be always at home and always far from home. Did it matter who was coming and who was going?

Michel, the downstairs neighbor, shuffled over and greeted me with his customary "I don't know if you recall." I've always wondered if he does this only with me or if the stroke five years back made it necessary to verify things before talking. It was good to see him, always charming and alert, teetering on the verge of fashion and ill health. It was good to see everyone, even the people I didn't know who came up to me and said, "Your father has told me a lot about you." To be told this by so many strangers! There wasn't anyone back in Washington he'd have talked to about me. But here, in Switzerland, he seemed to have freely indulged in fatherly pride. It was nice to know that.

I talked to Michel for a long time. Of course, I no longer recall what was said. I'll have to admit so next time I see him. I talked to lots of people. The apartment was packed. Somehow, not surprisingly, it had turned into a party. Shortly before midnight, I went out onto the balcony for some fresh air. The sky was clearing, the air was cold and dry. The sign flickered on the building across the street, a big orange letter *M*, which stood for Migros, the grocery store chain. The snow had stopped. The streets were empty. The tram came and went.

Fifteen years earlier, I'd sat out there with my father and asked what he planned to do in his Swiss retirement. "Smoke and stare at mountains," he said. The next day he came home with a dog, a snuffling, wriggling black puppy. He stood at the front door in a rumpled green track suit, scratching the stubble on his cheek and beaming as his little prize squatted and pissed all over the floor. "No. Not a dog!" Nicole groaned. "Please. Not a dog."

"She's not a dog." He scooped the overexcited animal up and cradled it in his arms. "She's a retriever."

I'd never seen that side of him. Was it a put-on? Or was I seeing something only a child can see in a parent who has suddenly and with embarrassing effort opted for light and joy and youth over plodding age and habit? Nicole played up her part as well. "You're going to clean up every mess. You're not going let it chew up the furniture. You're not feeding it from the table. Don't think I'm taking it out to do its business." She went on far longer than was necessary, and, naturally, every one of her stipulations was turned on its head within days.

All fathers have a Byronic streak in the eyes of their children. Some more, some less. Even the most conventional and domesticated preserve a core of mystery and dash that is both the source of their authority and the reason for its ultimate overthrow. My father's Byronic streak had less to do with his faithful hound and imaginary rambles through the mountains than with the smoking, drinking, two-courses-and-a-desert Byron—spiced with cayenne and easily unphilosophized. I was astounded at how much he enjoyed being led around town by that wriggling black smudge. How happy it made him.

When I returned inside, people were beginning to leave. In an hour, all had left but the seriously drunk, who were whittled down at last to a German academic who'd come from Bonn and an American named Blake, who introduced himself with bleary sincerity as "your father's oldest friend." He was dressed in a rumpled, once fashionable Italian suit and had brought with him two bottles of Gordon's gin and an enormous bouquet of flowers, which he had grandly presented to Nicole.

"Who is he?" I asked in the kitchen.

Nicole rolled her eyes. "I told him not to come, but he came anyway."

"But who is he?"

"An old colleague. He lives near Geneva. On the lake. Last time he was here I had to throw him out."

Nicole does not generally take a dislike to people. She tends in precisely the opposite direction, is the epicenter of an ever-widening circle of friends and is especially drawn to oddballs and eccentrics. Her gregarious nature was the driving force in the marriage, a force that over the years worked big changes. My father went from a per-

son who generally avoided socializing to being surrounded by ad-
mirers, people charmed by his gruff reserve, the sentimental tough
guy. He loved being *typisch Amerikanisch*—as long as typical meant
Humphrey Bogart.

Nicole lit a cigarette and began moving empty glasses from the
cluttered counter into the sink. She was covering her grief with a
get-to-work ethos and heavy smoking.

"Should I ask him to leave?"

"Don't bother," she said.

"You sure?"

"He'll be drunk soon. We'll call a taxi."

But he was already drunk and talking fluently in German to the
professor.

"Sie waren nie in Bayreuth? Das kann doch nicht wahr sein!" Blake
waved his glass at me as I entered the room. "He's never been to
Bayreuth!"

One wishes for clarity in such moments but must usually settle
for what might have been. Blake was baiting the professor, playing
the boorish American. It was a sophomoric bully sport passed down
through Foreign Service generations and always played for the ben-
efit of others in the know. The object was to build up and then suddenly demolish preconceived notions and prejudices, reducing the
victim to wondering how little he or she might really know and
understand; a bit of professional jujitsu adapted for the cocktail party.
My father had been a master. It was always embarrassing when he
got going. Had I been thinking clearly, I would have immediately left
the room and let the drunkards have at each other. Instead, I fell into
the role I'd always played and took sides with the professor. "I'm not
too fond of Wagner, either," I said.

"The man you can hate. But certainly not the music." Blake grinned, sipping his gin.

"Ach, Quatsch!" the professor spat back, rising unsteadily from his chair.

"But you agree with me," Blake pressed on. "The model of the German bourgeois interior that mixes history with myth." His smile had that turned-up quality that presages the opening of another front, but the professor stumbled against the corner of the table and nearly knocked over a lamp.

Nicole came into the room. "I've called a taxi," she announced.

"I'll walk." The professor tugged on his cuffs. "My hotel is just around the corner."

Blake called across the room, "You sure? I'm happy to share a taxi."

"I would prefer to walk," the professor said. "The fresh air will be good."

Blake raised his glass as Nicole escorted the professor from the room. He was sitting with one leg crossed over the other, shin exposed, clutching his scepter of gin, leering as if remembering me in diapers. I was waiting for him to start in with some sort of your-father-once-told-me comment—but he didn't. He seemed perfectly comfortable keeping silent.

"So. You're an old friend of my father?"

"That I am, yes."

"Retired?"

"Right again."

Nicole and the professor were talking in low tones by the front door. Blake was clearly aware that he was the subject of their conversation and, as some people do who know themselves to be unwelcome, settled back into his chair in an attitude of graceful quiet. I was sitting at the long dining table across the room, fidgeting. The front door closed as Nicole bade the professor good-bye. Rather than join us, she went back into the kitchen.

"So, where are you living these days?" Blake asked.

I ignored the question. "My father didn't have many friends."

Blake swished his gin.

"You say you're an *old* friend?" I pressed on.

"I think he would have put me in that category."

"I don't remember him ever mentioning you."

He frowned into his glass. "What can I say? He was the soul of discretion, your father was."

"You aren't surprised?"

"Surprised? By what?"

"That I have no idea who you are."

Blake took it in very calmly, then tossed back the remainder of his drink and glanced in silent debate with himself at the bottle on the side table. The vulnerability in his look softened me somewhat. I hadn't meant to attack the man, but I had no patience for the mysterious-stranger game he was playing. I didn't give a damn. The parlor aspect of the last decade of my father's life had worn thin. Since his retirement, the string of people who had trailed through this apartment could have stretched around the block. I don't remember when I began to find their eccentric friends and busy social life depressing, but I'd seen enough of the comings and goings during my visits to know better than to attach significance to anyone claiming deep friendship. Observing Blake as he reached for the bottle, I was struck by a weird irony. It was true that my father had never had any close friends. He was the type who would sit back and watch things unfold with a kind of wistful absorption that suggested an interest in, but not much time for, intimacy. The superficiality of the acquaintanceships that gathered around him made the appearance of someone claiming intimate friendship both impossible and curious. There was an error in the poor man's perception that was to be pitied, not exposed. I felt sorry for him. "Can I get you some ice?" I asked.

"Sure, if you've got it." As I left the room, he called after me, "An olive would be lovely, too. If you've got it."

It was a familiar errand and took the charge out of the atmosphere. As a Foreign Service brat, I'd grown up around the protocols of cocktails and drinking. Nicole was putting things away in the kitchen. "What did he tell you?" she asked.

"What is there to tell?" I took out the ice and the olives, expecting her to put some sort of time limit on the continued hospitality. But she didn't. She followed me back into the living room, where Blake was now sitting with his chin on his chest. His head jerked up as we entered. I handed him a fresh glass with ice and olives. He peered into it with drunken ceremony and said, "I'm not big in the friend department, either. Your father was the best one I ever had."

Nicole sat down, lit another cigarette, and swept away a loose strand of hair with the back of her hand. Her dislike was now as unpleasant as his presence. I felt a pang of shame for the seedy atmosphere that had overtaken the room. It wasn't just Blake. It was also Nicole, distraughtly puffing away at her cigarettes, the disorder of the apartment, the dreary winter weather, the shabbiness of lives foreshortened by cocktails and *weltschmerz*. I found myself wishing for a different setting, a different cast of characters, people who didn't pretend to know everything and who hadn't come into my father's life—and mine—so lately. Best of all would have been to go back to less sophisticated times, when everyone felt a little less secure of their place in the world. I was sorry and sad to see how it all had come to this.

"Nicole asked you not to come," I said.

Blake let the statement hang for a moment, then put his glass on the side table and sighed. "Yes. That's right, she did."

I looked at Nicole, who took a final puff from her cigarette, crushed it into the ashtray, and said, "No harm done."

Blake accepted this with a gracious little bow.

"I'll go see about the taxi," she said and got up to leave.

"I can't help it if she doesn't like me," Blake said when she was out of the room. "But I wasn't *not* going to come, my boy. I was never *not* going to come."

The patronizing tone demolished whatever sincerity he may have intended—and my sympathy as well. "You seem fairly accustomed to being unwelcome," I said.

Blake threw back his head and roared with laughter. It was spontaneous at first, but then he went on for too long and played it up, flourishing a handkerchief, wiping his watery eyes. "Your father told me you had a funny streak." He wiped his eyes again and shook his head. "Truer words were never spoken. You have no idea." He leaned to one side and stuffed the kerchief into his trouser pocket. I noticed he was far less steady than he let on, noticed also that what substance he had was made up entirely of puff and bloat, the sort of man who hides his infirmities in tailored suits and expensive cars, who is somehow finished in his being without ever having gotten started.

Nicole returned. "The taxi is here."

Blake rose slowly from the chair, regarded me with squint-eyed appraisal. "Lead the way."

I escorted him to the door, turned on the stairway light. He gripped the banister, took the steps carefully, one at a time. It occurred to me that I would never see him again, and I called down, "Mind if I ask you one last question?"

He descended the final few steps.

"Where did you meet my father?"

He put a hand in his trouser pocket, stood there jingling his change for a moment as if waiting for something to sink in. "It was in Laos. Yes. That's right. We met in Laos." Then, with a little wave, he left.

I could hear the idling taxi, the opening and closing of doors. The timer of the stairway light shut off with a loud snap as the taxi drove away. I lingered in the semidarkness for a moment. A faint light from the apartment shone through the stained-glass window set into the door. There was something oddly comfortable in being guest and host in this place where I was both foreign and at home. Nicole called from the kitchen, "I'll fix you a tea."

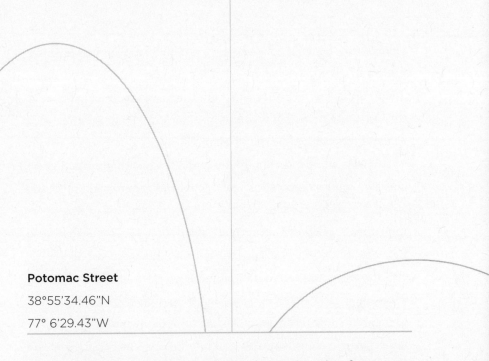

Potomac Street

38°55'34.46"N

77° 6'29.43"W

I am at my desk, which is set in front of a window that faces west-
southwest. It is an unusually cold morning. The wind is blowing in
gusts. Snow is predicted—a storm. It's the big story on television.
The meteorologists are calling for up to six inches. Reporters are
interviewing commuters and store clerks and school officials all over
the metro area. Federal employees are on liberal leave. My window
looks out onto a small patch of lawn shaded by mature oak, ash, and
elm trees. A leafy suburban neighborhood, well inside the Beltway, of
brick colonials and split-level ranches, many in various stages of re-
modeling and renovation. Along the property line, holly, evergreen,
and azalea bushes make for privacy and a sense of enclosure. There is
a pink dogwood in front of the house. Recently, deer have been
turning up in the yard. A new subdivision going up on some unde-
veloped land nearby has displaced the herd. They are disoriented and
wandering now through the neighborhoods. The last one was a buck
with a large rack of antlers. I watched him grazing in the yard for a

while, then opened the back door to see how tame he was. He lifted his head, looked over his shoulder. We had eye-to-eye contact for a good minute before he lumbered off. Later, I saw him lying down by the brick terrace wall in the neighbor's yard. We regarded each other again, and this time it was I who moved on.

I always sit at the window to work. My drafting table is there, cluttered with old notebooks, pens, inks, and pencils of all types and colors. Everything in its usual place. I am a mapmaker, a "geographic information scientist," in current jargon, and yes, I still draw and write by hand with pencils, pens, and ink. Although I use all the latest GIS systems and technology, I prefer to work whenever I can by hand and on foot and enjoy a reputation as a purist and a throwback to the days when those were the chief tools of the profession. For me, the point of mapmaking is to establish linkages and relationships on a terrestrial and a human scale, to see where one *is* in the fullest sense possible. Sure, it's a mistake to confuse a map with the terrain itself, or *where* one is with *who* one is. But they do cohere. And must.

When I returned from my father's funeral, it was difficult to return to work. By odd coincidence, I'd sat next to a professional grief counselor on the return flight. She had just finished a tour in Bosnia, having been sent there by the Red Cross to work with people still traumatized by the war in the 1990s. As we were settling into our seats, I broke into a bout of uncontrollable coughing. She offered me a lozenge, asked where I'd been, curious about the cough I'd picked up. I was too miserable for in-flight pleasantries. "A funeral," I said flatly. "I'm sorry," she said and shifted in her seat to allow me more of the cramped space we were forced to share. "My father's," I added, obliged by her kindness not to withdraw too rudely into silence. "I'm very sorry," she said. There was a moment of awkwardness. I leaned my head against the window, and she returned to her book. My coughing persisted. I tried my best to muffle it, but without much success. Later in the flight, she turned to me and said, "Grief often settles in the lungs." Then she told me about her work in Bosina. I remember little about what she said except that she was convinced that my cough was directly connected to the death of my father. She rejected my observation that the loss paled by comparison with the tragedy of Bosnia. I'll never know who she was, but I have her to thank for the insight into how strangely grief settles and unsettles us. I was still thinking about her and what she'd said to me as I walked above Canal Road a few days after I returned home. It was twilight, the afterglow of a brilliant sunset. I had been walking on the C&O Canal and was returning to my car, parked on Potomac Street, which runs along a ridge of the palisades overlooking the river. It is one of my favorite spots, a quiet residential street with an eclectic variety of houses on one side and clear views across the river to Virginia. In autumn, the colors are spectacular. At one end, a path leads down a wooded embankment onto an old railroad bridge that crosses the canal at Arizona Avenue, part of the old Georgetown Branch Rail Line that once connected Georgetown and Chevy Chase. In the early 1970s, the bridge was a rusting, graffiti-covered structure with a clear drop through the tracks to the road. Teenagers went there to smoke pot and run around in the woods. Now it is a restored and heavily bicycled part of the Crescent Trail, which links Georgetown with Bethesda and Silver Spring.

I'd just come up the trail from the bridge, was standing on the embankment for a last look at the pulsing sunset, when I heard the distinctive whoosh-click of a golf ball being hit. It wasn't a light chip shot but the solid crack of an earnest drive. In the vanishing daylight,

I could make out a figure. He bent down, placed a ball on the tee, straightened, and after a brief pause—crack—launched another ball. I glanced at the long stream of cars just below on Canal Road. Another ball was hit, a little less solidly this time, followed by a hoarsely muttered "Fuck!"

The man ignored me, went through the whole pantomime, wriggling hips and flexing shoulders. Just as I was about to interrupt, he drew back and—whoosh-click—the ball disappeared into the darkness.

"Don't you think that's a little dangerous?"

He set another ball on the tee without so much as a glance in my direction.

"Hey!" I called.

He relaxed his grip and turned to me with an expression of forced calm. He was well over six feet tall, with bunched athletic shoulders and a neatly trimmed goatee. His hair was cropped short, and he wore a red Washington Nationals baseball cap. My heart was thumping. "There's a busy road down there. You could cause an accident."

"You know what this is?" He held the club up, pointed to its absurdly outsized metal head. "Big Bertha. Titanium cup face, carbon composite body. Named after a forty-three-ton mobile howitzer. I can drive a ball three hundred yards with this sucker. Wanna try?"

I shook my head.

"Go ahead," he urged, as if my anger was priggish and unjustified. "The gun was named for Adolph Krupp's wife. It was fired for the first time on August 12, 1914, outside Liege. Took sixty seconds for the shell to travel the distance. Over nine miles. Then, boom! Fuckin'

World War I." It was dark now except for the glow of traffic below and a single streetlight farther up the road.

"The canal down there is a national park. I'm sure there's a law against littering it with golf balls."

"Who are you? The neighborhood watch?" He shook his head and yanked the tee out of the ground. Muttering, he stalked off.

I remained for a while, feeling as if I'd somehow earned rights to the spot. An airplane descended overhead, following the Potomac down to the airport. Across the river and through the trees, I could see traffic moving along the George Washington Parkway. Like many who call D.C. home, I am not from here but of here. I am not from anywhere, really, and yet I call this city home. It's a strange triangulation of geography, psychology, and fate and makes for great confusion, a confusion that calls for—no, demands—a map. Or many maps since, in cartography, a true one-to-one correspondence is impossible. The moment we begin to apply scale, we distort and alter our relationship to the world. Finally, I got into the car and drove home, listening on the radio as NPR reported on a missile strike against a Taliban guerrilla leader in Helmand Province.

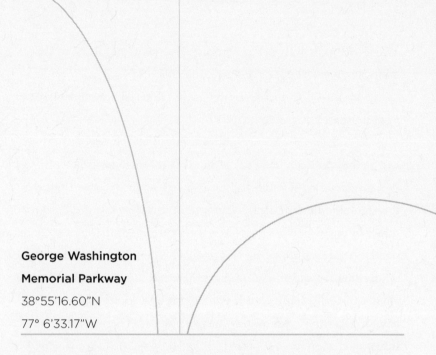

**George Washington
Memorial Parkway**
38°55'16.60"N
77° 6'33.17"W

Noel Leonard works at the Defense Intelligence Analysis Center, or DIAC, a complex of metal and glass blocks on Bolling Air Force Base surrounded by acres of mowed grass where the Anacostia flows into the Potomac. A new annex was built a few years ago, a sweeping brown glass facade with views downriver to Alexandria. Although it is joined to the old building, the new building stands apart physically and architecturally, as if it bears no relation. Noel's office is in the older, silver-skinned building. When the elevator doors slide open and he steps off every morning with that airy little puff of arrival, it is always as though he has temporarily exchanged identities with someone other than himself, a completely familiar alter ego who inhabits his body and will be buried in the same tomb with him, along with the details of the top-secret work he does for the Defense Intelligence Agency, which employs him to analyze data beamed down from satellites to create vivid and detailed maps and portraits of events on Earth.

His office is deep in the interior of the building behind cipher doors. It has no windows. At the end of the corridor is a large window with a panoramic view of the city. He pauses there from time to time to remind himself where he is. He can see the domes of the Capitol and the Library of Congress, the Washington Monument. On the hilltop in the distance is the National Cathedral. In the foreground are Haines Point and East Potomac Park, where he often plays golf; Fort McNair, the National War College, and the brand-new Nationals' baseball stadium. Immediately in front is the Anacostia Naval Air Station, where the president's helicopters are parked in an enormous hangar surrounded by double rows of high-security fencing. The president always travels in convoys of three, a pea hidden in one of the identically marked VH-3D Sikorsky Sea King shells.

It is snowing. A soft white blanket is coming down gently on the city and on the sprawling lawns of the air base. It has coated the three white radar orbs of the Naval Research Laboratory, the wings and fuselage of the F-105 Thunderchief that ornaments the traffic circle just inside the main entrance, *Foley's Folly*. Noel enjoys the incongruous quiet of the base. Falling snow makes everything feel ordinary, and life seem simple. Standing at the window, he is reminded of the famous photograph of Kennedy silhouetted against a window in the Oval Office, concentrated power invisibly served by bureaucrats and technicians staring intently at their computer screens—which is exactly what Noel is doing when Geoff Cowper, his first-level supervisor, comes into his office late in the afternoon. Cowper closes the door with conspiratorial gentleness. "It was a school," he says hoarsely.

"A school?"

"Investigation under way, but basically, we already know every-thing." He bounces against the door, holding the knob behind his back with both hands.

"A real school? With kids?"

A shrug.

"How many?"

Another shrug.

"Fuck!"

The light in the office is low. Noel prefers the incandescence of table lamps to high fluorescence overhead. In the corner is a light table for studying transparencies and a bank of high-res monitors. He leaves the light table on as a reminder that his existence is not all flickering fiery orange but may also be aqueous, blue and soothing. He is not without his refinements. Some time ago he taped a few lines from Wordsworth to the wall: *Listen! The mighty Being is awake/ And doth with his eternal motions make/A sound like thunder.* Noel enjoys poetry, especially Wordsworth, who offers consolations and reassurances—fits of joy, the charm of visionary things. And golf. Noel plays whenever he can. On summer evenings, he'll often stop at East Potomac Park and get in nine holes on his way home.

"We've got work to do," Cowper says, seating himself. He picks up a pencil, drums it on the table. Noel rarely sees him flustered. Cowper is one of the pioneers of drone air reconnaissance and came to the DIAC from the navy after the war in Yugoslavia. He is tanned and ruddy, a broad-chested Californian with a full head of silver hair, ten years older than Noel—though his good looks and easy humor often lead people to mistake him for the junior colleague. He has a thirty-two-foot Beneteau 323 sailboat that he keeps docked in Annapolis. He and his Texan wife, Ann, spend weekends sailing around the Chesapeake Bay. They are outdoorsy enjoyers of life and have no children.

"A little late, isn't it?" Noel mutters.

"You're goddamn right it's late." Cowper frowns, looks at his watch.

"I mean it's a little late for excuses."

"I'm not going argue with you." Cowper slides from the stool. "We gave the clear to engage. We need to have some answers ready before they've thought of the questions."

Answers before questions? Noel's impulse is to laugh. Typical Cowper: if not actually on top of things, then satisfied by his instinct to get himself there. The ever-prepared Boy Scout. Noel is not a Boy Scout. He prefers to wear his insignificance as camouflage rather than camouflage his insignificance. A message enters his in-box with an urgent ding. He knows all too well what it contains. It takes surprisingly little time for things to drift down to these lower depths. The bigger the catastrophe, the more leadenly it falls as the larger vertebrates swimming overhead voraciously consume responsibility while spitting out little pebbles of blame.

"We're not leaving here until it's done," Cowper says flatly.

They cue up the gun-tape footage and the audio feed and watch it over and over. Grayscale infrared picture fringed with instrument readouts. In the target hairs, a complex of square structures inside a walled compound, vehicles, and people—little infrared white grubs—moving between them. It's hard to look at, harder still to look away. A floating aerial camera view, circling steadily, keeping focus, command voices patched in, steady, circling, steady, then *flash*, white screen shock-wave shudder filtered zoom showing exploded bodies and slow-motion debris falling back to charred earth.

They craft the memo, couched in enough classified material to guard against its being released while leaving the requisite chutes and ladders open for the downward transference of blame. One of the reasons Cowper has survived for so long in the tense red-cell environment is the skill he brings to parsing and compartmentalizing the team's duties and after-action reports. His deftness in after-action jujitsu is an aspect of his athletic and competitive personality. He enjoys his victories and considers himself, in the office and out, to be a winner. Noel's pleasure is less gladiatorial. He thinks of it more like the action of bark-stripping porcupines, or of beavers on forests and wetlands: action from below with broad, far-reaching consequences.

After they send the carefully crafted memo into the chute, they linger in the office for a few minutes. The high-res feed runs in a soundless loop on the monitor. There are certain people, and Cowper is one, whose facial furniture gets completely rearranged when they begin to think. Frowns, creases, darkened looks are signs of deepest thought, which, like duty goods, must be declared upon arrival. He pulls his chair up to the edge of Noel's desk, slides his folded palms between his knees. Their eyes meet for a moment, then simultaneously avert. "Shit happens," Cowper says.

Noel understands his obligation is to be resigned to the mysterious engines that serve politics and fate. The other day, he overheard someone say, *The more that die, the sooner they're forgotten.* What a shock to hear Lenin paraphrased in the DIAC cafeteria. But it's the truth. One death is a tragedy, a million is a statistic. Nobody would openly admit it. In the world of full disclosure, certain things must not be seen, shown, or said. The same decorum that attends the arrival of flag-draped coffins at Dover Air Base attends those patriotic TV and newspaper-photo memorials to the fallen soldiers—desperate efforts to deny that the ego vanishes in history.

Snow has been falling all afternoon. He was hoping for a big storm, likes the idea of driving through it with snow swirling all around, sticking to the road, the grass and trees. He takes the South Capitol Street bridge, passes the new ballpark, and gets on the Southwest freeway. The Lincoln Navigator was made for just these conditions. It is late, and because of the snow emergency, the roads are nearly empty. He crosses the Fourteenth Street bridge, gets on the George Washington Memorial Parkway. After Arlington Cemetery, the parkway begins a steady ascent along the Potomac gorge. The river narrows here, and the banks on either side become suddenly darker. Noel is sure he is not alone in imagining, from time to time, plumes and towers of smoke rising from the city behind him, or, thinking forward, seeing cows and sheep grazing once again on the Mall. Why should the equalizing force of time that has made quaint archaeological sites of other great capitals spare Washington, D.C.?

He eases up on the gas and pulls into the scenic overlook at the top of Spout Run. He is intimate with the physiogeography of the area. The river gorge runs along the fall zone between the Piedmont Plateau and the Atlantic Coastal Plain. At Great Falls, the river drops seventy-six feet in less than a mile. How many Sundays has he spent climbing the rocks along Billy Goat Trail? Where he is now, on the very edge of the fall zone, the exposed terraces form steep bluffs that run along both sides of the river, which widens quickly just below Georgetown.

Noel steps into the chill air. Snow is coming down in great white sheets, is sticking to the trees. An airplane passes overhead, making its final descent into Reagan National. They come in low here, following the river. There has always seemed something magical to him about airplanes, the charm effect of kites and strings and flying arrows and other boyhood fantasies of projected power. Lately, he's begun to see a fuller connection between these fantasy forms of projection and what he calls "disembodied purpose." The gun-tape footage is lodged in his thoughts. He can't get rid of it. The sticking point is not the engineering of remote agency—which is just another fancy way of describing disembodiment—but the much larger question of purpose.

He opens the back hatch of the Navigator and takes a club from the golf bag he keeps there. Big Bertha. He fumbles in the pocket, grabs a handful of balls and a tee. A low stone wall runs the length of the parking lot, the WPA, National Park Service style of masonry that conjures visions of Buicks and Packards motoring along with all the time in the world. He steps over the wall and walks a few paces down the grass slope to where it drops steeply off. Through the swirling snow, he can just barely make out the black surface of the river below. With his foot he clears a small patch of grass in the snow, then, leaning on the club for balance, stoops and gently presses the ball and tee into the ground.

Another passing airplane distracts him, and he tops the first drive. The ball drops through the trees. He places a second ball on the tee, feeling a pleasant adrenaline flush, a foretaste of the perfect swing. He connects with a satisfying THWICK, sending the ball high and straight out over the gorge and filling his soul with deep, tranquilizing power.

He sets another ball onto the tee.

THWICK.

And another.

THWICK.

"Step back!"

A beam of light pierces the night.

"Step back!"

He turns into a milky blindness. A moment passes. The sound of a crackling radio sets his heart racing. Little white grubs skitter and pop in all the surplus light. Was milkiness the last thing they saw? He plucks ball and tee from the ground, then, with all the cheerful insouciance he can summon, strides toward the policeman, swinging Big Bertha like a walking stick. "Good evening, Officer."

"Drop the club!"

"It's all right, Officer. I was just—"

"Now!"

Noel drops the club.

"Put your hands up."

"I'm sure—"

"I am going to count to three." The caution is delivered with a precision that makes Noel smile as he raises his hands. The parking lot is lit like a stage. Snow falls gently through rose-white lights beaming atop the cruiser. The policeman steps over the wall, shining a baton of light directly into Noel's face.

"Officer, I can explain."

"Turn around."

Noel obeys.

"I'm going to frisk you. Keep your arms raised." The officer pats him down, removes the remaining golf balls from his pocket as well as his car keys. He runs his hands down each trouser leg, then steps back and says, "Okay, you can put your hands down."

A brief interrogation ensues. The cop is clearly a rookie. Noel can't help feeling both amused and irritated. He recognizes the text-book earnestness, the training sequences, the mock urgency—all misplaced and misapplied in this *real-world* situation. The Depart-ment of Defense ID sets the officer at ease. He allows Noel to fetch his golf club. As he picks it out of the snow and wipes it off, he wishes there were some way of telling the young cop about infrared white grubs, AGM-114 Hellfire missiles, and the dead schoolchil-dren on the other side of the world. Perhaps it would help both of them to see a little more clearly. Instead, he assumes the role of obe-dient citizen, thankful for being let off with a warning.

On the parkway, the Navigator's wiper blades beat time across the windscreen. The road is slushy, overly salted and sanded. It is cozy inside the enormous vehicle, protected against the elements. Noel's exact geographic location is mapped and displayed on the dash in degrees, minutes, and seconds. He loves the four-wheel-drive secu-rity, the three- hundred-sixty-degree visibility, and the pleasing sense of riding higher, heavier, and beyond all need. He'd joked about it— about heaviness, need, and middle age—in the doctor's office that morning. A bout of light-headedness yesterday and what felt like stabbing pains in his chest had gotten him an emergency appoint-ment. "Could be gas," the doctor told him after the EKG. "Gas? That high up?" The doctor assured him it was possible. "Could also be stress." He ordered the full battery of tests, the outcome of which Noel foresaw exactly. Diet, exercise. He wasn't a hypochondriac. The pains had been real. But like all the men in his family, he's always been stoic about aches and pains. You tough out the things you can't control. Pat, his wife, calls it dumb machismo, but it's really something homelier, a modesty that resists calling attention to private suffering, not to hide from but simply to acknowledge the fragility and finitude of the flesh.

An old Fleetwood Mac song is on the radio. *Thunder only happens when it's raining.* He switches it off. Fifteen minutes later he enters his Arlington house, a three-bedroom postwar brick colonial set among mature trees. They've been here since Hannah was three, when houses inside the Beltway cost a fraction of what they sell for now. A second mortgage is paying her tuition and fees at the University of Virginia. Regardless of what has happened at work, the peace of the neighborhood always makes him feel that he is returning to a parallel day here, a day he has missed.

"Pat?" He removes his wet shoes, hangs up his coat, finds her dozing on the sofa in front of the television. "Steve Kritsick called to see if he could ride with you on Saturday," she says, pulling the blue fleece over her feet.

"What did you tell him?"

"I said yes." She glances over when he doesn't respond. "I'm sorry. I didn't know what else to say."

"How about no?"

"I told him you'd call to confirm."

He goes into the kitchen as Pat wonders aloud why Hannah isn't answering her e-mail or returning her calls.

"I'm sure she has a lot on her plate." He takes a beer from the fridge. The Pottery Barn vase that appeared yesterday has already blended into the kitchen decor and now contains a bouquet of dried flowers. Pat is expert at introducing things into the house that seem always to have been there. It's in the kitchen that he feels they are truly cohabiting life partners. In bed, there are too many uncertain signposts en route to a good or bad night's sleep. The bedroom is too singular a place, whereas in the kitchen, preparing and eating a meal, he is always conscious of familiar settings and can sit down like anyone else to enjoy what is being served. Plus, there's no embarrassment about asking "So, how'd you like it?" afterward.

He puts the covered plate with his dinner into the microwave, punches the start button, and returns to the den.

"Did he say anything about tools?"

"No."

"Well, I'm bringing my own. The stuff they had for us last year was totally fucking useless."

Pat glances at him the way she often does when a remark strikes her as gratuitously cranky. He hadn't meant to sound that way. The microwave beeps. He goes to fetch his dinner. When he returns, Pat is surfing through the stations, remote control in one hand, holding the fleece at her neck with the other.

"Went in for a physical today," he says, sitting down.

Pat glances at him, contains her surprise by asking, "What prompted that?" equally casually.

"Just finally taking your advice." He smiles, imagines slipping an arm around her waist but knows how she would stiffen ever so slightly and turn away. He has always found her attractive. A little thicker in the waist, heavier in bust and jowl, but she's aging well. The same is said of him, in spite of the paunch.

They watch *The Charlie Rose Show*. There have been less even-tempered times, but they seem distant now. The big shift occurred three years ago, when Hannah left for college. It wasn't that he and Pat were drifting apart but rather as if a little patch of gray had opened up. She'd be embarrassed to know how much he loves and has always admired her. "Sometimes I wish I could trade places with you," he'd said to her recently in a slightly drunken, postcoital rush of emotion. They'd gone out to a bar in Clarendon for a Saint Patrick's Day drink, something they hadn't done in years. An early-spring breeze was blowing through the bedroom windows. What he meant was that he envied her direct, uncomplicated, open nature. She lifted the sheet up over her breasts. "Have you had these feelings for a long time?" The confusion that flashed in his eyes set her roaring with laughter. As he chuckled at her little joke, he added bawdy humor to the list of her admirable qualities. They lay for a quiet moment looking up at the ceiling. She was comfortable in her life and in her skin, someone who'd always understood that happiness is completely free. He turned his head on the pillow, looked at her, and felt the urge to embrace her again, but he waited instead to see if she came to him. The moment passed, and he realized it was not going to happen. When she got up and padded off to the bathroom, he felt a twinge of disappointment.

"I wish you hadn't told Kritsick I'd drive," he says, setting his empty plate on the table.

"I'm sorry. I didn't know what else to say."

Every March for the past three years, Noel and his neighbor have driven to a spit of land near the mouth of the Potomac where the church owns and operates a children's summer camp. It has become an annual all-men's parish outing, with Father Neale playing the role of host and foreman. The priest hustles about amiably, inspiring esprit de corps and providing continuity. It's impossible not to notice how conscious all are of their contribution. At the end of the day, a case of cold beer always appears.

"Why not just say you need to leave early?"

He doesn't respond.

The Charlie Rose Show has been the backdrop to dinner since the red-cell assignment started. It's been months since he was home before eleven o'clock. He takes his plate into the kitchen, opens the refrigerator to get another beer, and freezes up. He stands there for a moment, staring blankly at the haphazard topography of bottles, cartons, food containers—capped spikes and peaks and posts, plastic plates and foil wrapping. The interior light flickers as the motor cuts on with a shuddering whir. He takes out another beer, grips the bottle firmly, compressing the cold glass in his fist, and watches the interior light go off as he slowly closes the refrigerator door.

"I did something really stupid today," he says, standing in the doorway holding the unopened bottle. "Really, really, really inexcusably stupid."

Pat twists to face him. He becomes suddenly aware of the unopened bottle in his hand, returns to the kitchen. "What happened?"

He opens the bottle and, unsure, takes a long sip before returning to the sofa. "It was absurd. Plain fucking dumb. No other way to put it."

"Would you just tell me what happened?"

He takes another long sip, then says, "I was nearly arrested on the G. W. Parkway."

"What?"

He holds the bottle on his knee and releases himself to a mild alcoholic euphoria and the fuller world that he carries in his head.

"What were you doing?"

"Nothing, really. Taking in the view."

"For that you were nearly arrested?"

He turns to look at her squarely. "I was hitting drives."

"Golf balls?"

"At one of the overlooks. Right out over the river. In the snow." He traces an arc in the air with his hand. Innocent boyhood prankishness. Involuntarily, his eyes begin to tear and his stomach does a little roll. He lifts the bottle to his lips.

"And the police caught you?"

He nods, then chokes, sipping, as the wells of his eyes spill over.

Pat moves closer. "Want to tell me what's the matter?" She reaches up, but he turns away, wipes his cheek in the crook of an elbow, then stares dumbly at the television screen while Pat watches him intently. Weird. He hadn't. He didn't. It wasn't. In a minute it's over, and giddiness creeps in. "I really don't know what happened." He shakes his head with a mild chuckle. "It was just a prank. Totally spontaneous."

"You sure?"

He can only shrug. A blank look. The fuller world.

"You said he was going to arrest you?"

"No. He just told me to stop. I stopped. It was over, and I left. That was it."

"What on earth possessed you?"

He shrugs.

She continues staring. "Is everything all right at work?"

He shrugs.

"Maybe the bean-counting is starting to get to you."

He turns to her and smiles. "Not the counting. The beans."

On television, Charlie Rose coaxes and prods his evening guest as if each is satisfying a natural appetite for being fascinated. The ingenuous vigor of talk-show routine is difficult for him to watch. Is it that they know so much of so little? Or so little of so much? One day he will tell Pat everything. When the time comes. But what will he tell her? How will he begin? With the little white grubs? Beans? The dead schoolchildren?

FREDERICK REUSS

My mother lives in a condominium complex next to the National Geospatial Intelligence Agency. She bought the apartment when we returned from Germany and the house was sold as part of her divorce settlement with my father. The neighborhood was familiar, just behind the Little Falls shopping center where she'd always done her grocery shopping and also near Little Flower, the Catholic church she goes to, and the school of which I attended between the India and Germany phases of our Foreign Service life. In those days, the NGA complex was referred to as "Army Map." I had a friend, Bobby, whose father worked there. Bobby liked to brag that his dad put satellites into orbit. I remember thinking that Bobby's bragging was compensation for the disappointment of having a dad who merely put satellites up rather than get shot into orbit himself. My dad was in Vietnam. I may have boasted about it. If so, I'm sure Bobby understood it was to mask how much I missed him. It wasn't all that clear to us who had the cooler father.

Over the years, as Army Map became the Defense Mapping Agency and then the National Imagery and Mapping Agency and finally the National Geospatial Intelligence Agency, it has become an imposing and somewhat incongruous presence in the neighborhood, protected by high fences and an elaborate security gate at the main entrance. Soon it will disappear from public view entirely and move to Fort Belvoir, where a new and vastly enlarged headquarters is being built.

My mother's apartment is a roomy two-bedroom with a balcony that looks out over the woods surrounding the Dalecarlia Reservoir. She's become more and more reclusive over the years. When I arrive, she is usually either reading or knitting or in the kitchen, preparing a meal she will consume over the next several days, usually a soup or stew from the cookbook she brought back from a Trappist monastery in the Shenandoah Valley where she does a yearly retreat. She no longer plays the piano. Next to the Catholic Church and her divorce, music was once the biggest thing in her life. She used to say that Oberlin drove the music out of her, but it was marrying my father and becoming a Foreign Service wife that diverted her from the musical career she had aspired to at the conservatory. The Steinway she bought after the divorce is more personal totem than musical instrument. I can't remember the last time I heard her play it.

I let myself in, surprised to hear rock music coming from the television. She was knitting, glanced up when I came into the room, then returned her attention to the television.

"What are you watching, Mom?"

"A concert."

I couldn't help laughing. "Since when do you watch rock concerts on TV?"

She glanced up at me again, fingers working the needles, then over the top of her reading glasses at the television screen. "Is Roy Orbison rock?"

"One of the grandfathers."

"You wouldn't call it country?"

"Roy Orbison? I don't think so."

The song continued. I was too amused to know what to think. We listened for a few minutes. The stage was a who's who of rock 'n' roll luminaries. When Bruce Springsteen came into view, my mother put down her knitting and said, "I don't like that fellow."

"Bruce Springsteen?"

"Look at him. All preening and vain."

"Rock and vanity sort of go together, Mom."

She frowned and went on knitting. "Roy Orbison is the only artist up there. Look at him. He isn't jumping around."

She was right. Springsteen did seem a little stupidly overeager. I sat back and listened. "When did you become a Roy Orbison fan?"

"I like this concert. I've watched it several times."

She didn't elaborate and went on knitting. The concert continued. I settled back on the sofa, pleased by this little tremor in an otherwise unvarying routine. She was right about Orbison. The more the other idols pranced and preened around, the deeper Orbison seemed sunk into an autistic aloneness, which, I realized, was precisely what my mother most identified with. I wasn't so amused anymore and stood up. "Shall I make coffee?"

"I'll do it." She put her knitting aside.

We went into the kitchen together. I glanced through the newspaper while she put the kettle on. It was hard to tell which of us was more reluctant to talk. Her decision not to go to the funeral had come as a relief. Dad, which is how she still refers to him, is always an uneasy topic of conversation. After nearly thirty years, all I want is for her to put the divorce behind her and move on. A framed photograph of him stands on her dresser shrine next to photos of her dead parents and Padre Pio, a Catholic priest whom she has always been fascinated with. He was canonized by John Paul II. One of my earliest memories is of my father teasing her over the claims that the priest had performed miracles and received the stigmata. When she took offense, he became angry and said, "If you want to believe that crap, fine. Don't expect me to take any of it seriously."

She poured the coffee, fetched a bottle of Irish whiskey from the cabinet, and splashed a generous measure into her cup. She offered the same for me and was surprised when I accepted. I'm not a big whiskey drinker but felt a sense of nourishment in that sip, something careless and down to earth. We were quiet for a while, which is the natural complement to the aromas of booze and coffee. She held her cup by the handle, propping the rim with the fingertips of her other hand. Her gray hair was pulled back into a bun, and her eyes were a little bloodshot, but she was alert and present. For a moment, she appeared to me not as a mother or a grieving widow but as a linkage. The funeral seemed a small detail in a whole chain of linkages, and I understood for the first time how, in not going, she'd attended it in a more significant way. Still, it was with a twinge of guilty feeling that I described to her the planting of the tree outside Bern.

"What kind of tree?"

"I think it was an elm. A friend arranged it with a local farmer, who let us plant it on the edge of his field on the Dentenberg. It was one of Dad's favorite places to walk. There's a little restaurant up there where he liked to stop for a beer."

"Sounds nice." The disdain was muted, but only slightly; another reminder of things she felt cut off from. I'd said too much. We sipped our toddies and watched the birds at the feeder outside the window. Funny, the things we feel cut off from, how they so often turn out to be just the things we at one time deliberately rejected. My mother always complained about the superficialities of being a Foreign Service spouse. She detested the clubs, the cocktail parties, the bubbly charity of the wives, the pompous husbands. My father disliked all those things, too, but he protected himself with an ironic and often malicious sense of humor. He was a recognizable type: the wry, smart guy, likable but a little intimidating and best kept at a distance. The Foreign Service is full of them, always a rung or two down from ambassador, bearing all the institutional scars and grudges. My mother says she is happy to have left all that behind, is happy with her quiet life. I'm not sure I believe her.

We went into the living room. She picked up her knitting, and I listened as she began reminiscing. "I remember once we were in Aachen, walking through the cathedral there, and all of a sudden your father tells me there's something he needs to do and to meet him at the restaurant directly across from where we'd parked the car." She shook her head. "Right out of the blue. He's off. Just like that. I hadn't even noticed there *was* a restaurant."

"What did you do?"

"What could I do? I tried my best to enjoy the cathedral, then went to wait for him in the restaurant. I waited there for two hours!" She put her knitting down. "Can you believe it? Two hours! Then he comes in and plops himself down and says 'I'm famished,' as if there was nothing more normal in the world."

"What did you say?"

"I got right up and left. Are you kidding? The last thing on earth I wanted to do was sit there for another minute with him and pretend everything was just fine."

"Where was he all that time?"

"He said he had to call the office and afterward he'd done a little exploring and simply lost track of the time. Going home, he took one of his famous shortcuts that took us an hour and a half out of the way. We ended up stopping for dinner, anyway."

I always feel oppressed by her reminiscences. It pains me to see her so completely stuck in the past. She doesn't have to become a happy person, just live a little more fully in the present.

I stood up. "I'm going to have another toddy. Want one?"

"No, thank you." She smiled to let me know that she was happy to indulge this sudden immoderation on my part, in spite of all the lectures I'd given her about drinking. I went to the kitchen and poured the remaining coffee into my cup, taking note of what there was of whiskey left in the bottle. It was not to keep tabs but just to know. One of the phantoms of alcoholic behavior is always to take notice as well as to be alert to all notice-taking.

"Did you ever meet a friend of Dad's named Blake?" I asked, coming back into the living room.

"Blake?" She thought for a moment, knitting needles slowing. "Blake who?"

"I don't know." I sat down on the sofa, sipping the vaporous concoction. I tried to recall if any first names had been used, but couldn't remember. "He turned up at the memorial service and came back to the apartment afterward. Uninvited, it turned out—and pretty obnoxious. Nicole couldn't stand him. Claimed he was an old friend, met Dad in Laos."

She put her knitting aside, shook her head, and frowned. "That can't be. Dad was never in Laos."

"I'm just telling you what he said."

Her hands were folded in her lap. She stared down at them, the crease on her brow deepening. She can make herself look so angry when she becomes uncertain. It was hard to watch the Irish temper churning up. "No," she said firmly. "It's just not possible. He was never in Laos. I'd remember."

"Well, maybe I got it wrong," I said, wishing I hadn't brought it up. "I was just curious to know if you'd heard of the guy. It's not important."

The glare in her eyes was familiar and troubling.

"Look, Mom. Forget it. It's not important."

"I'll prove it, damn it," she said, and marched off to the bedroom. It came on too suddenly to protest. I knew she had saved all his Vietnam letters. She's offered to let me read them several times. I always decline. I settled back onto the sofa, resigned to going through the whole routine again. All these years of persisting in a worn-out relationship—not out of hope but out of hopelessness. It was too pathetic to think about, much less be shown the moldering evidence pulled from a dresser drawer.

She returned with an oversized manila envelope.

"I don't want to look at them," I said.

"Well, they're here if you change your mind." She put the envelope on the coffee table as if it were an extra helping of dessert I'd turned down. It was a provocation. The more indifferent I seem and the more she pretends not to be bothered in return, the more we prove to one another how deeply we both care. It's an uncalm, interior caring that needs to be guarded and restrained.

I was a little drunk when I left a short time later. It was late afternoon. She'd asked me to return some books to the library for her. It was a routine request. She typically has half-a-dozen overdue books lying around at any given time. Although she lives in Bethesda, she often takes books from the library in Georgetown, where her friend Marge Noonan works. Marge is also a divorced Foreign Service wife. She and my mother had been cordial in the Foreign Service wife way back in Madras. They became friends years later, in the context of their divorces. My earliest memory of Marge is of her dressed as a heavily bejeweled Indian bride, chain-smoking Salem 100s at a costume party at our house on Adyar Club Gate Road.

It was rush hour. A steady stream of traffic was flowing out of the front gate of the National Geospatial Intelligence Agency. The agency's motto is *Know the Earth. Show the Way,* which has always struck me as a peculiar variation of the Delphic injunction, *Know thyself.* I am also reminded of the lines from Rilke: *Nirgends, Geliebte, wird Welt sein, als innen*—Nowhere, beloved, will world be but within. To know the Earth is no simple proposition—but to be shown the way by a government agency? The inverse of the motto might be *Know Thyself. Find the Way.*

I drove down MacArthur Boulevard to Reservoir Road, feeling oddly mellow in the rush-hour twilight. It was more than just alcohol-induced well-being and had tinges of melancholy to give it ballast. There is a hidden traffic camera on MacArthur that has photographed me speeding several times. I always roll down the window and wave when I pass it. I also take note passing the mailbox at R and Thirty-seventh Street where Aldrich Ames made his drops. The original box is now on display downtown at the International Spy Museum—which speaks volumes about the legacy of the Cold War and the profitable cult of the secret agent. This part of upper Georgetown is a labyrinth of locations where secrets and watching have spilled over into history. There's Wild Bill Donovan's house on Thirtieth Street; Alger Hiss's various addresses on Volta Place, on P Street; Au Pied de Cochon, the restaurant Vitaly Yevchenko disappeared from when he redefected to the USSR. The restaurant is gone, but a plaque (also in the Spy Museum) once marked the table where he sat. There's the home of Amy "Betty" Pack, the OSS "swallow" who got her hands on the Vichy French naval codes by first getting them on Charles Brousse, the Vichy French attaché. Farther up Wisconsin Avenue is the apartment where the South African agent Jennifer Miles fucked her way through various echelons of the White House, DOD, and State Department. All are regular tour stops now, as much part of the quilt of Washington attractions as the monuments on the Mall, and perhaps all the more compelling for being so mundane.

The Georgetown library is a grandly sited neo-Georgian structure on the corner of Wisconsin Avenue and R Street. I was paying my mother's fine at the front desk when Marge Noonan came out of the History and Reference Room with an armload of books. "Come up and say hello," she called to me and pressed the elevator button with her elbow.

"I've been meaning to call your mother all week," she said as I entered her office a few minutes later. The room would be claustrophobic if it weren't for the enormous window directly behind her desk. The view is one of the best in the city.

"I was just returning some books for her," I said.

"How is she?"

"Fine," I said.

"Come in and close the door." I hesitated, unsure about the whiskey on my breath. "I'm sorry about your father," she said.

"Yes, well." I shifted my gaze to the window behind her.

"He was too young."

I nodded.

Marge pushed herself back in her chair. "I spent some time with your mother while you were at the funeral." She put her reading glasses on and glanced for a moment at her computer screen. Then she took them off again and let them dangle from the chain around her neck. "I worry about her."

"Well, you shouldn't." It came out sounding testy, but I couldn't help it. It wasn't just the busybody nature of the remark but the suggestion that my mother wasn't able to look after herself and I ought to be doing more to help her.

Marge took the tone of my remark as proof of her suspicion. "I think I have a right to worry," she said. "Your mother and I are old friends."

My resolve collapsed. I felt trapped. "What I mean is that she's— well, she is the way she is."

Marge's look softened. "It's been a rough time for both of you, I know." I was about to take this as my cue to leave when she perked up suddenly. "Oh, before I forget. You remember that elderly gentleman? When you were in here a while back? He came in recently and asked me to give you this." She rummaged through the drawer of her desk, then produced a card and handed it to me. It was an old index card, yellowed at the edges. "I have a map which may interest you." On the back were a name, address, and telephone number.

"Did he say anything else?" I asked.

Marge shook her head. "He just asked me to give you that."

I slipped the card into my pocket and only half listened as Marge mentioned the upcoming retreat at the Trappist monastery in Virginia. Evidently, my mother had invited Marge to join her. "I just hope she knows she's free to change her mind if she wants to," Marge was saying.

"Change her mind?"

"About me coming along."

I fingered the card in my pocket and glanced at my watch.

"Will you tell her?"

"That you changed your mind?"

"You haven't heard a word I've said, have you?" She rolled her eyes and waved me off. "Forget it. I'll tell her myself."

"When was he in here?" I asked, taking the card from my pocket.

"At least a month ago. I don't remember exactly."

It was dark outside. I crossed the library parking lot behind the building and stood in the little park that adjoins it. I never leave the library without stopping here to take in the view. I sat down on a bench, pulled my collar up against the wind. In the foreground, the rooftops of Georgetown slope down Wisconsin Avenue, quaint and tasteful and haughty in the Washington small-town way. Across the river, Arlington Cemetery, the Pentagon, and the skylines of Rosslyn and Crystal City spread out in their closed crucible of power. Vaulting into the sky just behind the Pentagon is the Air Force Memorial, a bouquet of chromium arcs meant to suggest the trajectories of soaring jets that looks more like an explosion tearing up the horizon.

The Pentagon
38°52'15.10"N
77° 3'20.51"W

Noel and Cowper have spent all morning at the Pentagon in meetings. Representatives from the offices of legal counsel were present at all of them—uniformed and civilian—chains of command going every which way. They each carried an armful of printouts containing all the relevant data. Rarefied stuff. Being the custodian of such material is its own reward—akin, Noel likes to believe, to knowing an ancient language or unraveling genetic code at the molecular level. Of course, Noel and Cowper are not the only ones who work with it, and a fair amount of possessiveness, jealousy, and conceit attends its use. Meetings can become great storms of silence as groups contend to have the greatest impact without overstepping their inner frontiers. Goals are spoken of laboriously. Everyone is circumspect. Today's meetings concluded with somber acknowledgment that the common mission absolves them individually. In the end, people don't kill, the state does.

As Noel is heading out to catch the shuttle back to Bolling, Cowper pulls him aside. "I thought it went well, considering."

"Considering what?"

"Well, considering how badly it could have gone." As ever, Cowper's reasoning is airtight. He fixes Noel with a look of aggrieved authority. "Look. There's nothing more we can do about it. Don't lose sight of the big picture."

Outside, in the big picture, plows have cleared the parking lots. The air is crisp and fresh. The Bolling shuttle pulls up, but Noel, in a sudden change of mind, waves the driver on. Pat is turning fifty-two next week, and he needs a birthday present. He heads over to Pentagon City Mall, navigating the unmarked network of sidewalks, shuttle stops, and parking lots. One can only feel out of place on foot here, either a threat to or threatened by the streaming traffic. As he is crossing Army-Navy Drive, his phone rings. He stops to answer, fumbling in the pockets of his overcoat.

It's Pat.

"Hey. I was about to leave a message. When are you coming home?"

"I'm running an errand."

"You sound out of breath."

"I'm walking."

"Noel? Can you hear me?"

"It's the traffic."

"I've been worried about Hannah."

"Me, too. We'll talk about it when I'm home."

"We have a bad connection. I can barely hear you. I'm going to hang up."

In Macy's, yellow signs warn of wet floors. Noel moves cautiously

FREDERICK REUSS

around them, through the polished glare. A display at one of the counters catches his eye: *l'Homme Fatal*.

"A new fragrance for men," a young woman says, materializing out of nowhere. She holds up a small glass flask. "Here, give me your hand."

He pulls up his coat sleeve. She daubs a minute amount of fluid on his wrist and, demonstrating, passes her wrist under her nose. Her black bangs are cut straight across and match the dark mascara on her lashes. A silver ring pierces her left eyebrow, and a stud is fixed just beneath her lower lip. She closes her eyes and sniffs in a suggestion of ambrosial sin. Noel follows her example, eyes fixed on her as he sniffs.

"Do you like it?"

"I'm not much of a cologne user." He passes his wrist under his nose again.

"But you like it, right?"

"The name caught my attention. Do you sell it everywhere? Or just here?"

"You can get it pretty much anywhere, I guess."

"I'm looking for a present for my wife."

"Give her this."

"But it's for men."

"Exactly," she says with a suggestive twinkle. "You work at the Pentagon, right?"

Noel nods, rolling his sleeve down.

"What do you do there?"

"I'm just a bean counter," he says flatly, then suddenly adds, "And I kill people."

She laughs, returns the sample bottle to the display stand.

"Why are you laughing?"

"I don't know. The way you said it sounded funny."

A pit opens in his stomach, the fuller world revealed. "Believe me, there's nothing funny about it."

She isn't sure how to take this.

Noel regrets the impulse and can see that she hasn't sold much, if any, *l'Homme Fatal*. "Okay. I'll take one," he says.

She levers a box from the display table with a practiced flair that is somehow sad to see, puts the overmanufactured box into an equally overproduced little satchel with a woven drawstring. "She's going to love it. I promise."

Noel reaches for his wallet, takes out his credit card, then changes his mind. "I don't have cash on me. Is there an ATM?"

"Out in the mall," she says, flashing a wry smile.

It doesn't take long to find a cash machine. The food court on the ground floor is busy. Underneath the glass-domed atrium, sparrows flutter down to pick up crumbs and fly up into the rafters. That they are inside is troubling; and strange that they should go about their scavenging unnoticed by the milling lunch crowd. Noel puts his card into the machine, recalling one of the more forgettable bromides from the first morning meeting. It was said that they were dealing with the law of unintended consequences, that it is often impossible to distinguish between innocent and nefarious infrastructure, and that their work must be performed with this constantly in mind. He wonders if such a thing is possible or if he is like the birds caught inside this shopping mall, trapped and living under false and artificial pretenses.

He returns to Macy's. In the men's department, he stops at a large display of belts. After browsing three full racks, he finally finds something. It isn't perfect but comes close enough. Black Fandango, not too wide, not too narrow, with a simple, nickel-plated buckle. He rolls it up in his fist, taking in the departmental landscape of racks and tables and headless, liveried mannequins. An elderly woman being escorted by a nurse steps in front of him on the escalator. He puts several treads between them, then steps on. Tock tock tock. He doesn't really need the belt. But the mindlessness of shopping makes him feel at ease, living serenely. At the bottom of the escalator, the elderly lady stumbles and is helped by her nurse. Noel veers around them, and all at once he knows that he must tell Pat everything. That very evening, as soon as he gets home. The way he just did with the girl at the perfume counter. Spontaneously. Or should he write her a letter?

Dear Pat: I am a killer. You would never think to call me that. Nobody would. In fact, you'd reject the notion and say I'm suffering from a guilt complex, or depression; that I need psychological counseling. And you'd be correct in all those things, because as long as what I do is done in secret and behind layers of abstract reasoning, is socially and legally sanctioned, it can't be THE WRONG THING TO DO. *I kill as part of a complex and vast political economy, and I have experienced a certain fulfillment in the excellence of my technical knowledge and find comfort and protection in a fully rationalized, hegemonic ideology. I consider myself a man of substance and many parts, am aware*

of the random inequities and the irrational contradic-
tions that we are born into and that life throws at us.
I also believe I am capable of putting these contingen-
cies into reasonable perspective and, in essence, that I
am a good person.

Will she be horrified? Or, in bringing the secret into the open, will he only horrify himself? That he will regret something is certain. One Sunday afternoon not too long ago, they went to the zoo. It had been a particularly difficult week, and he'd suggested they go have a look at the new baby panda. They stood in line and filed through the exhibit. It moved him to see how thrilled Pat was to watch those animals lolling idly in the grass, munching bamboo shoots. As they stood at the railing, Pat became quiet, as if her whole metabolism were slowing. She turned to him and said, "They seem so contented, don't they?" He agreed, but what struck him was not how the pandas seemed but their effect on the people who had come to look, filing through the exhibit to satisfy a craving for something simple that has been lost. Rather than lulled by those cute, cuddly bears, he began to feel abandoned. A little while later Pat went into raptures over the fennec foxes, curled up in their burrows. She put her arm around his waist and hugged him as if to draw them both into that homey scene, but his thoughts had turned to the MQ-1A Sky Warrior with the Synthetic Aperture Radar/Ground Moving Target Indicator system and the GBU-44/B Viper Strike GPS-aided laser-guided bombs tucked inside its weapons bay and he wanted to shout—*Listen! The mighty Being is awake!*

He heads for the cosmetics counter, anticipating the happy surprise of the perfume seller when he returns. *L'Homme Fatal.* Sure, it's a sick joke. But isn't it important to have a sense of humor about precisely the things one finds most unbearable? The perfume seller is not at her post. He glances around, makes a quick circuit of the brightly lit counter, looking for any sign of her. A plainclothes security guard is standing just a short distance away. The man has a shaved head. A wire disappears into the collar of his shirt. He puts a hand into the pocket of his blue blazer and takes hold of some concealed device, distracted by something streaming into his left ear. A group of women wearing brightly colored exercise clothes passes by, talking cheerfully among themselves.

Noel takes a bottle of the perfume from the display rack and goes to find a cashier. Even if he persuades Pat that he's a killer, will there be any change in who he is as a result? She'll object: "That's not *really* what you are!" Or maybe suggest he change jobs, do something different. What would that accomplish? Is it possible to stop being someone and become someone else? He wishes it were. But even in those clear-eyed moments—and they are rare—when one simply is, the world will usually see something else. It isn't a question of change. He can't say why, precisely, except that it evades the given, which is permanent and unchangeable, and thus addresses something less than what we are.

Besides, what is change when you're invisible?

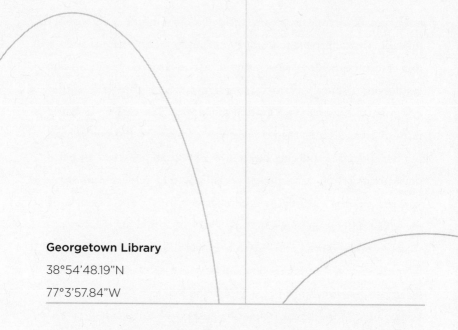

Georgetown Library

38°54'48.19"N

77°3'57.84"W

I took the old man's card from my pocket. He lived nearby. Dropping by unannounced seemed vaguely in keeping with some earlier custom. He would understand. Leaving my car in the library lot, I walked down Wisconsin Avenue and made a left on P Street.

I'd met him just the week before my father died. I had come to the library to do some research in the Peabody Room, which houses a unique archive devoted to the history of Georgetown. Marge introduced me to the archivist, explained to him that I was doing a book about maps and Washington.

"How did you know?" I asked, surprised.

"Your mother told me." She wrinkled her nose and touched my forearm in mock apology.

When the archivist brought out the map I'd come to see—a Civil War–era map that showed the location of all the Union forts defending the city—an elderly man sitting at an adjacent table asked if he might also have a look. I explained to him the map's historical significance. It was printed in 1862 by a commercial publisher to sell to tourists but depicts a secret, wartime landscape. The government confiscated all copies, destroyed the plates, and put the publisher out of business. "It's very rare," I told him. The man rubbed his chin and nodded as if he knew something more. I wondered if he was recalling the soda fountains and flophouses of a city I was too young to remember.

He lived in a small wood-frame house with red paint peeling off the siding in thick chunks. The shades were drawn on all but the top-story windows, which made the place seem minimally inhabited. The front door was on the second story. I climbed the cracked iron staircase, pressed the buzzer, and waited. I was about to give up and leave when a window just above me opened. "Yes?"

"Sorry to bother you. We met at the library." I took out the card and waved it for him to see.

"Oh, yes. Yes," he said. "I'll be right down."

By the time the door finally opened, several minutes had passed. He was much frailer than I remembered and was wearing a tie and jacket, which explained the delay. I apologized for not calling first. "I wouldn't have answered," he said and offered his hand. "Sales calls are all I get anymore."

The house smelled strongly of cigarette smoke. "You got my note," he said, closing the door.

"I was just at the library."

This seemed to please him. He ushered me into a dimly lit living room lined with bookcases. The musty smell of old furniture made it feel cramped, but in a cozy way. An old clock ticked loudly on the mantel above the fireplace. On a side table, mounted on a polished wooden block, was a stone head from a Hindu temple. When he saw that I was looking, he asked, "Do you recognize it?

"From India?"

"From a temple, I'm ashamed to say."

"Ashamed?"

"I bought it in Delhi. If I knew then what I know now, I would never have bought it." He touched his fingertips to the stone. "Pillaged works of art were for sale everywhere right after independence. Have you been to India?"

"I lived in New Delhi and Madras as a child."

"Well then you must know where Kanchipuram is."

"I do, yes. My mother has a sari from there."

"What were your parents doing there?"

"Foreign Service," I said.

"Well, it would have been well after my time." Looking slightly pained, he asked, "What do you think I should do with it?"

The question came as a surprise. I hesitated for a moment, unsure what was meant by it. "Give it back," I finally said.

He ran his fingertips over the figure, then turned to me and said, "Precisely what I intend to do." He stepped over to a staircase leading down to the lower floor, and motioned for me to follow. He took the steps one at a time, holding on to the railing with one hand and bracing himself on the wall with the other. At the bottom, he pointed to something hanging on the wall. "The map," he said and stood aside. It was drawn in ink on yellowed paper, about two feet square, mounted in a black lacquer frame protected by glass. I stepped up for a closer look at what appeared to be a diagram, heavily annotated in Japanese.

FREDERICK REUSS

"Do you know what it is?"

"Of course I do. I was there." He pointed to the land feature at the bottom. "That's Guadalcanal," he said. "And that's Tulagi."

"You were at Guadalcanal?"

"Yes," he said. "Right there. In one of those boats." He pointed to a small row of triangles. "Two Higgens boats and a tank lighter. I was in the middle one."

"Can you read the Japanese?"

"I can't. But I have a translation. Sit down. I'll get it."

The room was comfortably furnished with a sofa and a large easy chair. It looked onto a small, enclosed back garden lit by lights recessed in a high brick wall. The house had long ago come to a standstill and would remain exactly as it was until he was gone. The walls were hung with paintings that had the feel of works by friends. One, a whimsically rendered tropical bird, was captioned at the bottom in thick black paint: *This bird is native to Papua New Guinea . . . a rather hard to find variety but once in the hand it speaks, it squawks, it lives on foreign currency.*

"I can't seem to find it," he said, coming down the steps. "But if you like, I can tell you what happened."

"Only if you've got the time."

"I've got nothing *but* time." He laughed. "Speaking of which, it's time for my cocktail. Will you have one? All I can offer you is a vodka martini."

"Why not?" I said, still buzzing from the whiskey and coffee.

He carefully prepared the drinks and then served them on a little silver tray. "Cheers," he said and sat back down in the easy chair. As he sipped, he reached into the breast pocket of his jacket and took out a packet of cigarettes. "Care for one?"

I shook my head, watched as he produced a Zippo lighter. "You look surprised," he said.

"Don't see too many people your age smoking."

"Don't see too many people my age, period." He grinned. "I'm ninety-three. At my age, the effects of smoking are entirely positive." He held the lighter with both hands and lit the cigarette. "I was the press officer for the First Marine Division," he said settling back in the chair. "There was very little fighting on Guadalcanal when we landed. The Japanese had their main base on Tulagi, and there had been fighting there, but we could only get scattered messages by radio. First Division headquarters decided to send over a party to get firsthand info on what was happening. It was August 12, 1942. As press officer, I was one of the ones chosen to go. Japanese ships had free use of the channel between our island and Tulagi. They'd been shelling us quite freely. They had no opposition except guns and artillery, so they'd pop up and shell us. We knew the crossing would be dangerous and wanted to get started before sunrise and their planes started coming. But we didn't get off until after nine."

He took a puff of his cigarette, leaned forward. My eyes kept returning to the map behind him.

"I took a dunking getting aboard the boat. Soaked my boots, so I took them off. I think every time I got into a landing craft, I soaked my boots." He drifted off for a moment, then got up and went to the map. "We were in these three boats."

"It looks like six to me," I said.

"Yes. Three going and three returning. I told you it was a special map." He turned and smiled. "Anyway, we were three boats. Two Higgens boats and a tank lighter filled with drums of gasoline and supplies for the marines on Tulagi. It was a beautiful South Pacific day, sunny, clear. Except for the sound of the boats' engines, every-thing was quiet. After about an hour and a half, Captain Murray shouted to me, 'Take a look. Is that a submarine?' My glasses and binoculars were too wet with spray to make anything out. Just then it began firing. Shells splashed to the left and right. Ranging shots." He pointed to the diagram of a submarine just to the right of the boat convoy. The glass covering the map was smudged with finger-prints, years of pointing. He must have sensed what I was thinking because he turned to me, finger still pressed on the glass, and said, "My life didn't flash before my eyes or anything like that. But I was very absorbed in the moment."

There was a strange ambiguity in his expression, as if all the in-tervening years could be traced back to that single point on the map. I stepped in for a closer look and wanted to ask if he told this story often, but didn't want to risk insulting him. "What did you do?"

"There wasn't much we could do. The coxswain turned up the speed, but the old boat began to shake and shiver. Smoke was pour-ing out of the engine housing. Obviously, it wasn't going to last much longer. The other boat, seeing we were in distress, came along-side, and we jumped in. It wasn't easy with the boats bumping to-gether, shells exploding in the water. I left my field glasses, canteen, and pistol belt behind, tumbled into the boat like a sack of beans. And my boots! I didn't have my boots! I may as well have been na-ked. Just as we were aboard, a battery of marine artillery on Tulagi began firing. It was pure luck that they'd seen us and were in position to begin firing the howitzers. Anyway, the Japs submerged, and we made it to Tulagi safely."

It seemed a rather abrupt ending to the story. "And the map?" I asked.

"The map came to me on Guadalcanal a few days later." He sat down again, puffed on his cigarette. "Are you interested in history?"

"I'm interested in your story."

"My story? It's nothing but an old wartime tale."

"Isn't that history?"

He smiled. "Perhaps, perhaps not. I've always honored the Muses."

I had no idea what he meant. I don't think he was trying to lead me on, or to be oracular and pretentious.

"I've been lucky," he went on. "Over the years I've come to know other versions of what happened that day, in written accounts and from people I met years after the war who were also there. A dear friend and colleague whom I met back here after the war. He was attached to the battery of pack howitzers that fired on the submarine." He stubbed out his cigarette and chuckled. "We'd been friends for years before we put our stories together."

"He's in the map, too?"

He pointed to the two arrows drawn on either side of the submarine showing the direction of artillery fire. "If I remember, the Japanese reads, 'Received fire from Tulagi, 7 to 10 cm type.' Anyway, the significance for my friend was very different. They'd fired on the sub without orders. In fact, had gone against the wishes of their superiors, who didn't want them to give away the position of their guns. He was worried about facing disciplinary action."

"Did they sink the submarine?"

"No. It submerged, and we never saw it again." He pointed to a large block of Japanese text. "The Japanese had a completely different impression of events. They saw high-speed boats, fully loaded with men and munitions. Flying the British flag!" He laughed. "High speed? Our engines had conked out. And where did the British flag come from? We had a good laugh over that one."

He drifted off for several minutes in that unseeing way the elderly have of keeping you out of their thoughts and in their gaze. His blue eyes, clouded by cataracts, were like shrunken points of glass. The tear ducts were ripped and raw looking, as if something too large had passed through each socket. The only sound was the clock ticking on the mantel upstairs. I tossed back the remainder of my drink. "How'd you get the map?" I finally asked.

He sipped his drink before answering. "A few days later, back on Guadalcanal. The Japanese made some air drops to their troops just west of us. One of the baskets fell behind our lines. In it was—among cigarettes and candy and encouraging messages for the soldiers—an estimate of the situation. The map. It was translated right away by Pappy Moran. He'd been a missionary in Japan before the war, was our interpreter and prisoner interrogator. What struck me, of course, was the attention given to the encounter with the submarine. They'd gotten it all wrong. Completely wrong." He shook his head and chuckled.

"When did the significance of the map strike you?"

"Well, from the beginning, I knew it was unique. So far as I know, there isn't another one like it in existence."

"I mean, did you see the personal significance right away?"

"Personal significance?" The question seemed to amuse him. "I certainly didn't think in anything like those terms back then. Even now, I'm not sure 'personal' is the word I would use to describe its significance."

"What did you do with it after the war?"

"I put it away with the rest of my war papers and forgot about it," he said and set his empty glass on the table.

"But now you've got it hanging on your wall."

"Yes, I do."

"So why do you have it there?" I flushed as I said this, aware of the provocation in my tone.

He eased back in his chair, turned an appraising look on me, as if uncertain how much further he wished the conversation to go, and reached into his breast pocket for another cigarette. "I would say its significance for me is the opposite of personal. It has, in just about any way you look at it, nothing whatsoever to do with me." He put the cigarette to his lips with a shaky hand. "We live on a molten sphere with a thin crust orbiting the sun. Every event that occurs on it takes on a nearly infinite number of simultaneous meanings." The Zippo was produced. His hands trembled.

"But it's a key to a specific event. Something meaningful that once happened."

"Meaningful?" He thought for a moment, then shook his head—a little sadly, it seemed, as if he wished he could give a different answer. "From up close, war is always about nothing. For people who experience war, there is only confusion and forgetting. It's the ones who were never there, the ones who come later, who always decide what happened. They're the ones who write the histories, erect the monuments and memorials. Make up the meaning. The cliché that history forgotten is history repeated." He smiled and shook his head. "Well, the problem is often precisely what it is that is remembered. And who is doing the remembering." He began coughing, wiped his mouth with the back of his hand. "The past is a mental thing. It doesn't exist. The Pyramids and the great libraries, the Internet, are only the frailest scraps of physical evidence and will all disappear in time. Every night I have my cocktail, smoke my three cigarettes—this is my second. Don't think I haven't been counting. Later, I'll take my sleeping pill. I'm addicted and need it to sleep. And every morning, I wake up and, goddamn it, can't believe I'm still here!" He flashed a wry smile, something straight out of an old movie. There was something stagy about his manner. He seemed eager to make an impression on me. Age entitled him to the grand distance he took, the talk about meaning and meaninglessness, past and present. I wondered what he thought about GPS and Google Earth and a shrinking world confused by the technology of seeing.

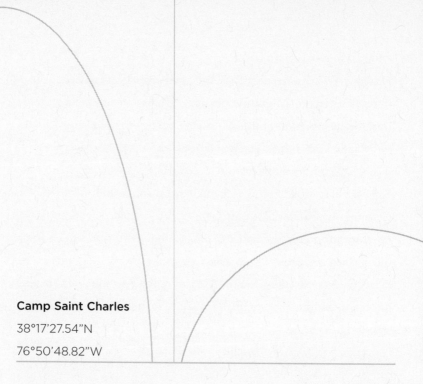

Camp Saint Charles

38°17'27.54"N

76°50'48.82"W

Seeing and shrinking and keeping his distance are Noel's main pre-occupations driving south on Maryland Route 301. It is just after eight o'clock, a chilly, overcast morning with winds from the north-northwest. Uncertainty over the weather has Steve Kritsick trying to locate Father Neale, who is not answering his cell phone. "I guess there's no coverage down there," Kritsick says after the third try.

"Or he's just not answering his phone," Noel offers.

"Why would he do that? He knows we're coming."

"Exactly."

Kritsick is a tall, easygoing, forty-five-year-old with a tall, easygoing wife named Margaret and three young children whose names Noel can never keep straight. They live a few blocks away in a house that has been expanded to the limits of the property line. Kritsick is an accountant at the General Services Administration and an amateur chef. He is also an active member of Holy Trinity, the church that Noel attends, and Pat has become close enough to his wife,

Margaret, to have compelled the men to a sort of diffident friendship. Kritsick, cramped even in the spacious Navigator, sits like a partially folded lawn chair jammed into the front seat. "I suppose we'd have heard if he was going to call it off."

"That'd be my guess."

"If it starts pouring, we're going to get zip accomplished."

Noel shrugs. "Accomplishment" is a big word in Kritsick's vocabulary, almost always used reflexively. Nobody is beyond the reach of his sincere approbation, the pride he takes in all humankind's achievements—scientific, artistic, athletic, political. He is impressed by all of it: Intel's latest microprocessor, a newly uncovered Mayan pyramid in Yucatán, the Human Genome Project, Picasso's Blue Period, the Iditarod. "So what's with the golf clubs?" He jerks his thumb over his shoulder. "You brought the hedge trimmers, too. Good going."

"Always come prepared," Noel says drily. It's the only way with Kritsick, whose good-natured enthusiasm always forces Noel into the role of curmudgeon.

They stop for gas at a Wawa station on Port Tobacco Road in La Plata. As Noel fills the tank, Kritsick goes in search of coffee. A van pulling a boat glides up to the next pump. The boat on the trailer is one that Noel briefly considered buying after 9/11. The exact model. The engine is a 90HP Evinrude. Noel wanted 120HP—with extra tanks to get him beyond the hundred and fifty miles he figured would be necessary. And at least a three-day water supply. The man with the boat whistles as he fills his tank. He is potbellied, pigtailed, decked out in biker gleam with a Harley-Davidson tee shirt and a silver chain looping into the rear pocket of his jeans. He catches Noel observing him and nods.

"Nice boat," Noel offers.

"Thanks." The man's voice is an octave higher than looks would suggest.

"What are you going for?"

"Rockfish."

The pump shuts off with a shudder. "Good luck," Noel says, twisting the gas cap back on.

The man nods, glances over his shoulder at his boat. The look causes a pang of envy in Noel—connected not to the object but to the pride itself. When did he lose contact with the humble sureties of having and being proud to have, of dreaming for things?

Kritsick returns bearing two large cups of coffee. They sit for a moment in the plush quiet of the Navigator, sipping through plastic lids.

"Whoever came up with a name like Wawa?" Noel says.

"Does sound a little funny, I guess."

"Not funny. It's baby talk. Wawa. It's a goddamn gas station."

"Well, they sell coffee and junk food, too."

Noel shakes his head, sips. "Ridiculous."

"Maybe it's an old Indian name."

"'Wawa'?" Noel laughs.

"What would you prefer? Joe's Garage?"

"Better than fucking Wawa." As the van pulls away, Noel says, "Almost bought one of those a few years back."

"I didn't know you were into fishing."

"I'm not."

"What would you want a boat like that for?"

"I don't know," Noel starts the engine, thinking of Cowper floating out on the bay with his cooler of iced tea—he quit drinking ten years ago—smoking cigars and listening to baseball on the radio. Ann would be below fixing sandwiches or reading a magazine. For a guy who grew up in working-class Cleveland, Cowper has fashioned himself into a credible Ivy League–NASCAR hybrid, a widely practiced modus vivendi in the agency. Tortoiseshell aviator slick. The teak shelves belowdecks are lined with political biographies and military histories, sports magazines, coffee-table books about cigar-making, sailing, and the Chesapeake Bay. Noel and Pat went out with them once. There was an emergency involving the mainsail that became a full-blown Cowper marital crisis out on the water. Strangely, rather than the episode quickening their bond, Cowper withdrew. He never invited them out again.

Glancing up at the gathering clouds, Kritsick tries calling Father Neale again. Noel sips his coffee, holding the steering wheel with one hand. His mood has been unusually good lately. Pat seems to be feeling a bit of an uplift herself. Last night, they took a walk through the neighborhood. It was late, and the air was crisp, on the verge of frost. Around the neighborhood, people were enjoying the last fires of the season. The smell of seasoned wood, their circumfused shadows as they passed beneath the streetlamps, made him feel at home and at peace—even with the next mission already well in the works. The Strategic Support Branch people had picked up a kid in Karachi over the weekend, have him in detention. He's giving them dates and places. The information won't be good for long—if it's any good at all. Like Noel's mood, it could become obsolete or superfluous at any moment.

Kritsick's phone erupts in a salsa beat. He glances at the display before answering. "Hello? Yeah—hi—I've been trying to reach you—just wondering about the weather—no—yes—about half an hour—do you need anything?—good—okay—well, it looks like rain here—they're both coming last I heard—no?—well, Nalker's supposed to be able to fix anything—nope—I hope so, too—pray for sun? That's your job, Father. Just leave the gate open—right. Yeah. See you shortly." He claps the phone shut. "We're on," he says and settles into his seat. He has a nervous leg that seems to bounce only during periods of silence. Noel glances at the GPS monitor on the dash, anticipating the next burst of commotional talking that will tranquilize the bouncing leg. Just as they are nearing the Rock Point Road turnoff, Kritsick's leg stops abruptly. "Have you been following this pet-food recall thing?"

"About the Chinese adding melamine?"

"They've got twenty million chickens quarantined on the Eastern Shore. All the feed is contaminated, too."

"Well, you're safe, then."

Kritsick's leg does a brief bounce. "I think it sucks."

"What sucks? That we're buying chicken feed from the Chinese?"

"Not just that. What about the people who can't afford organic?"

"I guess they'll have to stop eating chicken until the FDA gives the all clear."

"That's not funny."

"So what're you going to do about it?"

"I don't know," Kritsick says, gazing now out the passenger window. His leg erupts, then just as abruptly stops. "Part of me would like to do something."

Noel sucks the last drops of coffee through the little hole in the plastic lid, wrestling to contain his irritation. "Well, let the part of you that can *do something* feel bad." The words come out thick, stifled-sounding. His gaze is fixed on the road ahead. He grips the wheel in both hands. "And learn to goddamn live with the other part."

Kritsick is surprised by the anger. "What are you talking about, what other part?"

"The part that knows there isn't a fucking thing you can do." From the corner of his eye, he can see that Kritsick is pressing down on his knee to hold his leg still. "That's the part you *have* to live with."

"Is that the part you live with?"

"Yup."

"Come on, Noel! What're you all pissed off about?"

"Who says I'm pissed off?"

Kritsick eases back in the seat, crosses his arms over his chest. Rock Point Road is less than half a mile ahead. From there, it's another ten or twelve miles to where the dirt road begins. Noel pushes a button on the GPS, switching to satellite view.

"Well, I think it's possible to change things," Kritsick says. "I'm not cynical, and I don't feel as helpless as you do."

"Who says I feel helpless? All I'm saying is fix what it is you think is wrong, or shut up and stop whining about it."

"Being eternally pissed off is no different than whining."

"I'm not pissed off. I just accept the world the way it is."

"Yeah, right. Like Wawa."

An indicator begins to blink as they approach the turnoff. Noel slows, makes the turn onto Rock Point Road. A quarter of a mile beyond, he takes his foot off the gas pedal, puts on his emergency flashers, and coasts to a stop on the shoulder of the road. On the right is a large open field. To the left, about a quarter mile away, is an old farmhouse with a rusty silo.

"What are you doing?" Kritsick asks.

Noel opens his door and gets out. He opens the rear hatch, slides Big Bertha from the golf bag.

"What the hell are you doing?"

Noel fishes in the pocket of the golf bag for a ball and tee, then, leaving the hatch open, walks into the field. His feet sink into the newly upturned soil. The dirt is soft and pungent. After about ten yards, he stops, tamps down an area with his foot, then smooths it with the flat of his hand and presses the ball and tee into the ground. He gauges the distance to the line of trees that runs along the eastern edge of the field, adjusts his aim north by northeast, putting the woods at a distance of three hundred fifty to four hundred yards. The breeze is at his back, blowing south-southwest. He grips Big Bertha, addresses the little orb poking up from the ground at his feet.

"You're a nut!" Kritsick shouts from the car as the ball arcs high over the field, then falls shy of the woods.

He repeats the accusation a short while later as Father Neale helps him drag away a section of the tree branch that Noel is briskly cutting to pieces with a chain saw. "He's a nut, Father! Watch out."

The predicted rain hasn't come. It's nearly noon. They've been clearing fallen branches all morning, working their way around the perimeter of the tall fence that surrounds the camp's large, L-shaped swimming pool. High wind and last week's surprise snowstorm have littered the area with twisted limbs and branches. The debris is being dragged to a large pile at the center of the athletic field to be burned. In spite of his initial reluctance, Noel is glad to be here. He has worked up a pleasant sweat, sawing, shearing, hauling. Four other men from the parish are also helping. Noel sees them in church from time to time but hasn't made their acquaintance. They are working in teams of two, repairing the dock, clearing the grounds, fixing up the cabins.

"Everything all right?" Father Neale shouts.

Noel revs the saw's motor, smiles at the priest through the isolating hull of sound. The priest plucks a rag from his back pocket, wipes his forehead, points to the field, and shouts something else. Noel cuts the motor.

The priest adjusts his voice. "We're going to start the brush pile."

"I'll finish up here," Noel says. The tree limb lies in sections at his feet like a legless centipede. One last uncut branch leans against the fence just a few yards away. Father Neale tucks the rag into his back pocket. Bright red, perspiring, he fixes Noel with a sincere look and says, "Thank you for coming today. It's hard work, what you're doing." The priest pulls out the rag again, tamps his forehead. Noel understands this is meant as an opening, a little portal, and knows that not taking the opportunity merely adds weight to a later unburdening. There has always been a freighted superficiality in his encounters with the priest, as if each of them is waiting for the tap on the shoulder that will open the gate to something steeped in feeling. Coping with this tension is another aspect of the self-management Noel practices daily. It allows him to look Father Neale in the eye and, fingering the trigger of the chain saw, to smile and say, "My pleasure, Father. Always glad to lend a hand." A moment passes, with each of them appraising Noel's handiwork. Father Neale, without his collar and in working denims, has that silvery Society of Jesus sheen that comports easily with all varieties of worldliness. Among his flock is a cabinet member who arrives at church with a Secret Service retinue of black Suburbans and sits with his wife front and center at mass. There are also a few Pentagon higher-ups who come to church wearing army boots, a fashion that is said to have been started by Paul Bremmer at Little Flower in Bethesda when he was head of the Coalition Provisional Authority in Iraq.

"I'll get the fire started," Father Neale says and turns to leave.

"I'll be over as soon as I get through here." Noel tugs the cord, restarts the motor. His encounters with Father Neale always have this strange hand-to-mouth feel. He wonders if the priest would treat him differently if Pat attended church with him.

A thick plume of smoke rises from the middle of the field. Steve Kritsick and Father Neale are standing upwind, feeding scraps into the flames. Noel finishes the last branch, cuts the motor, and sets the saw down to cool. He loads the wheelbarrow, wondering why it is he always goes in dreading and ends up enjoying these occasions. It's similar to what he feels in church, a tired man partaking at a distance, enjoying the sight of others on holiday. He pushes the overloaded wheelbarrow toward the bonfire. The rubber tire is low on air. He weaves unsteadily over the soft, clumpy ground. Kritsick and Father Neale greet his arrival with playful enthusiasm. Sparks and embers fly. Smoke blows across the field in a nearly horizontal plume. They empty the wheelbarrow and retreat to watch the rising flames.

"You handle that chain saw well." The priest picks up a stick and flicks it into the fire. "Frankly, the thing scares me. I'm always afraid it's going to come loose, cut off a leg."

"They can be dangerous in the wrong hands, Father."

The priest acknowledges this with a smile. "In the wrong hands, anything can be dangerous."

"Law of unintended consequences," Noel says. Steve Kritsick has taken the wheelbarrow to fetch another load of wood. Noel gauges how far along he is and asks mildly, "Can sin be unintentional, Father?"

Father Neale bows his head in priestly consideration. "We are all born into sin," he finally says.

"I don't mean original sin. I mean unintended consequences."

The priest crosses his arms. "It's an old question. In recent years, the Church has taken a different tack. The focus isn't so much on sin itself. Some years back, John Paul put mercy forward as the more significant element in the whole question of sin and divine justice. He said love is the condition of justice—and justice is always done in the service of charity. In my view, it's a more positive way of talking about the issue."

Noel feels somehow as if he's been given a nonanswer. "I guess what I mean is, say, when you pick up a chain saw and cut off a leg by accident. Not your own, someone else's."

"Oh, that!" The priest laughs. "That's just plain stupidity. I'm afraid we're all at God's mercy there."

Noel smiles, tosses another branch into the fire.

"I'm being facetious, of course," the priest quickly adds, unaware of the mark he has hit. Kritsick is moving toward them now, absurdly overloaded and on the verge of tipping. "We have a group that meets every Thursday where we discuss these sorts of things. You might enjoy it. We're a pretty rigorous bunch."

"Maybe I will," Noel says in a noncommittal tone and tosses another branch onto the fire. He wonders how rigorously the priest believes himself when he speaks, how far from *via et vita et veritas* he is willing to venture.

"One more oughta do it," Kritsick says, dumping the load a few feet from the fire. He sets the empty wheelbarrow aside and surveys the scene. Noel grabs it and hustles off to fetch the last load.

"I'll gather the others. We'll have lunch over on the dock," Father Neale says.

"All we need are some marshmallows and we'll be set," Kritsick says, catching up to Noel.

"Marshmallows would make all the difference," Noel replies drily.

Kritsick lets him pace ahead, then shouts. "Better than smacking golf balls into the woods!"

Noel ignores him. It's a question of imagination. He once knew an analyst at Shin Bet, roughly his Israeli counterpart, who became a veterinary ophthalmologist. Helping animals with impaired vision. That was a higher order of thinking. You couldn't put it down to job discomfort. Midlife crisis. Noel loads the wheelbarrow slowly. His back is beginning to feel the strain. Kritsick has gone to meet the rest of the crew on the dock for lunch. The fire in the field is now unattended, which Noel decides will be his excuse for not joining them.

Bright sunlight is filtering through the trees outside my window. It is a light my father would remember well. And the sound of lawn mowers and garden bells chiming in the breeze. Those Bethesda afternoons he hated so much—personified by Mr. Falker, the de-licensed real estate agent and tennis bum who always had a thermos of martinis in his shoulder bag, carried a towel slung around his neck, wore a gold chain, and talked in a cackling voice. Falker died home-less, spent his last years in a tent in the woods behind the public tennis courts, drinking out of tennis-ball cans. He gave lessons to whom-ever came around and coached people as they played—whether they asked him or not. On cold nights, he slept in the basement at Little Flower. When I mentioned Falker's demise, my father smiled wist-fully. "Old Farkleheimer," he used to call him. It wasn't the poor man's pathetic end that made my father smile but the way it stood for something he'd narrowly escaped himself. I felt like an emissary from a pitiful country whenever I relayed news of the old neighborhood to my father—and, like him, in permanent conflict with the home office.

I couldn't help but think of old Farkleheimer as I filled out the Freedom of Information Act forms, wondering what, if anything, would come of it. The U.S. Information Agency, where my father had worked for thirty-three years, had been abolished by an executive order signed by President Clinton in 1998. Custody of all USIA records had been given to the State Department.

"Many inactive records were either retired or destroyed in accordance with their approved records disposition schedules. Unless otherwise noted."

"Files destroyed?" I asked.

There was a pause on the line. I was tempted to observe that destroying the files would be like destroying my father for a second time. Before I had the chance, the voice repeated, "Unless otherwise noted."

"Personnel files?"

"Personnel records were merged into State Department systems and given new names."

Throughout our brief conversation, I had the sense that the voice on the line was occupied with things far more urgent and diverting than my vague request. "Is there someplace I can go and have a look around? A public reading room?"

"We don't keep older personnel records here."

"Where are they?"

"NPRC. The National Personnel Records Center in St. Louis."

"St. Louis?" I had to redraw the map of just where the paper re-

mains of my father reposed. Not down in Foggy Bottom or in Langley or at the National Archives Building on Constitution Avenue or
out in College Park at Archives II but halfway across the country. I
have never been sentimental about graves and final resting places, but
traces left behind have always interested me deeply. I think it's largely
what drives me to mapmaking and keeping journals. I started the
habit of locking my journals and notebooks away as a kid, in a toy
safe I had received as a Christmas present. It had a combination lock
and a spring-loaded arm that set off a little alarm bell when opened.
I saw it advertised in the Sears & Roebuck catalog, which was where
all my impressions of American life came from until the age of ten,
when we left India and came to live in the United States for the first
time. I coveted the catalog, not just for the goodies it contained but
for the impression it gave me of what an American boy was supposed
to have and know and do. Hunt with BB guns, camp and canoe and
fish, race cars, supervise railroads, command armies of plastic soldiers
at D-day. Even the board games were alien—except for Monopoly
and Snakes and Ladders, which could be bought at Spenser's, the
British department store on Mount Road. But didn't all American
boys also have a telescope, a microscope, and binoculars? That year—
1967—it was invisible ink and the safe that captured my interest. I
remember the thrill when I opened it on that tropical Christmas
morning on the veranda of our house, took out the envelope stamped
TOP SECRET, and found inside a blank piece of paper, which my father
gently heated with his cigarette lighter to reveal the words "Merry
Christmas." I had to pretend to be surprised, but I had known I was
getting the invisible ink and the safe. The annual Sears shipment,
which came APO by sea, always arrived months before Christmas,

and the goodies were always hidden in my parents' closet, which was where I had discovered them, thereby deducing the truth about Santa Claus.

"Who should I contact in St. Louis?" I asked

There was another pause. "What are you looking for?"

"Anything I can get my hands on," I answered. Not wanting to sound too clueless, I added, "I'm especially curious to know if he was ever in Laos."

This time I interpreted the pause as sympathy and the advice as purely discretionary on his part. "Official personnel folders are kept by the National Personnel Records Center in St. Louis." Then he unleashed his "But!" like a blast of cold air.

"But what?"

"The records are the legal responsibility of the agency in which they were created, and access to all stored records is regulated by the authority of the creating agency."

"So what does that mean?"

"It means you'll have to submit a Freedom of Information Act request to the State Department."

"I think he might have worked for the CIA."

"The CIA, too, in that case."

"What about things produced in the course of his duties? Memoranda, reports?"

"I'm sorry," he said with a hint of pity. "You'll have to be more specific."

"How can I be specific if I don't know what I'm looking for?"

"I'm sorry," came the distracted voice again.

Desperate not to lose him, I asked, "What would you suggest?"

"Start with a FOIA request, and see where that leads."

It was back to square one. Tired, I thanked the voice and was about to hang up when he said, "Have you tried contacting any former colleagues?"

I don't know why this hadn't occurred to me. In part, I suppose it was just too obvious. I was interested not merely in learning what he'd done but in finding what was left of him in the oblivion of the records that hadn't made it to the oblivion of the grave.

That evening, when I asked to see the Vietnam letters, my mother reacted with a start. "What made you change your mind?" When she handed me the oversized manila envelope, I put it aside, and we talked about more current things. A fight was raging between the condominium board and a group of residents who were against making expensive upgrades to the building. "They're getting everyone all worked up. Telling us this is some elegant, glamorous place, and if we don't keep up appearances, it's all going to go down in value and we're going to lose money. Horseshit! I don't give a good goddamn about chandeliers and marble in the lobby."

I looked at my watch. The doors to the balcony were open to let in the evening air. In her agitated state, and because I had stopped in by surprise, she had forgotten her dinner, still heating in a covered dish in the oven. I've suggested she get a microwave. She refuses with a scorn that is equal parts fear, thrift, and snobbery. I kept her company as she ate, watching as she forked little mouthfuls of a vegetable-bean casserole between sips of white wine. Her mouth is ringed with creases that would trap lipstick if she still wore it. She has always been petite and at eighty doesn't seem diminished or shrunken as much as somehow free of her body. She sleeps a lot, and reads, and reads and sleeps. And drinks. She might still play the piano, for all I know. I hope she does. I always wanted to read as much and be as quiet as she can be, but loneliness is a formidable challenge, and now I am afraid of becoming like her.

I could tell she wanted to talk about the letters, was waiting for me to bring up the subject. She knew I wouldn't. Dad is the one subject on which she is defenseless. And the Catholic Church. But on that topic, she has literary and scholarly surrogates to speak for her—Czeslaw Milosz, Flannery O'Connor, and Raymond E. Brown being her favorites—so we can converse in her percolating way without having to mention either my father or the Church by name.

Her kitchen is always dim. She hates overhead light of any sort. Spaced along the countertops are reading lamps that spread disks of yellow light across the Formica surface. She also has an old-fashioned oil lamp with an adjustable wick that she lights proudly before sitting down to eat. Her eccentric taste in lighting has rubbed off on me. My house is also a cozy warren of lights and shadows.

"So what are you going to do with the letters?" she asked at last.

"Read them," I said.

She brought her empty plate to the sink. "I haven't read them in years," she said.

The lamp was beginning to smoke. I turned down the wick. "Do you want to go through them first?"

"There's nothing there I wouldn't want you to see." Then, with a chuckle, she added, "Darn it!"

I recalled that "darn it" when, later that evening at my desk, I removed the folded sheets from the envelope and began sorting them by date. Except for the first two, each letter was typed single-spaced on white legal paper and signed at the bottom in felt pen. The first was dated "Saigon, January 11, 1969. 6pm." A few had been sent from

Ban Me Thout. The rest gave no locale, just month and day. There were sixty-one letters in all.

It was all echoes and flashes over the next few days as I read and reread each letter. *Alone for a walk, a drink, and now lying in bed waiting for the opium to take hold for, I hope, 12 hours of sleep.* In Ban Me Thout he mentioned visiting the "Chieu Hoi" center: *A little spooky wandering around with all the ex-enemy. But they're just like any of the rest of the villagers, not only here but anywhere.* Chieu Hoi, or "Open Arms," was a psychological warfare and propaganda program aimed at persuading Vietcong to defect—in the jargon of the war, "rally"—to the side of the American-supported South Vietnamese government. What my father did at the Chieu Hoi center, other than get spooked wandering around, he never alluded to.

My mother's "darn it" meant something a little different with each re-reading. It wasn't that the letters were cold, but neither were they brimming with much love or longing. In fact, the word "love" appeared only in signing off, a perfunctory tenderness. "Love and kisses," with a signature scrawled underneath. On February 8, he crossed out half a paragraph in blue ink. After writing, *Arriving in Saigon was a feeling I'll never forget. Hard to describe, a spiritual experience I suppose,* the next sentence was just legible through the ink: *As a matter of fact, I guess I have one of those every night.* But the rest of the paragraph was lost beneath heavy blue scratches. The only emotion that got full airing was fear. It came through in letter after letter. And talk of sleep—not of how little he got but of where.

Feb 15. Even if I am a target its unlikely that they would get me with a rocket since I'm pretty well sandbagged and the house is pretty solid with difficult angles for clear shots. They're not likely to waste many men trying a straight out assault and only one or two would have a difficult time getting in and once in would likely be bumped off since they know Americans are armed to the teeth, which we are (even though I'm not sure how to use all the stuff). So I end up feeling pretty secure (during the day). When the noises at night start I wonder whether all the rationalizing during the day has been correct. There are lots of others who are much higher on the VC wanted list than I am. But I'm depressed by it all. Every day I compose, mentally, one or two letters of resignation. As far as I'm concerned now, all the opposition to the war is correct in spades. We don't stand a chance here in the long run, and the whole miserable effort, I think, is pretty much doomed. I think I'll be spending nights out at different places which are secure—or more secure—at least for the next week or so.

Some letters contained passages addressed specifically to me, which my mother at the time had wisely chosen not to share. Reading them for the first time these many decades later was like finding something underneath a sofa cushion that I hadn't known was missing. *I'm staring out the window toward the helicopter landing pad area watching helicopters going in and out. They are all kinds, great big ones that can lift up tanks and tiny little ones that could land in our garden. Then there's a thing called Spooky, or Puff the Magic Dragon, which I haven't seen at night yet, which sprays bullets and tracers, things that light up so fast it looks like a fountain. In one second it sends out enough bullets to completely saturate an area as big as a football field, so you can imagine how it looks at night. But I haven't seen it yet, and I sort of hope I don't.*

These were shocking images and swarmed over my memory like black spots. I studied the letters and suffered their mysterious weight by carrying them around with me for several days. One doesn't take in such material so much as absorb it through the heart. It wasn't clear to me if the boy to whom the lines were addressed was me or my father himself, an unconscious way of transfiguring his presence there by casting it in an innocent light. I was grateful to my mother for sparing me. That she had done so seemed further proof of their unconscious function. My memory of my father's Vietnam tour was composed entirely of his return from it, of being awakened at three o'clock in the morning and seeing him come into my bedroom wearing jungle boots, gaunt, unshaven. He seemed oddly to have grown younger, not older. He dropped to one knee. I jumped out of bed into his arms and knocked off his glasses, those thick black horn-rims of the 1960s. I found it funny that he couldn't see without them. After the big, fatherly bear hug, he groped around helplessly. I had to crawl under the bed where they had slid to get them. I went back to sleep, happy, and the next morning ran to fetch my friend Billy, who had recently moved across the street from Mobile, Alabama. We tiptoed into the bedroom for a peek at my sleeping dad, who woke up with a start when Billy's little sister exclaimed in thick Alabaman, "Ma Lord! He's *hayandsome!*"

There was no mention of Laos in any of the letters, but I plotted and dated each mention of a specific place on a map of South Vietnam. The result was meager and disappointing. I was hoping that the files I had requested through the FOIA might fill in some of the blanks, but I also knew that it was unlikely. In a sense, I was attempting to draw my own "Guadalcanal map"—or estimate of the situation—with my father coming and going in one of those little boats and me, the Japanese cartographer, seeing it from afar. I began to see that the map I was attempting to draw was nested in other maps, a way of projecting myself into a grid of hidden relationships and thereby assuming a place in a city I was both intimate with and completely cut off from at the same time. Washington, D.C., is built almost entirely on hidden relationships. I began seeing them, in evanescent cross-section, during my comings and goings; impressions in the human dough, each occupying a place in the collapsible distance between one and the next: standing on a Metro escalator, stuck in traffic on the Beltway, waiting in line at Safeway or Best Buy—or, since most of what happens in Washington actually transpires elsewhere, at departure gate C7 at Dulles Airport with a Starbucks coffee, a laptop, and a carry-on.

Noel looks up when the first-class passengers are called to begin boarding. A woman who resembles the News 4 anchorwoman is sitting next to him. She flips through a document while a man to her left idly opens and closes and opens and closes his cell phone. He is wearing a yellow polo shirt, jeans, and tasseled loafers. It seems he is awaiting confirmation of something important. Next to him, a grandmother cradles her handbag in her lap, eyelids drooping. A woman behind her is reading *Le Monde*, with occasional glances toward the departure gate. Parents preoccupied with two small children exchange knowing smiles with the couple just across from them, who are traveling with a small baby. A bald man dressed in black strides into the departure area, wheeling his carry-on behind him with practiced ease. He finds a seat next to a trim, salt-and-pepper-haired man drinking coffee with a laptop and a battered North Face day pack at his feet and a casual air of esoteric, technical knowledge. Noel is every bit a part of this cross-section and feels it the way he feels looking into a mirror. He can scale and proportion himself to a general idea but also knows that we are all as invisible to ourselves as to those whose paths cross and whose lives touch ours in ways we will never know.

On the shuttle bus going to Terminal C, he identifies the makes and models of aircraft parked at the gates. Even though the stoic impassivity of the refined air traveler comes naturally to him, he still feels a boyish excitement on takeoff, always chooses a window seat where, forehead pressed against the oval pane, he watches the ground fall away, feels the soaring banks and turns. His work doesn't call for much travel anymore. When he was told he was being sent at the last minute to attend the European Association of Remote Sensing Companies (EARSC) conference in Geneva, he accepted without argument. Arrangements were made quickly. Noel is attending the five-day conference under gray cover as a C2 program analyst with Mitre Corporation, a federally funded research and development corporation (FFRDC) based in McLean, Virginia.

Noel hasn't read through his dossier yet. He will do so before landing in Geneva. At the moment, he is preoccupied by a nasty quarrel he had with Pat yesterday. Her worry about Hannah's prolonged silence became an argument about his abandonment of Steve Kritsick and the summer-camp cleanup.

"You just went off and left everybody."

"I didn't just leave. I told them I was leaving. There wasn't a whole lot to do."

"That's not the point."

"What's the point?"

"The point is you just bagged out when you felt like leaving."

"I didn't bag out."

"You did. You just decided to leave and left!"

"Okay, I bagged out."

There was no point in arguing. He'd done all there was for him to do, had cut and piled every branch onto the fire while the rest of them ate their lunches on the dock. Nobody needed his help. What was he supposed to do? Stand around and join the gossip? When he came over to take his leave, they were discussing the new church organist, who was rumored to be a transsexual. Noel interrupted to say he was leaving.

"You're not angry, I hope," Kritsick said. His eyes narrowed in a friendly sincerity check. It was the unassailable good-guyness that was so hard to take. Not benignity but inanity. Where in the world had he earned the right to such hearty approval of things? Father Neale helped gather the tools and walked Noel to his car. The priest understood exactly why he was getting out of there. Jesuits have intuitive sense, don't play nice guy, are trained to take a hard look. There was room for anger, changes of mind and heart. And yes, it was private. All of it.

"I hope you'll drop in on our group sometime, Noel."

"I'll think about it, Father." Noel opened the back of the Navigator. The priest noticed the golf bag but said nothing. Noel liked him for that.

For Pat, there was no excuse. "You just left them and went off and played golf!"

"That's right, goddamn it. I did."

She left him in the kitchen, standing in mud-spattered socks in front of the open refrigerator. The East Potomac Park course, always muddy after the slightest rain, had been nearly impassable in places.

The rain that hadn't come to Charles County had stopped falling just an hour before he blasted his drive off the first tee, got onto the green with his nine iron, and sank the ball in two putts.

He made himself a sandwich and sat alone in the kitchen to read the paper. Pat busied herself in the basement with the laundry. She opened and let slam the washer and dryer doors. The echoless way he absorbed these signals only made her angrier. Trying each other's patience was one of those periodic tests that strengthened a marriage. The trick was not to mistake the test for a real emergency, not to waste valuable emotional energy. Pat didn't always cooperate. She needed to emit energy and released it in great bursts. He understood the need. But knowing that a certain amount of opposition was necessary didn't make it any easier to bear. Facts of life are never easier to bear simply for being constant.

Somewhere over the North Atlantic, he takes out the Mitre Corporation material he has brought with him. He'd gone straight home from the final briefing, where he'd received all his travel documents and a clutch of Mitre business cards with forward contact information. Someone from J-2 had come to the meeting to be briefed on the trip, an active reserve colonel. When intel guys from the Joint Staff were at a meeting, there were certain to be parallel, if not conflicting, agendas. It was hard for Noel not to feel somehow as if he were stepping into shoes that didn't quite fit. "Remember, we're just looking around," the colonel kept reminding him. "The joint interoperability workshop is your only must-show. The rest is all networking, getting to know people." The third time he said it, Noel had to force himself to keep his mouth shut. The revisit time with Joint Staff people always seemed shorter than with anyone else, some sort of organizational attention deficit disorder. OPSDEPS,

DEPSOPSDEPS. Regular army times ten. When he broke the news to Pat, he used the colonel's words almost exactly. She was more than a little surprised.

"A conference in Switzerland? Tomorrow? A little short notice, don't you think?"

"They just sprang it on me. Nothing I can do."

He hadn't been on an overseas trip in four years. The last one had been to Israel the summer Hannah graduated from high school. He'd taken the whole family that time. Three days of meetings at the Defense Ministry in Tel Aviv, then a week tour in the Negev, the highlight of which for Pat and Hannah were the three nights at the Queen of Sheba Resort Hotel in Eilat. The girls lounged around the seafront swimming pool while Noel slipped away for meetings at LOTAR headquarters, the Special Forces counterterror and hostage rescue outfit.

Pat followed him upstairs to help him pack. "I called the dean this morning," she said.

Noel had been expecting this. Hannah was now into her third week of total radio silence. He was surprised Pat had waited this long.

"I'm really worried, Noel."

"I know," he said.

"I don't understand. She just checked out. No warning. Nothing."

"She's asserting some independence. It's perfectly normal."

"God, I hope it isn't something horrible."

"Like what?"

"Like she's strung out on drugs or something."

Noel zipped up the garment bag hanging on the closet door. "She's twenty-two. We should leave her alone."

"What if she's depressed?"

"She's a grown-up." He went into the bathroom. "Grown-ups get depressed," he called back.

Pat was standing at the window when he came back.

"Why do you always do this?"

"Do what?"

"Make me feel like I'm all worked up over nothing."

There were times when he wished they could just communicate in letters, put their thoughts down on paper, leave them in a drawer to be read at some future date. What went back and forth as conversation always left too many residual trails of uncertainty. He was never sure if he'd understood or made himself understood. Half the time things were left half said. Given the half he couldn't share if he wanted to—if they could just write down what they meant and leave it in a drawer.

When he was packed, they went out for her birthday dinner to Central, a trendy and popular restaurant near the White House. The pretentious ambience, all light woods and marble and glass, was a welcome distraction. After they placed their orders, Noel reached into the pocket of his blazer. "Happy birthday," he said, placing the gift on the table.

She unwrapped the package. "La Home Fatal," she pronounced, "Men's cologne?" She removed the cap and sniffed. "Is it for me or you?"

"Exactly." Noel smiled, imitating the coy salesclerk. It didn't come off the way he'd hoped. She wasn't charmed. "I got it for the name," he said. "*L'Homme Fatal.*"

She put the bottle on the table and shook her head. "Thanks."

The mood soured. The timing was all wrong. He was unable to go through with what he'd planned, a lighthearted lead-in to full disclosure. They settled into their meal. At one point, there was a stir at the front of the restaurant. "It's James Carville and Mary Matalin," Pat said. A tremor of recognition spread throughout the room as the famous power couple was seated. Self-consciousness brimmed all around. Nobody wanted to be seen taking too much notice, and Jim and Mary were at obvious pains not to notice being noticed. Pat shared Noel's distaste for flamboyant personalities and preening connoisseurship. But, unlike him, it didn't make her cranky. He wondered why he couldn't be more like the Cowpers of the world. At work they played hard-ass and took a hard-ass stand on things. But in truth, there was nothing very hard-assed about any of them. They all wanted to be good, regular people, saved their money for retirement, bought cars and boats and recreational vehicles, had their kitchens done, collected useless junk just like everybody else.

"The doctor called today with my test results."

"What did he say?"

"Everything's fine except the cholesterol."

"What were the numbers?"

"I don't remember. The bad is too high and the good is too low. He wants to put me on a statin."

She took this in with a glance at the porterhouse on his plate and shook her head. "You need to watch what you eat, too."

"We're celebrating!"

"Are you going to do what he says?"

"I haven't decided."

"What do you mean, haven't decided?"

"All they do is push pills now. I'll try the diet and exercise route first."

She shook her head. "You'll have to do more than stop eating steak. And golf isn't exactly exercise."

"It is if you walk."

"And do you?"

"When I have time, yes."

"Well, I'm glad you're finally doing something about your health," she said archly and resumed eating.

"I feel fine," he said, wanting to have the last word and glad that he hadn't mentioned what had prompted the appointment in the first place, the tightness and the stabbing pains in his chest. He saw the two of them sitting there like those handsome, gray-haired couples in the TV ads who were always walking on beaches, holding hands, reading bedtime stories to freckle-faced grandkids while a friendly voice reels off adverse side effects, all the horrible agonies of the flesh. His vision of age isn't a picture or even a predicament but more like an interruption, suddenly not knowing what to say or do anymore. Soon there will be a drug to fix that, too. The medical business was really not much different from what he did. Both were very good at seeing. But then what? Nobody really knew. It was all a big crapshoot beyond that.

"Have you told Hannah you're going away?" Pat asked toward the end of the meal.

"I was going to send her an e-mail."

She took this in without looking up, working her knife and fork. Noel removed the napkin from his lap and gently placed it on the table. It took a moment for him to gather himself, and when he began to talk, it all came out at once. "For the past week, all you've done is criticize. You have no right to imply that I'm not concerned.

You can call the dean all you like, but Hannah isn't going to talk to you or to me until she's ready. Have you stopped for a second to consider what this is all about? For Christ's sake, give her some distance, Pat."

She was looking at him with hands in her lap, rigidly, waiting for him to go on, but he was out of steam and didn't know how to continue.

The little airplane silhouette creeps across the video map on the screen in front of him. Noel raises the window shade, watches the flashing light on the tip of the wing. The young woman sitting next to him has just put a mask over her eyes, wrapped herself in a blanket, and is trying to sleep. She is the woman he noticed reading *Le Monde* back at the departure gate. They exchanged a few polite nods as the attendants served drinks and dinner but have not spoken. She is about the same age as Hannah, but far more sophisticated and chic. Were her French parents worried about her? As they poked through their dinners, he considered striking up a conversation. *Are you a student? My daughter is at the University of Virginia.* He switches on the overhead light and begins to read. Senior information systems engineer, Defense Space Systems Division. Advises senior Department of Defense decision-makers involved in the development of strategies to guide acquisition of C2 capabilities compliant with DOD network-centric precepts, information strategies, and joint capability needs; assists in the development of strategies and recommendations consistent with the department's capability portfolio management initiatives.

It isn't at all hard for him to slip into the jargon of the job. He will float like a bubble through the conference. He puts the dossier away, picks up the *Financial Times*, and reads through the job advertisements. It isn't difficult to recognize himself in them, either. He knows who they are, where they live. The homes, the cars, the families and friends, the hopes, the fears, the desires—all familiar. An individuality among individualities. Why wouldn't their lives be interchangeable?

Dawn is breaking orange-pink outside his window. By the time he removes his reading glasses and switches off the light, they are approaching the coast of Ireland.

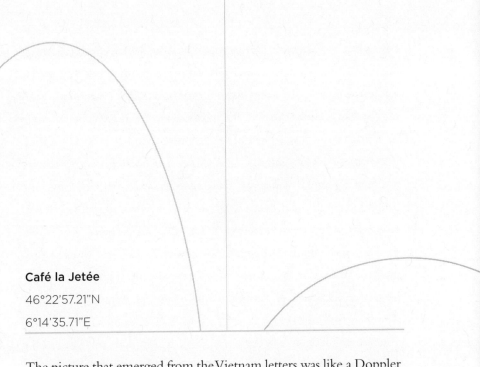

The picture that emerged from the Vietnam letters was like a Doppler image, receding in time and shifted to a part of the spectrum where light is absorbed in bands of memory. Two months after I submitted the Freedom of Information Act requests, I received a telephone call from a Ms. Barker of the Requester Communication Branch of the State Department. She told me that in order to process my request, I would need to provide a copy of my father's death certificate.

"But the State Department knows he has died. My mother and his second wife are receiving survivor benefits."

"We still need you to provide a copy of the death certificate."

"He died in Switzerland," I said.

"We will still need the certificate before we can release anything."

I wasn't surprised. It made a certain odious bureaucratic sense that I would have to furnish them with something before they would deliver the documents. Getting a Swiss death certificate posed a bit of a challenge. The CIA FOIA office was even more punctilious. My father had been born in Berlin and had come to the United States as a refugee with his parents in 1938. The CIA suddenly demanded to know the exact date of his naturalization as a U.S. citizen and gave me forty-five days to supply the information. Evidently, the fact that he had a thirty-year record of service as an employee of the federal government wasn't enough. It was hard not to feel that somehow, under the pretext of privacy, the government had buried him and rolled a giant boulder over the grave. Was it worth the effort? What could possibly be contained in the vaults and archives that could shed any more light on the man than my own memory? I was beginning to worry that this obsession with the details of his career might be better addressed and worked out with a therapist. The object wasn't to find out things I didn't know but to *re*find him and convince myself that he was the same man I had known and loved. The trouble was that the more I reread his letters, the more I began to see of a man I didn't recognize.

I'm in the CORDS thing, under Colby, and part of the province advisory team, in case that makes any sense to you. It doesn't make too much to me.

"Does it make sense to you?"

Blake stopped walking and turned to me. "You came all the way here to ask me that?" He was slightly out of breath, and his face was flushed. He looked more or less exactly as I remembered him from the night of the funeral. A little thinner, maybe, and wearing the same checkered Italian blazer. He shook his head in disbelief and resumed walking. "CORDS stood for Civil Operations and Revolutionary Development Support. It was a program that coordinated military and civilian advisory programs. William Colby—you do know who he was, don't you?"

"The CIA director."

"Not then he wasn't. In Vietnam, he was head of CORDS, came in after Bob Komer, and took the heat from Congress and the press when everything went all to hell. It was known as Phoenix, and they started calling it an assassination program in the press. For Christ's sake. Assassination? We were in the middle of a goddamn war!"

I'd found Blake in Nyon, a small town on the lake just half an hour's train ride from Geneva. We were walking along a paved footpath that runs along the lakeshore. It was a clear and unusually warm spring afternoon. The marina was quiet, a small forest of bobbing boat masts in the foreground. In the distance across the lake, Mont Blanc stood out in postcard clarity. Blake lived in a fisherman's cottage at the water's edge. A shack, really, with boxes of geraniums underneath the windows. Wire fishing cages were stacked in piles all around. Blake's place stood between a boathouse and a tiny fish restaurant with a chalkboard easel and two small tables set outside. I passed it several times, certain that Nicole had somehow misdirected me. "What on earth do you want with him?" had been her reaction when I'd called to ask for his address. I walked to where the footpath ended and joined the main road, then back into Nyon along the Quai Louis Bonnard to the ferry dock. Finally, I went into one of the boathouses and asked if anyone knew an American who lived someplace along here.

A shirtless man looked up from the boat he was sanding. "In the red house," he said in English.

"Merci," I said and turned to leave.

"You want to buy a painting?"

"A painting?"

"Forget it, my friend. He don't sell." With a friendly wave, he resumed his sanding.

"Merci," I said again and left, wondering if we were talking about the same person or if there was another American living out his retirement in a tiny fishing shack on the shore of Lake Geneva.

I walked for a little while to collect my thoughts. A group of teenagers was kicking a soccer ball and listening to loud music in a small, grassy park. I watched them for a time, delaying the inevitable, feeling bent under some mysterious weight. When I finally knocked and Blake opened the door, bleary-eyed, like a man from another era, it felt as if something foreordained had finally come to pass.

At first he didn't recognize me. "What do you want?" he asked in French.

"Ed Blake?"

The grogginess vanished. "Who are you?"

"We met last February. In Bern."

A moment or two passed. He was on the verge of closing the door. When I told him who I was, he took it in with no show of surprise, apologized, and asked if I would wait a few minutes while he tidied up. I thought he meant tidy up the house, but when he opened the door fifteen minutes later, he was washed and combed and wearing that familiar blazer. "Shall we walk?" he asked.

Of course, I had done some preliminary research. It wasn't just the letters I was working from. I knew that CORDS was a component of the Phoenix Program, one of the more notorious CIA operations in Vietnam. I had read several histories of the program and also what I could find of declassified government documents. But I'd decided not to let on what I knew. There were too many unknowns to risk putting Blake on the defensive. I flattered myself that being quietly one-up on him would be a way of leveling the playing field, a chance to beat an old spy at his own game.

We were coming to the jetty, where the ferry from Lausanne was just docking, when Blake turned to me and said, "I know you didn't come all the way here to talk about Vietnam." He gestured to a café across the street. "Let's cut the crap and have a cognac."

In fact, I had come all that way to talk about Vietnam. In my backpack were my father's letters and a list of the specific questions I wanted Blake to help clarify. I'd brought a tape recorder, which I was hoping he would consent to let me turn on. We sat down at one of the café tables in the small plaza. Blake was a regular. The waiter already had his cognac and coffee when he came to take my order.

"Great view, isn't it?" Blake adjusted himself on the narrow chair and pointed to the jetty where passengers were disembarking. "The ferry's a wonderful convenience. I often take it instead of the train. To Lausanne, Yvoire, Vevey, Montreux. Your father liked taking the ferry, too."

"My father came here?"

"Many times. This very café, in fact."

The waiter set down my espresso. Blake lifted his cup. "To your father," he said and sipped. He produced a silk handkerchief and patted away the film of brown foam from his upper lip. A mix of tourists and office workers were coming and going in the small plaza. The light was very clear, and everything seemed fringed with a sharpness and singularity that cut into my sense of urgency and purpose. Blake sat across from me, one leg draped over the other, fingertips idly turning the base of the cognac glass. He blended into the background, vaguely seedy, neither restless nor bored nor even especially present. I imagined him coming daily to this table, sitting with his newspaper, nodding politely at familiar faces as they passed by. What I could not imagine was my father sitting here with him. He would have mocked Blake's adopted European mannerisms. I tried to imagine them exchanging confidences. But I couldn't.

"Are you in Switzerland on business?" he asked.

"I came here to see you."

He took this in with a faint smile, turning the cognac glass in his fingertips. I opened my backpack and took out a manila folder. "I have some letters. I wonder if you could help clarify some things for me."

"I'll do what I can," he said and lifted his glass.

"This one is dated Dalat, February 1969. 'My chief is a languid Mandarin type who is absolutely incompetent. Interesting but incompetent. I think I've maneuvered to transfer him to Hue.'"

Blake laughed. "Wonderful! That's just wonderful! Your father through and through."

"Any idea who he's talking about?"

"Well, it certainly wasn't me. He never got me transferred to Hue." He smiled fondly. "I'll be goddamned. It gives me the shivers, hearing you read that. Mind if I have a look?"

I was about to give him the letter, then changed my mind. "I'd better not. It belongs to my mother."

"Understood," he said and sat back in his chair. The waiter passed by, and he ordered another cognac. "I wasn't in Dalat," he said. "I was in Nha Trang, which was the headquarters of II Corps. The chief he's referring to in the letter would have been one of the Vietnamese province chiefs who reported to him. Your father got there in '68, after Tet and long after the whole 'quiet American' phase was over, the star ideologues were gone, and the nation-building business had melted down. We were doing accelerated pacification, which meant getting as many of the provinces under South Vietnamese government control as possible. The Village Chief Program, we called it. It boiled down to arming the villages so they could shoot back at the communists and trying to persuade those who weren't willing to do that to change their minds. The ones who refused would fall under suspicion of being either communist sympathizers—not in itself a big problem, we could live with sympathizers—or part of the Vietcong Infrastructure, the VCI. They were the ones we were after. The military targets. We rated every village and hamlet according to how secure it was, that is, how free from Vietcong control, and trained the Vietnamese in how to manage the whole business from top to bottom so we could begin to pull out our troops. Trouble was, lots of those village chiefs were on the take, and we ended up with a program of self-perpetuating corruption that only turned the local population against the very South Vietnamese government we were trying to build up support for. But I don't need to tell you any of this. That's the whole fucking war in a nutshell. Oceans of stuff has been written on it. Pro and con, right and wrong. Read it all and decide for yourself."

The waiter put Blake's cognac on the table and took away the empty glass.

"I'm really only interested in my father's experience there."

"Ah, you want war stories."

"Not war stories, necessarily. I would like to know more about what he did while he was there. He never talked about it."

"So what makes you think I will?"

There are certain people for whom intimidation is a way of drawing people to them, of seeking affection. My father did it, and I was very young when I understood that the only way to pass the test—and it was a test—was to refuse it. I returned the letters to my backpack. "I won't take up any more of your time," I said, put ten francs on the table, and stood up.

"Sit down, goddamn it!" He picked up his cognac, swirled it, and looked meditatively into the glass. Pretentious but also somehow deflated. I sat down so that we were both looking in the direction of the lake, with our backs to the café wall. "I'm not going to talk to you about Vietnam," he said at last. "I have nothing to say about it. I'm not interested in playing the deranged veteran or the slimy spook. That stuff is all very entertaining and makes people think they understand what went on there, and good for them. I'm all for myths and movies."

The Lausanne ferry was preparing to depart and people were lining up at the dock. The waiter paused on his way inside. and Blake looked at his watch and signaled for another drink. "But Vietnam isn't what you came here to talk about, is it?"

For the third time, my answer was the same.

"So tell me." Blake leaned toward me, elbow propped on the table between us. "If your father never said anything to you, why should I?"

"My father never told me about you, either," I shot back. "But here I am."

"You've seen too many movies." He grinned.

"Will you at least confirm a few things for me? As a favor?"

"All right. Shoot."

I didn't understand why he was mocking me and decided to ignore it. He'd downed three cognacs and was already drunk.

"Was my father in the CIA?"

Without hesitation, Blake nodded.

"Was he with the CIA in Africa and India, too? Or was he really with USIA in those places?"

"That's entirely likely."

"What? That he really was career Foreign Service?"

"Yes."

"In Germany and Switzerland, too?"

"Correct."

"He was in Dalat until June 1969. With CORDS."

Blake nodded.

"You said he was also in Laos."

"Did I?"

"You told me so in Bern. At his funeral."

Blake shrugged. "I don't remember."

"When would that have been?"

"December '68. Very briefly."

I was about to continue but he held up his hand and stopped me. "Look. I'm not going to say any more, understand? I'm not trying to frustrate you. It's nothing hush-hush. I'm retired. I'm old. I live alone. Your father and I were friends. Good friends. I know it's hard to believe, but it's true. Vietnam isn't terribly important. Certainly not to me. Neither of us were very important when we were there, either. Yes. We did things. But it's water under the bridge. Read the histories, the big picture. That's important. There's a whole goddamn academic industry around it. Find out all you can. My guess is you're already doing that. You've done your homework, am I right? I'll bet you have. Well, I don't have anything to add. Neither would your father. We were a couple of young bureaucrats out there doing what young bureaucrats do. Running around and fucking things up." He leaned his back against the café wall, crossed his spidery legs. "Forget about Vietnam," he said.

I got up and left him there. I walked up the hill into the center of town. It was too early to go back to my hotel room for the night. It had been a mistake to think I'd be there for more than an afternoon. The shops were closing up. I wandered aimlessly up and down the side streets, which only added to my sense of being shut out. I began to feel stupid for leaving in a huff. I could have waited him out, let the cognac do the talking. I'd wanted to be straight with him, even to the point of being naive. Of course, ingenuousness, calculated in advance, is disingenuous, but I'd thought Blake might play straight with me out of respect for my father. I suppose in refusing to talk, he was doing just that. But there was more to his refusal. He wasn't trying to hide anything. He said it was just unimportant—which was odd, even for the sort of man who masked his regrets and disappointments with smooth unconcern.

I walked along the promenade to the big château overlooking the lake. The sun had set, and it was getting dark. Some tourists were photographing the view from the terraced walkway. Their effort was more charming than any image they would come away with. It didn't take an expert photographer to see that there was not enough light. In a funny way, it mirrored my own hapless effort, trying to achieve an imprint of something, the essence of which can never be captured. Even if Blake had cooperated, the best I could have hoped for would have been some unscripted recollections delivered in an alcoholic blur, his version of the war stories he mocked me for wanting to hear. But I wasn't after war stories. All I wanted was to triangulate a location in the confusing topography of who and where and when.

Geneva Golf Club
46°13'18.06"N
6°11'33.37"E

The ninth and eighteenth holes share the same green at the Geneva Golf Club. Just behind the green is the main clubhouse, which evokes the era in which it was built with a broad stone terrace overlooking the course. It is a great surprise for Noel to find himself playing here, two days into the conference.

Clubs and caddies are lined up and waiting when they arrive. Noel reminds himself not to be either too over- or underwhelmed. His partners for the afternoon are executives from BAE Systems, Siemens, and Telespazio. They are a worldly group, very present to themselves, relaxed and reserved in the way of men accustomed to having things done for them. In some places, this reserve might pass for thoughtfulness, but Noel recognizes it as a variation of a style carried over from the military: illusionless tough guys, steeped in the world's rigging.

Noel is pleased to be there. Before the surprise invitation, he'd toyed with the idea of renting a car to drive up to Crans-sur-Sierre, a course in the Alps where the European Masters Tournament is played. He knows it from satellite images. Some years back, he worked up a little presentation for a joint procurement seminar comparing the agency's then current high-res capabilities with the Geo-Eye 1, a commercial-use optical land satellite with a resolution of 0.41 to 1.64 meters and a fifteen-kilometer swath. The demonstration had been a big hit, and the three-dimensional fly-throughs of the ninth and the sixteenth holes (ball's-eye view) had been dubbed the "Tiger Woods video."

He is happy for the chance to play, although he feels slightly off-the-rack and can't help noticing the difference in cloth and leather. He will be using a rental set of Pings. The others had their personal clubs delivered in advance by a driver. Siemens, a barrel-chested, cigar-smoking German in a purple Bobby Jones shirt, has a set of custom clubs worth half of Noel's annual take-home and a brand-new digital range finder, the merits of which he is quietly discussing with his caddie.

Noel's cartmate is a balding, freckled Australian from BAE Systems. Noel has overheard him referred to as "Slam Man" in a conversation about the firm's development of applications for simultaneous localization and mapping (SLAM) for UAVs in GPS-denied environments. He introduced himself to Noel after the first panel: Interoperability: Toward a Single Information Space.

"It's what we're here to do, mate. Interoperate." As they head over to the first tee, Noel finds himself recalling the standard agency memo: *The propriety of attendance by DOD employees in their personal capacities at incidental social portions of this event shall be determined by the individual DOD employee's Ethics Councilor based on standards of conduct and community relations requirements.* He wonders just how incidental this event really is. Maybe everything has all been somehow rigged. Net-centricities all around. He must remain vague, not just because it is his mission but because it was the role handed to him in the car ride over when Siemens asked, "So, what's your background?" and his answer, "Technical," drew looks of appraisal.

The course has a more park-like feel than the plainer public courses he plays around Washington. It is a cloudy spring afternoon, the mountains obscured by a gauzy veil. They listen to a jumpsuited caddie crisply describe the hole and spell out the distances and approaches in French. Noel understands just barely enough to follow. A par four—with two traps at the inside bend of the right dogleg and four more surrounding the front two-thirds of the green. Last to tee off, Noel hits his drive straight up the right side of the fairway, clearing both traps at the bend and landing dead center in the fairway beyond. The others exchange nods, as if to say they are pleased he has slipped in among them.

Noel is keyed up but also strangely relaxed. He feels visited by something, scaled to the terrain, in harmony. He pars the first hole, is first off the second tee. His drive arcs high and lands with a pleasing series of long hops on the left side of the fairway just beyond the two hundred fifty–meter mark. Languidly, he stoops, plucks the tee from the grass, rolls it in his fingertips, and waits by the cart as the others tee off. Toweling his hands, he takes in the surroundings, in tune, in possession of something.

At the fifth hole, he is five strokes ahead of Siemens and can't believe what he is bringing off. Congratulations have stopped. He listens to the conversation as it ranges across topics familiar (the radar satellite TerraSAR-X launch from the Russian cosmodrome at Baikonur in Kazakhstan) and unfamiliar (a three-star restaurant in Cer-

niat that serves food made only from ingredients taken in the wild).
The casually serious tone seems appropriate to this city of trade talks
and peace accords and makes him feel even more like an interloper.
There is little substance. Just pompous self-consciousness—the way
people in art museums feel they must talk about art, or tourists at the
Pantheon are stimulated to reflect upon the ancient past.

Siemens has put away his range finder and swears loudly at a
badly topped drive off the sixth tee. Noel realizes that, without in-
tending to, he has messed up the chemistry of the game and drawn
attention to himself.

"You didn't tell us you were a scratch player, mate," Slam Man
says as they cruise down the fairway. There is an accusatory hint in
his tone. "Where do you play in D.C.?"

"Do you know Washington?"

"Five years in Potomac. Played at Congressional."

"Nice."

"Played there?"

"Nope. I play nearby, at Falls Road." He smiles, watching for a
reaction at the mention of a public course.

"Don't know that one," Slam Man says flatly and stops the cart.
They wait for Siemens to hit. Slam Man takes out his BlackBerry
and scrolls through his messages. He looks up just as Siemens slices
the ball into the rough at the upper bend of the dogleg. Noel grips
the seat handle as they speed down the fairway. The mood has turned
competitive and unpleasant. He feels suddenly exposed and vulner-
able, waits in the cart as Slam Man draws a club from the bag and
marches over to his ball with the wide-hipped gait of a man comfortable throwing his weight around. Noel can see him pressing the
flesh at Congressional Country Club, roaring around Sydney harbor,

nose daubed with white zinc, in a flashy speedboat. Motherfucker. He can't stand these industry guys. It's not envy. It's more than money and smug realpolitik patriotism. There is something brutal about their peace of mind. The bastards don't bear the burden of actually having to use the things they sell. Noel wants nothing more now than to go quietly back to DIAC, disappear into the buzzing hive of American power.

Slam Man hits his second shot with just enough whip at impact to send it high over the trees on the inside curve of the dogleg. It lands on the right of the fairway about eighty meters beyond where Noel's drive landed. A straight line to the green.

"Nice shot."

"Thanks," Slam Man mutters, wiping the dirt from the head of the club. The other cart passes by. If only Noel could hear what they are saying as well as he can smell the Monte Cristos they are smoking. Slam Man climbs behind the wheel, punches the accelerator, and drives ahead without speaking. Noel doesn't mind being silent. He's not so sure about the gristly redhead next to him, who seems one of those for whom silence is a form of aggression. He brings the cart to a stop a short distance behind the ball. Noel hops out, takes his five iron. Up ahead, the caddies have positioned themselves to the left and right of the fairway. Noel squats, sights the ball. A hundred-meter line to the green with two sets of bunkers left and right. Directly behind the green is a tall hedgerow. He can try for the green and risk landing in some Vandoeuvres tea party on the other side of the hedge, or he can drop it short and risk landing in one of the traps. He takes three practice swings, decides to go for the green, and steps up to the ball, flattens the grass with the edge of the club head. The world is all planes and surfaces. The air is still. An inner sense of the physical order among bodies and objects. Everything in precise location. Rolling lawn in the foreground, Cologny and Vandoeuvres estates in the middle, mountains in the distance, overhead a pewter sky, wispy clouds. At the top of his backswing, everything registers. The whoosh of the shaft cutting the air, the click of the ball leaping out of the sheared grass. It isn't with his eyes that he sees it soar to the top of its arc, then descend. He knows where it will land, how it will bounce. How far it will roll.

At the green, the caddies are waving and making hand signals. Noel puts the club in the bag without cleaning it and gets in the cart. The caddies race to meet them as they drive toward the green. "*Super! Incroyable!* A perfect shot!" Expressions of amazement all around. Siemens pulls up, shaking his head and rolling his cigar between his fingertips. "*Unglaublich!*" he bellows, the way one would at a clever magic trick. Telespazio, the quiet, professorial one, flashes a discreet two thumbs up. Noel's pulse races. He struggles to contain his glee.

"That was fucking unbelievable!" Slam Man says.

Noel shakes his head in modest disbelief, all too aware that he has done something he will have to answer for later. *Well undone!* An expression from the Kosovo war. After General Clarke's press-conference mea culpa showing gun-camera footage of a JDAM hit against a passenger train crossing a bridge. Now, with superior misprecision, the schoolchildren. Well undone.

Noel waits for the others to finish putting. Goodwill has suddenly broken out, gruff camaraderie. "Go ahead and call it a hole-in-fucking-one, mate. You're going to be telling your grandchildren about that one!" Slam Man claps him on the shoulder. Noel triangulates his new position, calculates how this is going to play out over the next two days, suddenly thinking of Hannah and whether Pat has heard from her yet. Will he find time to get her a present? Where should he go? Rue du Rhône? Rue de la Confédération? All too intimidating. He prefers good old Pentagon City. Or Tyson's Corner. Will he have time after the morning panel, Confirmation Bias in Remote Sensing? Then get his things and out to the airport. What about Dominique Martin from Spot Image? She seemed actually to be flirting, made him feel awkward and un-with-it.

When the hole is finished, they gather for a moment at the edge of the green. Siemens takes one of the caddies aside and dispatches him on an errand, then pats Noel on the shoulder. Important etiquette is being observed. They must remain faithful to the game, to sportsmanship in general. The spirit is collective. Noel understands they are not singling him out for admiration as much as breathing in the spirit of the event together, sharing a moment of excellence. At the edge of the green a cloth-covered table has been set up. On it, a bottle of Dom Perignon in a silver bucket and four crystal flutes lined up in a row. The caddies drive the carts away as a white-gloved waiter pops the cork and ceremoniously fills the glasses. The manager who met them at the entrance is looking on. Siemens steps up to make the toast: "Gentlemen. Our caddy has informed me that the last confirmed albatross here was hit on March 19, 1960. Today's is the third in the history of the club." He lifts his glass toward Noel. "Bravo, gentlemen. Prost!"

"Salut!"

"Cheers!"

Noel hoists his glass and sips, bemused. The manager takes a photograph. What the fuck is an albatross? Never heard of an albatross. It was a double eagle on a par five. But he keeps quiet. The haze lifts. The light is clear. Red-tiled clubhouse roof, blue lake, Alps, white tablecloth, green, green grass, pale, effervescing champagne. It all comes down on him like a butterfly net. He stands slightly apart from the others. If he could interrupt the sporty cheer flowing all around, it would be to say that he doesn't belong here, is not one of them, does not want to be. He bows his head as if listening carefully to what Slam Man is telling them of a recent adventure in Chile. In fact, he is just looking at his grass-stained shoes, present and absent at the epicenter of attention. It is the essence of his work, and the only way he knows how to be. Present and absent at any given moment. He suspects each of them feels the same way. Only partially here.

Ever, only partially here.

I wandered around Nyon for another hour, had a sandwich in a café before returning to the hotel to call Nicole. I told her about finding Blake, his strange little shack on the lake, and that he'd refused to talk to me about Vietnam.

"I'm not surprised," she said. "I wouldn't believe anything that man told me."

"He said Dad came often to see him here."

"I wouldn't call it often. Three or four times, maybe."

"When was the last time?"

She lit a cigarette. "At least two or three years ago."

"Did you ever come with him?"

"He never asked me. Anyway, I wouldn't have wanted to go. Your father knew I couldn't stand the man. He didn't like him much, either."

"So why the visits?"

There was a pause. I could see her tilting her head slightly away from the mouthpiece, exhaling a blue cloud up at the ceiling. "I don't know. To talk about old times, I suppose."

"Didn't you ever ask?"

"I didn't especially care. You know how hard it was to get your father to do anything. I was glad anytime he stopped his reading and got out of the house."

"He was getting paid to read."

"He needed exercise and fresh air. I even had to remind him to walk the dog."

It was true, if a little hard to hear from a two-packs-a-day smoker. All talk of long walks in the mountains was forgotten when he began reading for a local publisher, recommending books for translation into German. It was the perfect retirement job for him. The publisher couldn't supply him with books quickly enough. In the very first season, two of his recommendations became best-sellers in Switzerland. I wish I'd saved some of the reports he shared with me, astute and insightful with flavors of Mencken and Perelman, his heroes in wit and style. He never talked much about books and was generally put off by literary conversation, but I think of him as a serious reader, one of the few I have known for whom reading was never an escape but an expression of creative aloneness. The belly laughs! Lying on the sofa. His whole body would shake. Tears would stream from his eyes. As a child, I loved his hilarious explosions, saw that there was a connection between brains and humor, and aspired to being smart enough to find things as funny as he did when I grew up.

Nicole talked about her upcoming move to a smaller apartment.

Did I want her to keep anything for me? No. There was nothing I cared to have. She was disappointed that I wasn't coming to see her. I explained that this trip had been a last-minute thing and that from Nyon I was going on to La Corbière, an artists' residence on Lac de Neuchâtel where I had made arrangements to spend some time putting what I'd gathered into some sort of coherent form. I wanted to decompress, reflect, recover some of what had been lost in the fog. A map is what I had in mind, an annotated historical map depicting my father's career and the family peregrinations. I'd brought all the documents I'd managed to assemble in Washington—letters, assorted memorabilia, books, monographs, declassified and heavily redacted CIA documents with bold-typed titles: VIET CONG PLANS FOR THE DECEMBER PHASE OF THE WINTER–SPRING CAMPAIGN IN DALAT and VC PROCEDURES FOR DETAINING AND EXECUTING PRISONERS IN TUYEN DUC PROVINCE.

Not having foreseen how uncooperative Blake would be, I now faced the prospect of having no additional material to work with. "How frequently did Blake come to Bern?" I asked Nicole. "Do you remember anything about his visits?"

"Not much. He was usually drunk. I left the two of them to themselves."

"Did Dad ever say what they talked about?"

"Never."

"Come on. Weren't you even curious? You must have wondered why he kept turning up."

There was a pause on the line. I could hear her lighter click, another cigarette lit. Nicole and my father were married for twenty years. She and I were comfortable with one another, friends, but I wondered if she might be pulling back, retreating. "Sorry to be so pushy," I said. "I'm just trying to get some answers. It's all been very frustrating."

"And I'm sorry I can't be more help. He never told me anything about his work. He always brushed off my questions, so I stopped asking. It wasn't until after he retired that I began to get a sense of things. You know how bitter and full of resentment he was at the end. Talking about his career was the last thing either of us wanted to do."

"When did you first meet Blake?"

"Oh, a long time ago. Shortly after your father and I first met."

"Tell me about that."

"My first impression wasn't good, as you know. Of your father, either, when I look back on it. He invited me to lunch at that *beiz* in the Rathausplatz. You remember it?"

"Sure, I remember. He took me there the first time I came to visit. Right next to the fountain with the knight."

"The Vennerbrunnen. We were regulars. Seems like another life-time. Just shortly after he arrived in Bern. It was during the Iran spy business. The Schweitzerhof, that's the hotel where the negotiations were going on—the same place the hostage negotiations went on the year before. It was all secret. Of course, I had no idea. Your father would call me at the strangest times to ask if I wanted to meet him for a drink. Always at the Rathaus. You remember the picture of him in the newspaper?"

"Of course," I said. As she talked, I rummaged through the suit-case on the bed. I had the clipping. February 12, 1981, *International Herald Tribune*. It was captioned *U.S. free-lance writer Cynthia Dwyer, who was held in Iran nine months as a spy, arrived at Zurich airport Wednes-*

day on her way home after being freed. Photo shows her with a bodyguard.
The only other newspaper photograph I have of him was taken in
Nigeria with Edward R. Murrow.

Nicole continued, "I was about to give up and leave. My lunch
hour was almost over when he finally came in. And that was the first
time I saw Blake."

"You had lunch together?"

"No. I needed to get back to work. Your father said they'd been
held over in a meeting. Blake was very courtly and correct in that
artificial, old-fashioned way that only certain types of Americans
bother with anymore. He immediately ordered a bottle of champagne, insisted that I stay and have a glass. It was all show. I don't
know why I stayed. I should have said good-bye and left."

"Why didn't you?"

"Well, because I was attracted to your father. I was young, and
here was this handsome American diplomat—and not typical in any
way at all. For one thing, he was single. And his German was perfect.
That alone set him apart from all the other Americans I had met.
Also, he didn't put on airs. A quiet type. If he hadn't had the diplo-
matic plates on his car, I would never have known. It wasn't until the
third or fourth time I saw him that he said anything to me at all
about being with the embassy."

"So you did have lunch together."

"No. We didn't. I had to get back to the office. Blake kept insist-
ing that I stay. 'Have another glass of champagne, have lunch.' He
wouldn't let me leave. It made me very uncomfortable. I felt he was
doing it on purpose. Trying to humiliate me. Finally, your father
ended it by offering to walk me back to the office. On the way, he
apologized, told me Blake had turned up unexpectedly, was leaving

later that day. He called him an asshole friend. What an odd thing to say. I couldn't understand that."

"He had a lot of asshole friends."

We both laughed. I said I'd try to get to Bern before going back to Washington, but the truth was that I didn't want to go back to Bern at all.

La Patriarche de Ferney

46°15'23.68"N

6°6'34.05"E

The temperature has been falling steadily. After some fumbling with the latch, Noel manages to close the window of the room in which he has just been installed at a hotel in Ferney Voltaire, which is right next to Geneva International Airport. He'd considered going straight to the airport, getting on the next available flight, but switching hotels and waiting out the end of the conference seemed more prudent.

His room overlooks a small patio. Beyond it is a grass lawn bounded by trees and tall shrubs. The hotel feels like a place with a regular clientele. Sales reps and budget tourists. There is a tiny bar just off the lobby. Down the block are some cafés and restaurants. Voltaire's house is a five-minute walk. Maybe he'll pay it a visit. There is virtually no chance of running into anyone out here. All he can hope is that his sudden disappearance will go unnoticed.

He switches on the television set, takes off his shoes, and settles down on the bed with the remote control. The Real Madrid–FC Barcelona game is in the final fifteen minutes. Being alone isn't something he is particularly adept at, but he feels as if he both deserves and has earned it. Maybe tomorrow he'll check out Voltaire's house, visit his statue, buy a copy of *Candide* to read, do nothing until his return flight, thirty-two hours away. And he'll write a report summarizing everything he knows of current trends in geospatial imaging, photogrammetric engineering, and remote sensing, down to the specifics of multiparametric sensor fusion and integration, data smoothing, noise removal, pattern extraction—and evaluate the European firms at the forefront of the new technologies. He still doesn't quite understand why he was sent. Doesn't get the point. Maybe there is none except to keep doing what he's told to do. He had a wordless conversation with the taxi driver who brought him to the hotel. A Bosnian Muslim, he guessed, from the driver identification on the dash. Their eyes met once or twice in the rearview mirror. There was something in the way the man hauled Noel's luggage out of the trunk and set it down on the sidewalk and stood there in his cheap counterfeit designer jeans and red Adidas warm-up jacket. He accepted the tip with a modesty that verged on trauma.

Noel had erred badly on the golf course. All he'd wanted was to flow with whatever vital force had touched him out there, some sort of incubated energy spontaneously cut loose. He hadn't meant to show off, but that was what it amounted to among the alpha dogs. All he could do was go in reverse, try to avoid killing them. On the tenth tee he'd sliced his drive into the adjacent fairway intentionally, then continued through the next four holes with a string of bad shots and missed putts. When his drive from the sixteenth tee splashed down into the water hazard, Siemens flicked his cigar stub aside with undisguised contempt. Noel shrugged meekly and forced a grin. The others exchanged glances, but it was clear they agreed with the German.

"What's he pissed off about?" Noel asked as Slam Man drove up the fairway.

"He's pissed off because he thinks you're fucking with him, mate." He cut the wheel and hit the brakes a little harder than necessary pulling up to his ball.

At the end of the eighteenth hole, the German took his ball from the cup and stalked into the clubhouse without another word. The caddies took their tips and hustled away. Noel followed the others into the clubhouse bar. When the German refused to shake hands, Noel quietly asked the bartender to call him a taxi. Back at the hotel was a note from Dominique Martin. An invitation to the dinner Spot Image was hosting at the Athénée Galerie Café. "Forgive the last-minute invitation. I sincerely hope you will be able to attend and look forward to seeing you there." He went up to his room, booked another hotel on the Internet, and checked out. Absurd situations beget absurd outcomes. What else could he do? Stick around and pretend nothing had happened? Siemens was sure to be asking around: Who was that *arschloch* from Mitre?

Real Madrid scores a goal. The room has warmed up. Noel gets off the bed and goes to the window. Below, the patio lights are on but the umbrellas are down and the chairs are all stacked along the wall. He'll have a quiet breakfast there tomorrow morning if the weather cooperates. Some coffee, a croissant. He's glad to have found this place away from the push-button City Center with everything rolling around on castors. He'll even try reading the complimentary copy of the *Neue Zürcher Zeitung* that came with the room. He was almost sent to Germany at the start of his career. In spite of repeated efforts, the posting never came through. How differently would things have turned out had they gone overseas? Would he and Pat have more to reminisce about? Would Hannah now be part of the restless global youth culture striding through airports and hotels with cell phones pressed to their ears speaking six different languages? Like Dominique Martin, PR-ing away in the Antibes office, or in London, Brussels, Shanghai? He ought to have called Pat by now but still can't bring himself to pick up the phone. Should he tell her about his trip? Whoever decided to go gray on the goddamn thing in the first place? And why Mitre? An FFRDC? Whose brilliant fucking idea was that?

His watch is five minutes faster than the alarm clock on the bedside table. The game is in its final minutes, 2-1, Real Madrid. He sits on the edge of the bed, more distracted by his own presence in the room than by the game. He watches the ball passing among the players. The voice of the game announcer mingles with the sounds of hotel plumbing, footsteps in the corridor. A single rose pokes from a bud vase on top of the television set. He looks again at the clock. The Spot dinner is getting under way. He won't get to hear Dominique Martin say how happy she is to see him. She knows her business, this professional spokeswoman in her thirties; what Spot can do for Mitre and Mitre for Spot. The smooth, willfully fit senior vice president she'd certainly introduce him to will know still more about what they can do for each other. And he'll be a golfer. And ski, and sail, and paraglide. And he'll have that Antibes tan for sure, and be familiar with the miseries of flying into Heathrow, De Gaulle, Kennedy, Dulles, the horrors of congestion on I-66, the beauty of fall foliage on Skyline Drive, and the pleasure of eating blue crabs on the Eastern Shore. The briefest mention will be made of Mitre's START project, the stereo-view, relief-mapping capabilities of SPOT 5, before conversation is abruptly halted, cards exchanged, and they move separately toward the bar, where a loud, sunburned German will be describing an amazing albatross made out at the Golf Club that afternoon by an American who was obviously a spook.

Uninterested in the game and still less interested in the prospect of staying locked in the room for the rest of the evening, he decides to go downstairs to the bar. He'll have a beer, stroll to the restaurant, have dinner, then come back and go to sleep watching CNN.

"Ouvert?" Noel asks the woman at the front desk, pointing toward the bar.

"Oui." She smiles. "What can I get you?"

"You're English!" he says, surprised.

"Yes, that's right."

It isn't much of a bar, just a dark room with a few tables and a counter with five or six stools. "I'll have a beer. *Une pression.*" Noel pronounces, pointing to the tap. "You double as a bartender?"

"Not usually. Our man is late tonight for some reason." She sets the glass on a coaster and looks at the clock on the wall. "He'll be in any minute. I'll be out there if you need anything." She points to the front desk.

The empty bar is unnerving. He drinks quickly, conscious of the pathetic figure he cuts sitting there all alone. Was it wrong to run away and hide? Okay, then. Right. He'll deliver a full report, complete with tables and indices. He glances at his watch. Lunchtime is just ending in Washington. If Pat isn't eating at her desk, which she does to avoid the hospital cafeteria fare, she's out race-walking along the Custis Trail. She took up race-walking to lose weight, is training for a ten-kilometer across the Chesapeake Bay Bridge. When he tells her about his albatross, she'll react to the silliness of the term the way he responds to the comedy of race-walking. Another thing you have to do to appreciate.

On his way through the lobby, he asks the woman at the desk to recommend a restaurant. She suggests a place just down the street. "It's quite good for pizza, that kind of thing." She pronounces it *pitza*, and that is just what Noel orders—*quatro staggioni*—and eats American-style, with his fingers, not with knife and fork, recalling as he finishes the peculiar way the German turned away and refused to shake hands. His dainty petulance now seems as stupid and miscarried as Noel's bungled bungling.

Back at the hotel, the barman is at his post, but the Englishwoman is no longer at the front desk. Noel hesitates, then goes in for one last drink. There are customers now. Music is playing. Noel takes the same seat as before. *"Une pression,"* he tells the bartender. At the other end of the bar, a woman is busy with her iPhone. Smoke curls from a cigarette in the ashtray at her elbow. The bartender sets Noel's beer down.

"Merci."

"You are American," the woman says.

Noel turns to her. "Yes, I am."

She sets her phone on the counter, takes the cigarette from the ashtray, and puffs. She is probably younger than the business suit makes her look. A flight attendant, perhaps. Noel worries for a moment that she is from the conference.

"I like your country. But I hate your president," she says.

Noel appraises her for a moment, then says flatly, "Well you're going to have to hate me, too, because I work for him." He looks away. A Dutch couple is having a serious conversation at a table in the rear of the room. The logic of the situation would seem to call for him to pay and leave without another word. But too many seconds have ticked by, and Noel can feel his nerve beginning to fail. The woman says something in French to the bartender. The man takes a bottle of cognac from the top shelf, pours, and sets a glass down in front of each. The woman raises hers and says, "An end to hatred." She keeps her glass raised. "It was not my intention to offend you," she says. "My apologies."

"You're Swiss."

"Not Swiss. From Slovakia."

"I wouldn't have known. Another thing to hate about Americans. We don't know languages."

She lights another cigarette. "I think if you go to Pittsburgh in Pennsylvania, you can hear Slovak in the street. At one time there were more Slovaks in Pittsburgh than any place besides Bratislava. You've been there?"

Noel shakes his head, takes another sip of cognac.

"It is very famous in my country. Every child learns about the Pittsburgh Agreement."

"Pittsburgh Agreement?"

"It is like your Declaration of Independence. Signed by Tomas Masaryk in 1918. It created the state of Czechoslovakia."

"I'll be damned." Noel chuckles, in part to hide his embarrassment, in part because he finds her attractive and wants to keep the conversation going. Her phone erupts in a swirl of electronic tones. Her French sounds completely native to him. He checks his watch, finishes his beer. He should go back to his room. In an hour Pat will be home. He'll call her. He should have two days ago.

The woman puts the phone down.

"Traveling on business?" Noel asks.

"I am a businesswoman, yes."

Noel pretends not to notice the eavesdropping bartender. "What kind of business?"

"Hospitality business."

Noel takes a moment to register.

"You seem surprised."

"Well, what can I say?"

"It's quite legal. I pay taxes." She takes a card from her handbag. "My license and health certificate. Excuse the terrible picture." She offers it to Noel. "As you can see. All up-to-date. Also, I take Visa."

He waves them off. "I believe you," he says.

She takes a business card from her handbag, offers it.

"Doctor of Erosophy?"

She smiles.

Noel wishes he had a clever response but lacks the urbane flounce necessary for such a conversation. The closest he can come to taking it in stride is to be as frank and direct with her as she has been with him. He gives back the card. "Sorry, but I'm not interested," he says awkwardly. "No offense." He lifts the glass, half turning to her but looking at the golden dot of reflected light in his glass, afraid of making himself look stupid. He gestures to the bartender for the check and tosses back the cognac. "Thanks for the drink."

"What do you do for your president?" the woman asks.

"Pardon me?"

"You said you work for the president. What do you do?"

Noel takes a bill from his wallet, slides it across the counter to the bartender. "I'm his literary adviser," he says.

She laughs. There is a spark in her eyes.

The bartender returns with change. Noel leaves the money on the counter. "Well, actually, I'm not the only one," he adds. "I'm in the agency that handles the Romantic era. The Wordsworth division, to be exact." He feels overtaken by a suave virtuosity, an alternate nature asserting itself. Another albatross? He presses against the counter with the splayed fingertips of both hands, stalled in the effort of departure, ambivalent. He can see himself in the mirror behind the bar, and the woman, too, a brighter spark. Suited up for business. Polite, refined, discreet, with a portfolio of regular clients, an Audi, a well-furnished apartment with a retractable awning over the balcony, a view of the lake, a cat, a bird in a cage. She is more than pretty; she is beautiful in the way that hides in-woven suffering. A real person, unashamed of what she must do.

The Dutch couple have paid their bill and gone. Minutes later, Noel has moved down the bar and taken the seat next to her. He gestures to the bartender, stirring a circle in the air with his index finger. *"Encore de cognac,"* he says.

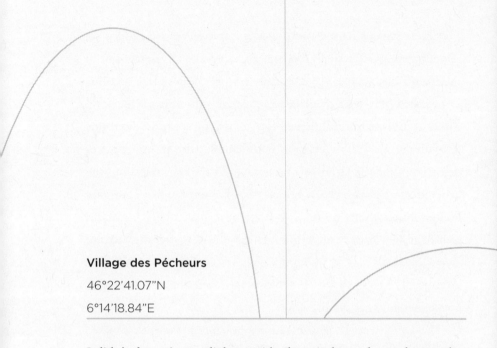

Village des Pécheurs
46°22'41.07"N
6°14'18.84"E

I didn't sleep. A streetlight outside the window, a loose shutter, the intermittent clicking of a dog's nails on bare floor were the background of my wandering thoughts. In 1884, a conference was held in Washington for the purpose of fixing a Prime Meridian and a Universal Day. The conference proceedings, which I had recently read, became a spiderweb in which far-fetched ideas about mapping and the keeping of secrets became caught, struggled for a time, and expired. Wonderful, the associations the drowsy brain can come up with. At one point I took out my notebook and tried to put into sentences some of what was racing through my head: *A secret is a negative space in a life that must mirror the negative space that opens up in the soul of one who keeps it. Secrets date and become old the way people do. A secret is not a fact but only the deteriorating condition for its own keeping.*

The nocturnal ramblings seemed less coherent when I reread them in the morning. It was shortly after seven o'clock when I left the hotel. I had coffee and a croissant in the café at the train station

The platform was packed with commuters. It was nice being part of the morning flux. After all the sleepless cerebration, it was reassuring just to watch schoolkids and office workers coming and going on the trains. I bought a newspaper and ordered a second coffee. Public transportation is often cited as one of the main differences between life in Europe and America. I would refine it further. It is the presence of backpack-toting schoolchildren on public transportation that makes the difference. My friend Werner told me that one of the images he carries in his head of America is a yellow International Harvester school bus. In the early 1970s, he and a group of musician friends managed to buy one that was being surplused at a U.S. Army base someplace near Munich. They drove it all the way to India, giving impromptu concerts along the way. The only problem they encountered during the yearlong trip happened in Iran, where they were jailed for several days and interrogated by SAVAK, the shah's notorious secret police. After failing to extract money, they made them play a concert for local youth on a soccer field behind the jail.

When rush hour ended, I was still in the café, a day ahead of myself and not in any particular hurry to get to La Corbière. Haste was antithetical to the whole philosophy of the place, summed up in its motto, *Jour par Jour*, a project dedicated to artistic living that brought together people from a diversity of nationalities, callings, and disciplines: musicians, painters, filmmakers, circus performers, cooks, poets, and gardeners. Werner, of the bus journey, and his Japanese wife, Ayako, were cofounders of the project and lived on the grounds of the estate in a circus trailer heated by a wood stove. I was attracted by the freewheeling artistic lifestyle and felt comfortable, if self-consciously American, in what was generally a very friendly milieu. My subject matter could not have been more removed in time, place, and sensibility. I was a little wary of the prospect of discussing it in too much detail.

Now, since Blake had said essentially nothing to me, I wouldn't have to.

With half an hour until the next train, I left the café. There was a *boulangerie* across the street from the station. I went in to buy a sandwich to eat on the train. It was a modest little shop with a bell on the door and doilies, bread-laden shelves, glass cases filled with pastries and sandwiches, and two little cream-colored tables in the rear. A matronly woman with a singsong voice and a starched apron waited on me, but I was distracted by a painting hanging on the wall behind her. I recognized it, a French landscape, an identical copy of which was still hanging in my father's apartment in Bern.

Ten minutes later, I was knocking on Blake's door. When there was no answer, I went around and knocked on a window at the side of the house. Finally, I heard an angry "All right, goddamn it!" He came to the door in his robe and slippers. "Oh, it's you," he grumbled, rubbing the stubble on his cheek. I began to apologize, but he cut me off. "Come in," he said. "I've been expecting you."

Inside was an artist's studio, well lit, dominated by a paint-crusted easel, shelves of pigments, brushes, and solvents. A large light table took up the center of the room, partitioned by a set of low bookshelves and a musty reading chair. Along the back wall was a cluttered kitchen counter and cabinets. Blake excused himself and went into the next room to get dressed. The canvas on the easel was painted in patches of dark and light hues. An underpainting, I guessed. On the light table was a large transparency. I stepped over for a look as Blake emerged from the bedroom.

"Dürer. *Self-portrait at Twenty-eight.*" He switched on the light table. I'd never seen a painting so finely photographed. The rich tones and subtle hues, even the brushstrokes. The transparency was nearly the same size as the canvas on the easel. "You're a copyist," I said.

"You could say that, I suppose." He switched off the light. "I like to think of it as being apprenticed to the masters."

"The painting in the *boulangerie* across from the train station, you did that, didn't you?"

"Well, yes," he said, surprised. "That's right." He padded across the room. "Would you like some coffee? I make a passable café au lait."

"I saw it just as I was about to catch the train."

He filled a kettle at the sink, set it on a two-burner cooker, and turned the burner on. "Propane," he said. "You wouldn't believe what it took for me to be allowed to have a propane stove down here."

"Do you do it for a living?"

"Do what?"

"Copy paintings."

"Not sure how to answer that. If you mean money, yes. As far as satisfying the Muses, well, that's a different story."

I watched as he carefully measured out the coffee, then filled a saucepan with milk and set it on the burner next to the steaming kettle. His hands shook, but only slightly. Uncombed and unshaven, he cut a completely different figure from the man I'd left at the café the day before. He took a wire whisk from a drawer and, after beating the milk into a frothy foam, poured it into the coffee. We drank from large white bowls at a small table. A window, curtains parted tidily and a box of geraniums hanging outside, looked directly onto the footpath. Just a few steps beyond, the dock was piled with fishing traps. Sailboats, the lake and mountains. It all created a feeling of openness to the elements. We sipped our coffee. People passed by—

close enough for us to hear their conversations. Blake seemed content to say nothing. He was savoring the start of the day. I wondered how long the sobriety lasted and when he did his painting. I could feel, in spite of his deep and obvious degeneration, that the little cottage-studio was an effort to hold on to something. I don't know what to call it, exactly, but it was on display, something unoriginal and also entirely unique. I wondered what was painted on the canvases turned to the wall. Da Vincis? Van Goghs? More Barbizon landscapes?

"Were you really expecting me?" I asked.

"Yes." He drew his chair up closer to the table.

"If I hadn't gone into that *boulangerie*, I'd be on a train now."

He smiled, looked out the window. "Okay. How about hoping? Does that satisfy you?"

I regretted my remark and blushed.

"Your father always said you were a blunt little bastard."

"He did?"

"Annoying as hell," Blake shook his head and sipped his coffee.

I couldn't think of anything to say. Thrust and parry seemed to be the only mode of conversation possible between us. This giving and taking of offense was not what I'd intended, but it seemed unavoidable.

"So then, what is it that brings you back? The painting you saw?"

"Partly."

"It was a gift to Madame Juliet. I buy all my bread and baked goods from her. She takes nice care of me."

"You gave one to my father, too."

"It's a marvelous painting, don't you think? Daubigny. A favorite, one of my more successful efforts." He regarded me for a moment, then stood up and fetched the saucepan from the stove. "Is that what you came to talk about?" He divided the remaining milk into the bowls.

"Not really."

"So why did you come back?" He sat down and looked at me with an earnestness he had not shown before.

I could only repeat what I'd said the day before. "I want to know when my father joined the CIA and what he did in Vietnam."

He drank the rest of his coffee, then stood up. I remained sitting as he cleared the cups and saucepan from the table. "Do you know Bettina Lüneberg?" he asked.

I shook my head. "No. I don't."

"Have you ever heard the name?"

I shook my head again. "No."

He began stacking dirty dishes in the sink.

"Well?" I called over the clattering. "Who is she?"

"Your half-sister," Blake said and turned on the faucet.

part two

Only when I'm disguised am
I really myself. And around
me all unknown sunsets, as
they die, gild the landscapes
I shall never see.

—Fernando Pessoa

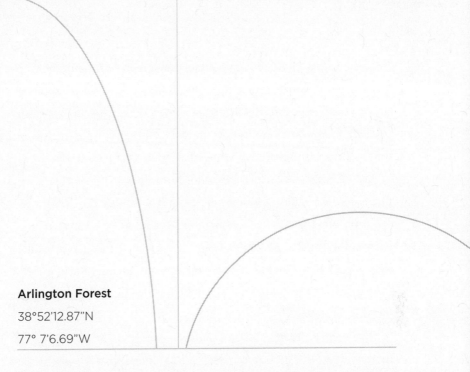

Arlington Forest

38°52'12.87"N

77° 7'6.69"W

On transatlantic flights, he likes to sit with a view toward the pole. Westbound, this means being on the right side of the aircraft, preferably in front of the wing. At forty thousand feet, the curvature of the Earth is visible on the horizon. The wakes of ships and tankers stand out in clear relief, long Vs etched onto the ocean surface. Land and ice and water form and re-form to create an infinitely changing coastline that finally resolves itself into North America over Iqaluit, Nunavut, over Kuujjuaq and Northern Quebec, skirting the far western boundary of Newfoundland Labrador; then, in little more than a few hours, into the populated quilt that becomes the eastern United States. The descent begins over southeastern Pennsylvania, passes over the easternmost Blue Ridge Mountains of western Maryland, crosses northern Virginia, and finally, in a puff of burned rubber, drops onto the runway at Dulles International Airport.

These changes in scale are exhilarating and have mathematical as well as psychological dimensions. The mathematical changes are easily plotted. As a game, he enjoys calculating distances to both the true and the visible horizon from his window seat. The human implications, what is stirred in the heart, are more problematic. Seeing from on high dazzles but also misleads, and his confusion on landing has as much to do with where he has been as with what he has done.

It is a muggy late-April afternoon, and he is starving. He's gone nearly two days with nothing but water. The shuttle trawls through the economy parking lot, a woman's automatized voice announcing each color-coded, numbered stop. He's worried that he won't be strong enough to lift his suitcase off the bus, dreams about a fully loaded double cheeseburger and large fries. The image keeps floating into his thoughts.

He hadn't planned to go without eating. The circumstances merely evolved. The idea of fasting had the appeal of a penance he could impose on himself while contemplating his various predicaments. So he didn't eat. He didn't go to see Voltaire's house or buy a copy of *Candide* to read, either. All he did was work on his report. At some point, he began to fantasize about entering a Carthusian monastery. The Chartreuse de La Valsainte was just a hundred kilometers away in a secluded alpine village called Cherniat. He peeked down on it using Google Earth. Carthusian architecture is plainly visible from space.

His phone, which he'd left in the car, is dead, and the battery charger he always keeps in the glove compartment is missing. This is bad. It means arriving home without a single call, not even to say he's landed safely and is on the way and should he pick anything up? The dead phone replaces the double cheeseburger as the focal point of his thoughts—and guilt, the hunger in the pit of his stomach. The steering wheel feels enormous in his hands; the span of the windshield and the hood, vast; the driver's seat, plush and cavernous; the glass office buildings along the Dulles corridor, monstrous, false, and unwholesome. He puts on the radio, but the chattering show hosts, the soft-drink advertisements, even the Beatles' "I Am the Walrus," sound foreign and unfamiliar. He isn't frightened. He isn't even hungry anymore. Just hollow and in a hurry.

He pulls into the driveway and sits for a time looking at the house. It seems important to sit quietly and recall their first married summer there, the long, hot evenings drinking beer and talking about the future on the louvered-glass side porch. The white oak that once stood next to it had to be taken down ten years ago. It shaded and cooled the house during the day, hummed with cicadas at night. The dogwood that replaced it blooms pink every spring and looks lovely but doesn't cool. Central air conditioning was installed shortly after the oak tree came down. In the early '90s the porch was enclosed to make the library/den where he and Pat watch television at night.

It would be tempting to say those were simpler times. But that would be wrong. There isn't much difference between then and now. He still drives forty minutes to and from work. Except for Starbucks and a new Thai restaurant, the local shopping center still features the same dry cleaner, ABC Liquor, and Giant Food. The trash is still picked up twice weekly, except that now the county recycles and everything is lifted pneumatically into the back of a truck instead of hauled off in large burlap sheets by graying black men in tattered overalls. Although cable television is ubiquitous, the local broadcast stations are still numbered 4, 5, 7, 9, 20 and 26, and satellite dishes have replaced telephone poles as the most conspicuous communication infrastructure. The names of the bank and phone company have changed, but the account and phone numbers have remained the same for twenty-five years. The neighborhood still feels asymptoti-cally empty.

After a while, Pat comes tiptoeing down the flagstone path in stocking feet. "What are you doing?" she asks. He unbuckles his seat-belt and opens the door. All he wants is to take her in his arms, hug her tightly, go inside, pop open a beer, and catch up on what has hap-pened on the home front, all the ups and downs, every detail, then go upstairs and, with bags half unpacked and gifts bestowed, tumble onto the unmade bed together, and fall soundly to sleep. The tele-phone rings. "I've got to get that," she says and hurries back inside the house.

He drags his bags from the back of the Navigator, astounded by how heavy they feel, how weak he is, yet fizzing with alertness. He is still unsure what to say to her, what to tell and what not to tell. A horn sounds. "Welcome back!" Steve Kritsick calls to him, then speeds off with a wave. When he drops his bags inside the front door, all his ferment and anticipation collapse into the murmur of Pat talk-ing on the telephone in the kitchen.

He carries his suitcase upstairs to the bedroom and flops down on the bed. Pat's voice is clearly audible from downstairs. The con-versation is friendly, intimate. Maybe she's enjoyed her week alone. It's all he can hope for: to have not been missed, or in any way remiss, and thereby not obliged to make excuses, ask forgiveness, or confess things.

"Do people often tell you their secrets?" he'd asked back in the hotel room.

"That's all I ever hear," she'd said.

The moment seemed to call for it, but by asking, he had ruined whatever chances they may have had to make the encounter unique.

He sensed she was also disappointed. The room was dark except for the glow of the television, on which an old French film was showing. She undressed in front of it and then undressed him as he lay on the bed, beginning with his shoes and working her way up. Last to come off was his shirt, which she carefully hung on the back of a chair. It was so deliberate and precise. He couldn't help but smile, seeing in the protocol a whole cargo of implications, the clientele she served and was a product of herself. There was tenderness in her efficiency. Or maybe it was efficient tenderness. He was quickly aroused, but all the cognac prolonged things to the point that he considered giving up. She showed no signs of impatience, and he thanked her for that afterward, then made his first confession, which was that he'd never been unfaithful to his wife before. She was sitting on the edge of the bed, fastening her brassiere. "All the faithful men I've led astray," she said over her shoulder.

The sarcasm stung. He felt foolish. "It's true." It suddenly became crucial that she believe everything he said to her. "What I said in the bar is also true. I really do work for the president of the United States."

"Yes. The Romantic Division," she said.

"Would you like to know what I do?"

She didn't answer and continued dressing. He covered himself with the bedsheet, embarrassed but also feeling a twinge of desire. "I'm a part of a covert operations cell that tracks and captures or kills suspected terrorists around the world. We are part of the Joint Functional Component Command for Intelligence, Surveillance, and Reconnaissance and work out of the Defense Intelligence Analysis Center at Bolling Air Force Base." It came out just that easily. He shuddered with the blissful delight of transgression. "Not even my wife knows that." He sat up, not caring how foolish or deranged or pathetic a figure he cut. It wasn't empty pomp. He wanted her to understand the significance of the moment. Two major infidelities in a single night—adultery and a class-one felony he could go to jail for.

"You're a real James Bond." She smiled.

He rose from the bed, took one of the brochures from the briefcase—a technical sheet describing an Eads/Astrium satellite. It was silly to think of it as any kind of proof, but he was determined to make her believe him. She glanced at it in the blue light of the television, then handed it back. For the first time, she seemed uncomfortable. He put the brochure away, returned to the bed, and pulled the sheet up. "How much will it cost for you to stay all night?"

"I am not available all night," she said.

"Then for another hour."

The movie had ended, and the room darkened as the credits ran on the screen. He switched on the bedside light.

"The charge is the same as before," she said. "But only if you promise no more secrets."

"I have no more secrets to tell."

He pulled her onto the bed. This time the light stayed on. There was no choreographed undressing or artful folding of clothes. She seemed to respond differently as well, returning his gaze, then afterward gently stroking his arm. "Do you mind if I smoke?" she asked.

"I would love you to smoke." He jumped up to fetch her an ashtray and lay there watching her smoke, immensely happy. He tried to imagine what it would be like to have her as a mistress, a confidante, or even just a friend. Would he leave Pat for a midlife love affair? Divorce and remarry? "Why don't you like hearing people's secrets?"

"I am people's secrets," she said.

The weariness in her voice was heartbreaking. For a moment, he was afraid she was going to get up and leave. "Do you have . . . ?" He stopped himself.

"Do I have what?"

"A family?"

She took a long drag from her cigarette, blew the smoke at the ceiling, and shook her head. "No. No family."

An awkward silence followed. There was simply nothing left to say. She finished her cigarette, then went into the bathroom. He counted out and left the cash on the dresser. Handing it over would have been too uncomfortable. She spotted the money right away when she came out of the bathroom and put it into her handbag without counting. He was grateful for that little gesture of trust and asked if he could have one of her cards. She made him wait until she was completely dressed, then handed it to him with a businesslike flourish.

"Dora. As in Dorothea?"

"No, as in Pandora."

"Is that your real name?"

"No, my professional name."

"May I ask your real name?"

"Sorry. That's my secret." She blew him a kiss and left.

"Noel?"

He opens his eyes. Pat is standing at the foot of the bed, wearing a red warm-up jacket and black spandex pants that accentuate the contours of her hips and thighs. She's done something to her hair, streaked and lightened it. Her eyes seem bluer.

He sits up, disoriented but alert.

"I'm going to the gym. We'll eat when I get back." The way it comes out all packed together tells him right away she is holding something back.

"Have you heard from Hannah?"

"We'll talk about it when I get back," she says and leaves the room. He sits up and listens as she skips downstairs, jingles her car keys, slams the front door. He watches from the window as she drives away.

The dogwood and the azaleas are all in full bloom. Knots of fresh new grass have sprouted in the yard. All through the neighborhood, the trees are tinted with spring. He takes off his wristwatch and adjusts it to local time, then goes into the backyard to look at the tulip beds he planted last September. The blossoms—red, yellow, white, purple—are beyond their peak, exploded heads sagging on weakened stems, finished and fully discharged of purpose.

Yverdon les-Bains

46°46'53.25"N

6°38'26.94"E

Changing trains in Yverdon les-Bains, I went onto the station café to get a cup of coffee. A brochure on the counter caught my attention. *L'Expo qui rend fou*, an exhibition of unspeakable things at the Maison d'Ailleurs, a museum of science fiction, utopia, and extraordinary journeys. The train to Estavayer le-Lac was not due for half an hour. I ordered a coffee and stood at the counter to read the brochure, which described an exhibit of "things better left unspoken" inspired by H. P. Lovecraft's *Commonplace Book*.

I was a day late getting to La Corbière, having stayed another afternoon in Nyon to drink cognac with Blake at his favorite café. It wasn't time lost. Such afternoons are never lost. They leave their watermarks in unretractable barings of soul. Blake had certainly shared such occasions with my father, had sat with him late into the night at tables strewn with bottles, overflowing ashtrays, and delusions of significance that lingered for only as long as the next morning's hangover. Bleary-eyed good times.

We left the house toward noon and followed the same path along the lakeshore. It felt different this time, like strolling with an elderly uncle. Blake seemed happy to play the part. The suspicion and guardedness of the previous day had dissolved. Locking the front door of the cottage, he dropped the keys into his blazer pocket, turned to me, and said, "Maybe he wanted it to happen this way. Makes a certain sense, doesn't it?"

"'Sense' isn't the word I'd use."

The lake was calm, the surface glassy. We walked without talking. I stopped at one point, having forgotten my tape recorder. "Want to run back for it?" Blake reached for his keys. "I'll wait here." I took the keys, then changed my mind and handed them back.

I watched a flock of sparrows pecking at crumbs on the station platform and finished my coffee. My questions to Blake were like little crumbs. I'd pecked here, pecked there, but the pile only grew bigger, more daunting, with each crumb I took. My first question— does my mother know?—could have gone unasked. I knew the answer and would gladly have exchanged it for a blank spot. What about Nicole? There was the briefest urge to get on the telephone. Break the sensational news. Sit down, you won't believe this. But this wasn't news to telephone and pass along. It wasn't even news but more like something given clandestinely, slipped in among matters at hand.

The train slid into the station. I didn't notice until moments before departure and ran from the café with all my gear, made it onto the train just as the doors were closing. I found a rearward-facing window seat. Gauzy afternoon sunlight filtered through the tinted glass. The muted greens and browns of empty fields and pasture rolled by and disappeared in the distance.

"Before he came to the U.S., your grandfather worked for the Reichsbahn in Berlin," Blake had explained. "The German railroad. The OSS interviewed him in New York. July of 1943. They were compiling lists of German refugees who had worked for and were familiar with the German railroads, identifying those who were implicated with Nazi politics and ought to be eliminated after the war. Your grandfather worked in the Reichsbahnrat, the legal office, until 1935, when he was fired for being a Jew. He arrived in the U.S. in 1938. At the time of the interview, he couldn't have known that his own parents had been transported and had died in Theresienstadt earlier that very year. He found out after the war. Many former Reichsbahn bureaucrats were recruited and sent back to Germany to work in denazification. Your grandfather refused, for understandable reasons."

It had come out as if it were all just yesterday's news.

"Did you know my grandfather?"

Blake shook his head. "Never met him."

"He never talked about Germany or his life before the war."

"It's all in the transcripts. He describes things pretty clearly and in detail. Anyway, that's what brought me to your father. His name came up on a list." Blake put his nose into the cognac snifter and took an appreciative sip.

"What kind of list?"

"A list of U.S. Foreign Service officers born in Germany."

"Did he know he was on a list?"

"Everyone is on some sort of list at one time or another."

We settled into our chairs, the same place as on the previous day. Again, Blake had immediately been brought his coffee and cognac, exchanged pleasantries with the waiter. I was hungry and asked for a glass of beer and a *croque monsieur*. The day before, I'd been unable to imagine my father and Blake ever sitting in a café together. Now I had the sense of following footsteps. I took out my notebook and retractable pencil, set them down on the table. "Can I get a copy of the interview?"

"I would think so. Most OSS stuff was being declassified in the early 1990s, when I retired."

I jotted this down, a little self-consciously. The note-taking seemed to amuse Blake, who paused to let me catch up.

"Where did you first meet my father?"

"In Vietnam. Dalat, a town in the central highlands."

"You said it was Laos."

"Did I?"

"I remember distinctly. You said you met in Laos."

"I was in Laos briefly. Not with him. With Ted Shackley. That's probably it. Shackley was working on the lists before he came to Laos from Berlin. Anyway, I'll never forget meeting your father. He invited me out with his entire office staff to have lunch at the zoo. Horribly depressing place, emaciated animals, the whole thing. Nothing like the Saigon zoo, which was magnificent in its day. Anyway, they had venison on the menu. God knows what it really was— wildebeest or water buffalo or something. Your father said he'd eaten there, which turned out to be a complete lie. We all had the shits for three days afterward. Everyone called in sick. He joked that he'd planned the whole thing. The next day I found him relaxing down at the BOQ, the bachelor officers' quarters, reading a John Barth novel. *The Sot-Weed Factor.* I remember because he was laughing hysterically and gave it to me afterward. It's still one of my favorite books. Your father always liked to brag that he discovered John Barth before any of the rest of us. We had a good afternoon together. He described what it felt like to be crapping around in a job that had no chance of success, overstaffed and overtasked with a big red target painted across his ass." Blake laughed, reminiscing fondly. "Right from the start, I knew we were going to be friends. He was very much his own man. Never forget what he said when I asked how things were going. He said rooting out VC in Vietnam was like trying to root out Republicans in the South. They're everywhere."

"Did you go there looking for him?"

"To the BOQ?"

"No. To Vietnam."

Blake forced a smile. "Not exactly, no. But I knew who he was before meeting him. In those days, you kept mental track of people. Things were smaller, more personal, tightly knit. People knew one another, or at least knew of one another, generally. I'd been in Berlin working on the Runge case and was looking for native speakers to bring to Germany."

"Runge case?"

"Evgeny Evgenievitch 'Max' Runge—a KGB colonel who came over to us at Berlin Base in October '67. A big deal. He'd been living in West Germany from the mid-1950s, was giving us the names of KGB illegals living all over West Germany. A major defection. Read up on it. Anyway, there were all these young Foreign Service officers over in Vietnam working as provincial advisers, doing their one-year tour in CORDS. It made sense to get to know some of them, see who might be useful later on down the road."

"Useful how?"

"Lots of ways. We were working hard to get Bonn to go public with support for the war—and looking to send German-born case officers to help."

"So you recruited him?"

Blake shook his head. "It's more complicated than that."

I regretted not having brought the tape recorder and proposed running back to fetch it, but this time Blake would have none of it.

"I don't want to miss any details."

"Fuck the details!" Blake said. "I'm just giving you a little background."

I pushed the notebook aside and took a bite of the rapidly congealing *croque monsieur*. "Why didn't you tell me any of this yesterday?"

Blake smiled wryly but said nothing. I didn't press him, recognized the pattern of silence and disclosure, the bureaucrat compensating for his insignificance by withholding. But knowing this didn't help me wrest from Blake any more than Blake was in the mood to tell. He swilled his cognac just as he had the day before, waved greetings to the occasional passerby, and digressed with pompous little asides. Flemish painting technique. The efficient use of time. Cola de Renzo, the fourteenth-century leader of a popular rebellion in Rome, tried by the papal court in Avignon and an object of fascination to Blake for obscure reasons. Just as I began to lose patience, Blake said, "Anyway, we knew all about your mother's drinking problem. And that the marriage was headed for the rocks."

It caught me completely off guard.

"Don't worry, my boy," Blake went on airily. "I'm not being critical. I've lived way too long in my own glass house to take up stone-throwing. Consider it a mark of character. Drinking and divorce are an occupational hazard. Practically to be expected. But when your parents split up in Düsseldorf, nobody could have predicted that your mother would refuse to leave the country, that she'd dig in and insist on staying in the house until the tour was over."

"That was because of me," I said hotly, feeling somehow implicated, intruded upon. "I wanted to graduate from high school, not leave in the middle of my senior year. She stayed in the house on my account."

"Well, as it happened. the timing couldn't have been better." Blake stopped himself. "I'm sorry." He leaned forward and gripped my forearm. "We can stop now if you like."

"No," I said, withdrawing my arm. "Go on."

Blake looked at his watch. "It's back to lists again," he said. "Not just ours. Your father was on an East German list, too. The Stasi were fantastic list-keepers, and particularly interested in tracking émigrés, especially those who'd fled with their parents right before the war. They were interested in your father from the day he arrived in Düsseldorf."

"Did you know that? Is that why he was sent there?"

"Are those two separate questions?" Blake flashed one of his superior smiles. "No association with an intelligence agency is ever forgotten. It can be revived and revisited anytime, no matter how unfortunate the circumstances."

The waiter delivered another cognac to the table, took away the empty glasses. "Aren't you going to eat anything?" I asked.

"I don't eat during the day," Blake said.

I considered breaking off before things started going downhill. My bags were at Blake's, which meant walking home with him—or at this rate, escorting him back, then having to decide whether to catch the next train out. Blake had already offered his sofa for the night.

"Your father was in Düsseldorf when I caught up with him again. You were supposed to move to Beirut. Then to Tel Aviv, but the Yom Kippur War broke out, so you ended up in Düsseldorf. The posting had more to do with bureaucratic screwing around than anything else. 'Restructuring,' it was called. Regrouping along functional lines, or some such bullshit."

"You didn't know he was being sent there?"

Blake laughed. "I didn't even know he was there until the station chief in Bonn called me in to discuss what we ought to do! Your father was running around town with the arts editor of a fashion magazine—who also happened to be an East German intelligence agent. One of the illegals Runge had given us, as a matter of fact. She'd been around for a while, not a conspicuous presence but well connected."

"Ursula," I said.

"You knew her?"

"I met her once. When they started living together. I wasn't very friendly."

Blake took this in with a look of slight regret. I excused myself and went into the café to find the bathroom. I wasn't sure how much more I wanted to hear. What had happened was clear enough. I stood at the sink and splashed a little water on my face, glanced in the mirror. The airless, bottomless past. Thursdays were the worst. Every Thursday we drove down Cecilienallee to the consulate. My mother would wait in the car while I went up to the office to get the envelope with our cash for the week. The windows of his office overlooked the rear parking lot. You could see her waiting down there in the blue Peugeot 504 station wagon. The family car. Frau Schiffman, his secretary, always greeted me with a mildly pitying smile. I'd go into the office, close the door, go through the *what's new, how's school.* But it was clear to both of us that there was nothing to catch up on, nothing to say. Then he'd hand over the envelope, and that was all I'd see of him until the following week. If there had been ATM machines back then, we wouldn't have seen each other at all.

Back outside, Blake was reading a newspaper, chair turned to the side, legs casually crossed. I sat down, let Blake continue his perusal of the pages, then after a few moments asked, "Did he know what he was doing?"

Blake folded and put the paper aside. "Good question." He was drunk but still in possession of himself and wanted to demonstrate as much. "I suppose it depends on how you view it. Does someone having an affair ever really know what he's doing?"

"I mean did he know that she was a spy?"

"Not at first." He fidgeted for a moment, as if focusing. "She approached him—I should say, they met—in connection with an art exhibit at the Düsseldorf Kunsthalle that your father organized. Part of the bicentennial. The Hudson and the Rhein. A fantastic show. Paintings from all the major U.S. and German museums. World class."

"The CIA organized art exhibits?"

"No. USIS did. Anyway. She was covering the show for her magazine. They ran a feature story on it. That's when they began seeing each other. It went on for a while before anyone found out." Blake paused. "On our side, that is. We only found out what was going on when a guy at the Bundesamt für Verfassungsschutz, the West German counterintelligence outfit, tipped off our station chief in Bonn."

I watched him sip his drink, feeling some of the chill of the first encounter. "How did my father find out?"

"That he was being romanced by an East German professional?" Blake gave one of his worldly smirks. "As a matter of fact, I was the one who told him."

"When?"

"Well, let's just say much later than he would have preferred."

DIAC
38°50'56.78"N
77° 0'40.34"W

The sun has just set when Pat returns from the gym. He is in the backyard, dozing on a lawn chair. It's his favorite time of day. The yard feels completely enclosed, self-contained. He's proud of it. The bushes he planted along the fence when they first moved in twenty years ago are full and block the view on either side. The wooden fence at the back is covered with wisteria, which he's trained along the top and chops back every year. It started blooming while he was away, and now the pendulous clumps of purple flowers are at their peak. The little back lot is the closest thing he has to a refuge. The whole neighborhood seems distant, and everything seems further away back here, even the sound of barking dogs, lawn mowers, leaf blowers, the traffic on Route 50.

He can hear her getting dinner ready in the kitchen. The smell of food is tempting and nauseating at the same time. He isn't sure he wants to eat, or even if he can. Everything feels a little wobbly. She calls to him, thinking he is still upstairs, and is startled when he appears at the back door. "You've been outside all this time?" Her face is flushed from exercise. The evening news is on in the next room.

He takes his usual place at the kitchen table. It's clear that she's waiting for him to say something first. She doesn't seem angry or tense, merely to be going about the evening routine. However and whenever he chooses to join her is completely up to him. He has the impression that he could say anything to her and she would take it with perfect equanimity and a sip of wine. It isn't at all in character, but it is nice for a change. The longer he sits there, the more he wants to see how far they can take this new thing together.

"I don't think I can eat," he says. "My system is all off."

She regards him for a moment, then shrugs and continues eating. "Tell me about Hannah."

"You're suddenly curious?"

"Look, Pat. I'm sorry. I know I should've called. I meant to, but—"

"But you didn't," she cuts him off. "I left three voice messages, sent you an e-mail and got back an automatic reply. Why, Noel? Automatic reply. What was that all about?" She shakes her head, the color in her cheeks deepening. "Unbelievable. Just unbelievable."

"I'm sorry." There is nothing else to say. In the brief span that follows, it becomes clear they are beyond apologies. She is moving on. Her blitheness is meant to demonstrate this, and no pecking away at details is going to restore things to the status quo ante. She has rights as the injured party and thus the upper hand. He is perfectly happy to concede both. What remains to be seen is how it will hold up in the face of what he is about to tell her.

"Is she all right?" he asks.

Pat nods.

"When did she call? Or did you call her?"

"She called."

"And? What did she say?"

She chews with forced calm. "Why don't you talk to her your-self?" She struggles with herself for another moment, then her eyes fill with tears. She gets up and leaves the room.

He finds her in the den, sitting in the corner of the sofa with legs tucked up, chin on knee, staring at the television. He returns to the kitchen, dials Hannah's number. Failing to get an answer, he leaves a voice message and hangs up.

"I'm sorry you're upset, Pat. There's something I need to get off my chest. It will help explain a lot."

She doesn't respond. He drops down in the opposite corner of the sofa, struggling to find the precise words, a way to begin. Pat wipes her eyes, sniffles once or twice, determined not to speak, while phrases flit through his head: There's something you need to under-stand what I'm telling you is you're not going to believe but you know, my whole career, intelligence, surveillance, target acquisition and recognition.

All of a sudden, a map flashes onto the television of Pakistan's northwest frontier, and a banner headline appears behind the news anchor's head: "Missile Strike Against Al-Qaeda." He grabs the re-mote, punches up the volume. "American military officials, speaking on condition of anonymity because the subject involves covert op-erations, said the attack against a safehouse in North Waziristan was not carried out by a Pentagon-operated Predator. A spokesman for the CIA declined to comment on the missile attack."

He stands up, points to the television with the remote, heart rac-ing. Pat has not changed her position except to turn her head slightly. He turns down the volume, tingling in every nerve. *I'm part of that,* he wants to say. *That's what's been going on all this time, what I'm trying to tell you.* But then it suddenly occurs to him that, no, he wasn't part of it. Not that one. Definitively not. Thought it had been settled before he left. The Pak Frontier Corps was doing recon all around there. There was talk about a flyover with F-15 Strike Eagles in a show of force. But the house they wanted to target was the site of a possible *jirga* between the Pak government and Waziri leaders, the *maliks*. Good sources on the ground there. Don't hit it, he'd said. Too risky. Not worth it, was his final call. The Mehsuds were hemmed in on three sides—Jandulla, Razmak, and Wana. Baitullah and his boys weren't anywhere near there.

"So what is it you need to get off your chest?" Pat asks. The high emotional color of earlier has given way to a blotchy paleness, as if she's already decided how little it will matter.

He switches off the television and sits down again, hearing his own words being pitched back sarcastically in the beat of her question. "I'm involved in that whole business, Pat. That stuff, right there. That's what I've been wanting to tell you." He says it looking straight ahead at the television screen. "I don't know how else to put it."

"Put what?"

"Well, what I've been doing. I'm not allowed to talk about it. And lately there have been problems, and I can't discuss them, either. It's hard to deal with sometimes."

She eyes him for a moment, more suspicious than curious.

"But don't worry. I'm one of the good guys, Pat. It's just that things get a little messed up now and then."

She stands up. "You amaze me, Noel. I'm not stupid. What did you think? I know you don't measure draperies for the Pentagon! Don't flatter yourself. You're not one of the good guys. Or even the bad guys." She pauses for a moment in the doorway. "You're just an asshole."

An asshole.

It was true.

Speaking on condition of anonymity.

Not carried out by a Predator.

This is true, too. With Cowper's fingerprints all over it. A good sound byte, perfectly literally true and with the standard *no comment* from Langley that looked, for all the public cared, like taking the Fifth. "You're right. I'm an asshole."

He gets in the car and leaves. And just like a real asshole, it isn't until he is on the George Washington Parkway that it occurs to him where he is going. Speaking on condition of anonymity, his abrupt departure was further proof of a harsh truth: an asshole nature. He should have laughed. But he is reeling with the news from Pakistan, realizing he'd been sidelined, sent off on that stupid junket. It's more ridiculous than anything else, really. And true, true, true. Good guy, bad guy, the metaethic that underpins everything, an efficient practical reason of light and dark. A good guy only has to think he's right. A bad guy needs a dark, immodest agenda. An asshole just needs simple instructions and a gun.

Pat has it exactly right. When he gets back home, he'll expand on the whole asshole thing and explain to her that, yes, it was all true: No attack against a safehouse by a Pentagon-operated Predator. But, in fact, an attack from about thirty-five thousand feet by an MQ-9 Reaper equipped with a Raytheon AN/AAS-52 multispectral targeting suite, wide-area surveillance sensors, and two five-hundred-pound GBU-38 GPS-guided JDAMs with warheads containing BLU-97/B combined effects bombs that provide armor-defeating capability, a fragmenting case for materiel destruction, and a zirconium ring for incendiary effects.

It is exactly 21:13 when he arrives at Bolling. The guard, a young woman with hair tucked up and trigger finger extended on the M16 belted diagonally across her chest, scans his ID, then asks him to wait a moment and disappears into the smoked-glass sentry booth. Wait? He's never been asked to wait before. He's up-to-date, with new embedded ID chip. She reappears a moment later, hands back the card with a no-nonsense "Proceed." Is something wrong? He's about to ask, but she is already moving toward the car behind his.

He finds a parking space near the front entrance and sits for a moment before getting out of the car. There is a faint electrical hum in the air and, from across the river, the sound of airplanes taking off from National. The clustered buildings seem dim and distant, silver-skinned facades reflecting the orange glow of the lamplit parking lot, a place haunted by itself. Entering, one never has the sense of arriving but of being absorbed. The additional checkpoints and the soaring lobby decorated with one of Saddam's SCUDs add to the feeling of being drawn into an impervious realm of complex hierarchies and obscure grammars.

Waiting for him is a youngish lieutenant colonel from J-2 and a civilian contractor holding a cardboard box.

"You've been retasked, no longer cleared to enter the section," the colonel says straightaway.

Noel is distracted by the man with the box, who seems unsure, waiting for instructions from the colonel, who, in spite of his brisk-ness, has a friendly, open face and blue, almost aquamarine eyes. He can see him coaching kids' soccer on the weekend. "The assistant deputy director will brief you tomorrow."

The man with the box steps forward and offers it, sealed with yellow tape. "From your desk," the colonel says. "Should be all there."

"I don't understand."

The colonel flashes a sympathetic look. "Apologize for the surprise. You weren't expected to report in today." He glances at his watch. "The assistant deputy director will bring you up to speed at 09:00 tomorrow, put everything in context."

"Understood," he finds himself saying, although he doesn't understand at all. The colonel turns and leaves him there holding the box.

He wanders across the lobby, sits down on a bench along the wall. This is the only part of the building that could be considered public space, but he feels self-conscious and out of place sitting there, empty stomach gurgling, with a cardboard box in his lap, staring dumbly at the chain of hexagonal brass plates inscribed with names and dates. The Patriots Memorial. He wanders over to read them. Nearly half are women, most recently those who died on 9/11, working in the Office of the Comptroller.

The security guys let him leave without asking to look inside the box. The scrubbed contents of his desk. He puts it into the back of the Navigator, next to his golf clubs, pausing to consider their significance, and tries to think of the perfect Joseph Helleresque response to what has just happened. But he can't.

La Corbière

46°51'41.85"N

6°51'49.49"E

A flock of sheep was being driven across the lawn when I finally arrived at La Corbière. I sat on my bags and watched them pass, forty or fifty, all heading in the direction of a grassy field. The setting wasn't quite what I'd expected, but it made sense that a place calling itself the *laboratoire village nomade* should also be populated by sheep. Blue neon letters reading *ce moment n'est ce pas le même* had been affixed to the side of the house. This moment is not the same. A Zen motto? I wasn't quite sure what it was supposed to mean. Undoubtedly, somebody inside would enlighten me.

The walk from the train station had taken longer than I'd been told it would. I felt conspicuous dragging my bags through the town's narrow cobbled streets. The whole thing felt like a stupid mistake. I asked directions and found myself heading out of town on a main road that ran through open fields. Cars and tractors whooshed past. Nobody stopped. It took me an hour to find the old house, which was hidden behind a large stand of trees at the end of a long drive. It had been built in 1856 by a French captain who'd married the daughter of Georges-Antoine Endrion, an officer in the court of Louis XVI who'd played a role in the monarch's bungled escape from Paris. Legend has it that he fled the city himself under a hay cart with a barrel of Louis d'Ors, sank the gold coins in the lake, then later retrieved and reburied them at La Corbière.

A child's voice startled me. *"Etes-vous l'organiste?"* A little girl approached, no more than six or seven years old. She looked Japanese. I was about to answer when she pointed to my bags and asked, in perfect English, "Is that your music?"

"My music?"

"Pour l'orgue. Want me to show you where it is?"

I didn't know what she was talking about. "What's your name?"

"Mariko."

"Is this La Corbière?"

The little girl nodded. She was barefoot and wearing a print dress over long pants. "You speak English and French," I said.

The girl nodded again. "Is that your music?" she asked, tracing her finger along the dust-covered suitcase.

"You could call it that."

"The organ is in the chapel." She pointed to a little spire behind a stand of trees near the house. The sheep were now grazing all around us.

"Do you live here?"

The girl nodded.

"Can you show me where everyone is?"

Before it was turned into an intercultural artist's residence by a local philanthropist, the house had been a boy's boarding school.

In spite of renovation, alterations, and impromptu art installations throughout, a stifled schoolhouse feel still lingered about the place. The terms of residence were as simple as they were generous—six weeks of free room and board in return for sharing the fruits of a creative project. I was shown to the tower room by a photographer named Dieter who chuckled and said. "This is where we put the writers."

"Did Res say I was a writer?"

"Aren't you?"

"I suppose in a way, yes."

The room was bare and very bright, with windows on all sides. It had a bed, a sink, a desk and chair, a small bookcase and wardrobe. Some of the windows had been left open. Fresh bird droppings on the floor were the only sign of recent habitation. "Looks like you won't be quite so alone," Dieter laughed. We chatted briefly about the daily program. There wasn't any—except for an evening meal which was served promptly at seven. "Just relax," Dieter said, taking leave. "If you'd like to have a swim, just follow the path down through the woods. The water is a little cold but quite refreshing."

I unpacked, made the bed with sheets and a blanket taken from the wardrobe, and tried to settle in. The whole thing felt incongruous—the quaint room, a view over the fields, the lake framed by hills, and on the desk a stack of official documents and reports I'd hauled with me from Washington: Phoenix 1969 End of Year Report. Saigon. CORDS PP&P. Phung Hoang Results Due Directly to Psyops. Phoenix Directorate. They didn't belong, were unsettling and made no sense. Images flashed in my mind, of exploring this very part of Switzerland with my father in the early 1980s, a car ashtray full of cigarette butts, his liver-spotted hands on the steering wheel and a ribbon of smoke being sucked out of the cracked window at 140 kph. My project had come off its wheels, had become a neurotic father-project. I'd come here thinking I would somehow use what I'd gathered to construct a fuller world in my head. Now that fuller world seemed to open onto a succession of new voids and emptinesses. Bettina Lüneberg. But it was only a name, nothing else, and no more substantial than State Dept. Telegram 271149Z, Special Phung Hoang Campaign in Dalat.

I made a list of the things I would need for a basic plane-table survey: a two-foot-by-two-foot board; a tripod, a compass; a level; a simple Alidade, which I could make from a box ruler with raised sights joined with a length of black thread; a measuring tape; graph paper; pins; a set of retractable pencils with leads of varying colors and thickness; an eraser. As the sun dropped below the horizon, I sat down at the desk and made a rough sketch of my location, using the road leading to the house as a baseline. I scaled my position following a system of triangulation that referred as much to the visible landscape as it did to a tangled, interior chain of my own belonging. The estate sits on top of a forested ridge that runs along the southwest shore of the lake. In the distance, I could make out the rounded, medieval towers of Château d' Estavayer. In the morning, I would begin a series of traverses to measure lines and calculate azimuths by angle closure. And since the room was a perfect observatory with a clear view of the sky, I could check all my calculations at night by the stars.

On a map, the user fills in empty space with his own imagined presence. This imposes important restrictions for the mapmaker, who must strike a balance between filling in necessary detail and leaving room for the user to locate himself and become, in the words of Tim

Robinson, my mapmaker guru, "the irreducible nub of topographicity." It was Robinson's work in Ireland that, over the years, has inspired and kept me with both feet on the ground. Never mind GIS and GPS and all the new technology, he is the greatest cartographic theorist of the twentieth century, a true philosopher. According to him, a map is a one-to-one encounter between a person and a terrain, an existential project. The best maps are mostly blank and make locating oneself easy, which was why I didn't want to insist on unnecessary detail. Blake had provided me with more than enough to navigate by. On the other hand, what I'd learned from him also meant having to ascertain a new azimuth, and getting and fixing points required new measurements. Everything hinged on his lists. "The spreadsheets in my head," he called them.

"So. Ursula was an East German spy."

"Kundschafter," Blake corrected. "That was the HvA term. They didn't say spy. They called themselves 'purveyors of information.' She was also an 'illegal,' which was the term of art for East German operatives who'd been settled in the West under assumed identities—usually the name of a dead person or someone who'd emigrated. As far as we could tell, she'd been in Düsseldorf since the mid-'60s. Started out as a freelance journalist covering the fashion industry. Around '71 or '72, she became an editor at one of the fashion monthlies. Romeo spying was a specialty of East German intelligence. Mostly, they used men and went after lonely secretaries in government and party offices. By the '70s they were using women—Juliets—with, we now know, amazing results. When we learned about the affair with your father, we saw it as an opportunity."

"Opportunity for what?"

"For more lists," Blake laughed. "Lists of lists of lists. Opportunities always turn into lists and lists into opportunities. Even a list that leads completely in the wrong direction is an opportunity if you know how to use it. The East Germans put their lists together and came up with one thing: young, German born, native speaker, USIA, Vietnam. But we had our lists, too, and put them together our way and saw opportunities as well."

"So he was with the CIA in Germany?"

"He was now." Blake grinned.

"And in Vietnam?"

"In Vietnam, certainly."

"Africa and India, too? His whole career?"

Blake waved the question away. "Why is that so important to you? I don't get it."

"Whatever happened to Ursula?"

We had left the café and were making our way back to Blake's place. He was drunk but remarkably lucid. "Nobody knew. At first we assumed she'd been pulled back. They did that with their people anytime things got even the slightest bit sticky."

"Did my father know why she disappeared? I mean, they were living together."

"Yes, they were. And we wanted them to keep living together. We were expecting a recruitment pitch any day."

"Recruitment pitch?"

"We were hoping for one, yes. But the timing had to be just right. Pitches are always risky and extremely dangerous." Blake grinned. "And we didn't know what she'd do because he actually was love-struck and careless. And evidently she was, too."

"I don't know what you mean."

"They were having a real, bona fide love affair, for Christ's sake. He loved her, and she loved him."

Oddly, I wasn't uncomfortable hearing Blake talk this way. I'd hashed through the emotional wreckage of those years so thoroughly with my mother that this new twist was almost refreshing. I could also not imagine sharing any of it with her.

"We were glad the way things were going," Blake continued.

"My dad wasn't, I bet."

"No, he wasn't, at first. Then the shock wore off. Mainly he felt jerked around and was pissed off. But it didn't take much to make him to see it not as a lapse, something that would fuck up his career, but as an opportunity. A fantastic opportunity. We had her right where we wanted her. But then she was gone before we could get started with anything serious."

"Serious with what?"

"Oh, we were going to blow all kinds of smoke up her ass," Blake said with a chuckle.

I detected a tinge of bitterness, as if he harbored some sort of grudge. "What sort of smoke?"

"I don't remember anymore. Anyway, it's not important."

We arrived at Blake's cottage. It was just after five o'clock. A man was setting tables in front of the fish restaurant next door and waved to us.

"I eat there three or four times a week. Fish right out of the lake. It's like having a private chef."

We went inside. I still couldn't decide whether to catch the train or take up the offer of the sofa and spend the night under the gaze of Albrecht Dürer. When Blake announced that he was going to

freshen up for dinner and retired to his bedroom, I decided on
the sofa.

Two hours later, he was shaking me awake. "Dinnertime, my boy.
Georges is saving his last two filets for us. And I've been saving this."
He flourished a bottle of wine, was freshly washed, wet gray hair
combed straight back over his head. With his tortoiseshell glasses, silk
cravat, and the ubiquitous Italian blazer, he resembled a European-
ized Robert McNamara.

Georges greeted us with an impatient glance at his watch. His
restaurant, twenty feet from Blake's front door, consisted of four tables and a steamy little galley kitchen where he cooked the day's
catch and served it with boiled potatoes and whatever vegetable he
had on hand. He was short and barrel shaped, a Lebanese from Beirut
who'd been eking out a living by the lake for almost twenty years.
Blake introduced me as his "godson."

"Why you never visit before?" Georges demanded, wagging a
finger at me. "Your godfather is living twenty years here."

"You remember Peter?" Blake asked with a nod at me. "His
father."

"Peter? Your father?" Georges gripped my shoulder, looked me
in the eye, and shook his head somberly. "Your father was a good
man," he said and went inside.

We sat quietly for several minutes, listening to Georges clattering
in the kitchen and the gentle lapping of water under the dock. The
tables outside were lit by red and yellow bulbs hanging from a wire
strung overhead. The stripped-down atmosphere was cozy. I could
imagine my father sitting for hours there over a bottle of wine. It was
exactly right.

Georges brought out our dinners and set them down with a

flourish. Broiled fish, potatoes, and green beans. "Keep him company," he said to me. "He always eat alone if I don't sit with him."

"That's just so you can drink all my wine." Blake smiled.

"He never buy from me. Always bring his own wine."

"Your wines are lousy, Georges!"

The bantering was for my amusement, but it was also clear that they were taking the opportunity to demonstrate a fondness not generally aired. I wanted to get back to Ursula, and when Georges finally returned to the kitchen asked, "What was it you were planning to use her for? Some sort of disinformation campaign?"

Blake was enjoying his fish and nodded.

"Was all this going on while they were living together?"

Blake nodded again.

"Did my mother know about any of this?"

"No, she did not." Blake pointed with his knife for emphasis. "The situation between your parents was strictly private. An extramarital affair. Everyone knew, and it was devastating, of course. We were all worried he'd fly off the handle, do something stupid. But he kept his cool. Considering how badly things could have gone, that he managed to keep his wits about him and continued living with her for as long as he did. Some pretty amazing tradecraft. Ursula, too, for that matter. They were a couple of very cool cookies."

"Did she know that he knew she was a spy?"

"I don't know. Certainly, there was no way we could know for sure."

"Isn't that likely why she was pulled back?"

"I have no idea what the real reasons were. There's no documentation been found. Anyway, being pregnant would certainly have been enough."

"Did my father know she was pregnant when she left?"

Blake shook his head. "I know for a fact he didn't."

"When did he find out?"

"Not until many years later, after the wall came down. She got a message to him through the State Department. As it happened, he was in Bonn."

"What did she say?"

"I don't know."

"Did they meet?"

"Twice, I think. Your father was pretty vague. He was in shock himself, trying to figure out what to do. Remember, in the months right after the wall came down, people were scrambling madly, especially those with any kind of baggage. Nobody knew what to do."

"What about Bettina? Did they ever meet?"

Blake shook his head. "No. Not directly. She still doesn't know. For your father, that was the hardest part. It really tore him up. We talked it over endlessly, what he should do. Remember, there was nobody he could talk openly to about the full picture except yours truly." He gave one of those cornball smirks straight out of a Cary Grant film and returned to eating his fish.

"What about Nicole? Does she know?"

"No."

"Are you certain?"

He dabbed his lips with his napkin and nodded.

I took it all in with a hollow feeling, not sure how much more of Blake's calm self-assurance I could take. "So why didn't he just find Bettina and tell her himself?" I asked. What I really wanted to know was why Blake seemed to take such special pride in being my father's sole confidant.

"Because Ursula had asked him to stay away from her. She didn't want anyone to know. Period. Financial help was welcome, but only from a distance." He picked up his wineglass and said, "It was in her last note to him. Her dying wish. The next we heard she was dead. An overdose of sleeping pills."

I watched him sip, then put down his glass. It was suddenly quiet except for the water lapping on the shoreline. Georges appeared, pointed to my untouched dinner. "What's the matter? You don't like the fish?"

I picked up my fork. "We're having a difficult conversation," Blake said. With glances at the two of us, Georges refilled the wineglasses and went back inside. I pushed my plate aside. "So he never tried to get in touch, or to meet her?"

Blake hesitated. "There was a memorial service, a gathering of friends and family somewhere in Prenzlauer Berg, where she lived. He went to it. There were uncles and cousins there. Bettina must have been fourteen or fifteen. He couldn't bring himself to approach her and left after the service without talking to anyone. He called me when he got back to Bonn. He was really shaken up. We spent at least an hour on the phone, deciding what to do. I helped him set up the money transfers. The uncle she went to live with got a letter explaining that an account had been opened in a Swiss bank in Bettina's name by a former colleague of her mother who wished to remain anonymous." He shook his head. "A former colleague. Funny little twist. But what else could he do?"

Indeed, what else? It was what I spent the rest of the night asking myself. Bright moonlight shone through the curtains as I lay on Blake's lumpy sofa. The room shimmered. Albrecht Dürer's unfinished face organized itself in a conglomeration of hues on the easel at the far end of the room. I wondered what she looked like. If she was dark- or light-haired, if she resembled her mother or her father. That was the only way I could frame it, the father of Bettina being, in a sense, a man I had never known. Where had she gone to school? What was she doing now, this very minute? She was born in 1977, the year I turned seventeen. What was her birthday? Where had I been on that day?

Before retiring for the night, Blake had handed me an envelope. "About a year ago, I received this. It was forwarded by the bank. My name is on the account. *Privat.* We set it up that way as an extra precaution."

> *Dear Sir,*
> *I write regarding regular deposits being made into*
> *my account. Is there any way to track the source of*
> *these funds? I would appreciate any information you*
> *can provide.*

The return address was Munich. I handed back the letter, but Blake refused. "Keep it," he said.

I wasn't sure I wanted to. It was too much like hearing a voice. "Did you show it to my father?"

"He didn't want to see it."

"Did you reply?"

"I sent a letter to the bank saying that the depositor wished to remain anonymous. Secrecy is a religion here."

"Did you contact the bank after he died?"

Blake shook his head.

"What's going to happen now?"

"Well, the deposits have stopped. Eventually, I expect I'll get a letter from the bank when she closes the account. But maybe not. She doesn't need my signature for that. I was merely the trustee until she turned eighteen."

"And she'll never know where the money came from or why it suddenly stopped?"

"Isn't that pretty much how it is with everything?" he said and shuffled off to bed.

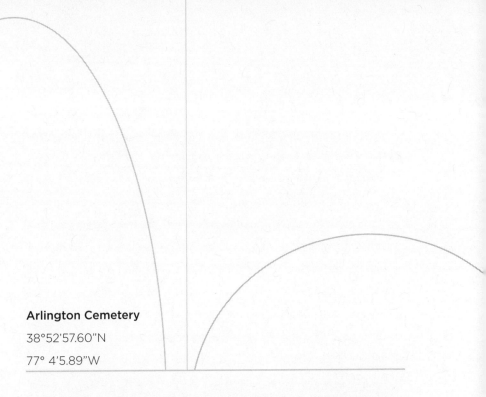

Arlington Cemetery
38°52'57.60"N
77° 4'5.89"W

Noel detours from his usual route home, down the Mall, which on Sunday nights has all the desolate majesty of a well-lighted but empty cathedral. It isn't mawkish patriotism or a sense of having been wronged, nor to be reminded of his humble place in larger turning wheels. He is simply embarrassed, can't bear to go back home and face Pat holding the contents of his emptied desk in a sealed box.

He crosses the Potomac on Memorial Bridge. Arlington Cemetery is closed. He pauses for a few minutes to take in the procession of monuments and statues and the symbolism of this enormous graveyard on the doorstep of the Pentagon, and also of his last performance evaluation, written by Cowper. At the time, he hadn't been particularly bothered by it but should have recognized the red flags.

Such close association with much higher-ranking officers tends to inhibit somewhat the development of, or the necessity for, independent initiative, resourcefulness, and acceptance of responsibility, such as might be much more important factors for a senior analyst at the same grade level.

Or:

*Although a competent organizer and unsurpassed in intellectual equip-
ment and the competence he brings to technical analytical work, I have found
several of his reports overbrief and less than complete, and although his work
productivity is high, the morale of team members would be higher if he paid
more personalized attention to the significant accomplishments of the team.*

He's always enjoyed bureaucratic poetry; how in marvelous dis-
tortions of language so much can be made of so little, and so little of
so much. Like statues, in a way. He wishes he could be more original,
but there isn't anything new to be said about the absurdities and
paradoxes of bureaucracy. To begin criticizing would only be a sign
of bitterness. The fact is, he has enjoyed his career. He is proud to
have been in close proximity to big events. He even enjoys the charge
of lethal combat—at least as much as can be felt without actually
being in a firefight on the ground or flying sorties over the enemy at
mach speed. He likes working in a SCIF, a Sensitive Compartmented
Information Facility, just a few steps from direct presidential control,
going after the bad guys in the service of his country. There is a
downside, of course. People and relationships become ambiguous,
inside and outside the SCIF. But there's also comfort in the nonde-
scriptness that comes with this kind of employment. Over time, being nondescript becomes a personality trait. In good light, you are
self-contained, modest, or shy. In bad light, you are distant, aloof, or
vacant. An asshole.

He's determined now to tell Pat everything, to lay out the trajec-
tory of his entire career, beginning with the grad-school thesis on
partial differential equation–based modeling of geometric boundaries and topological structures that got the attention of DARPA, the
Defense Department's Advanced Research Projects Agency, right

down to the dead schoolchildren, the Geneva junket, the hotel hooker. But when he finally gets home, she's gone to bed and is already sound asleep. He can't bring himself to wake her, so he undresses quietly and slips under the covers.

He lies there briefly, mind racing, stomach gurgling. When Pat begins to snore, he goes downstairs, sits at the computer, and starts composing his letter of resignation and request for early retirement. The beginning is easy enough. But after the opening lines, he begins to sputter. Indignation gives way to uncertainty. Maybe he should wait, not jump the gun. In a twinge of self-disgust, he goes to the kitchen, opens the refrigerator, and stares dumbly into the lighted interior. It occurs to him that perhaps he's delusional from hunger. If so, perhaps he should continue without food for another day just to see what happens.

Pat's cell phone is on the counter. He picks it up, thinking now might be a good time to try to reach Hannah. She'll be up late studying for finals and think it is her mother calling and maybe answer. He scrolls through the call log, surprised to see not only that Pat talked to Hannah just a few hours ago but that they talked frequently the whole time he was gone. Two, sometimes three times a day.

He wanders into the den, drapes Pat's pink fringed fleece around his shoulders, and lies down on the sofa. Incredible how much noise an empty stomach makes and how quietly a head full of thoughts races; how minuscule purposes coincide in the world with enormous ones, like a foot falling among a line of ants struggling with a crumb or bombs into a compound filled with infrared grubs. All he ever really wanted was to be a good husband and father. Even next to his job, he always felt these were the important things. One might be president of the United States, but true worth as a human being comes from the commonplaces of family and friends; how you are regarded depends entirely on your regard for others. Okay, so Pat and Hannah had been talking the whole week he was in Switzerland golfing and having sex with a hotel whore, and his job in Washington has been reassigned, and on the other side of the world in Pakistan a jihadist and his family have just been obliterated in a targeted strike he argued against right before leaving. Somehow it all coheres, not in flashes of illumination but in a vast grayness that only becomes duller and less distinguishable the more he contemplates it.

These are the hard facts. There are soft ones to consider as well. The domestic agenda. When Pat and he were getting started in married life, how convinced they were of the need to do certain things a certain way: to find a decent house in a decent neighborhood near a decent school; to make decent friends and volunteer in the community—Pat at the Fairfax County Hospital, where she works, he at Holy Trinity, where he attends mass; to eat a healthy, balanced diet and exercise and pay for tutors and piano lessons and summer dance camps and family vacations that didn't just mean going to Rehoboth Beach every summer but were edifying, too, like hiking the Appalachian Trail, visiting Mayan ruins in Yucatán, seeing the Holy Land. When Hannah got into UVA, they felt they'd done everything right. By her and by themselves. He was the one who'd choked up on the drive back from Charlottesville, not just at how quickly she'd grown up but at how lucky he was to have such a great wife and daughter to ground him and make the world seem sensible and whole. As a reward for all his dedicated work, he was promoted through the ranks, finally ending up as lead GIS analyst in a top-secret red-cell operation under Cowper, whom he'd looked up to at the beginning, but whose trick of seizing on every insignificant detail—a shoe style

FREDERICK REUSS

or the title of a book—and referring to them as if they were highly symbolic of something significant he finally came to see as a bully tactic to mask his own insecurities. Cowper had always put him on the defensive. From the very first day. *So I'm wearing oxfords. I'm reading a book of poetry. My reports are brief. Isn't that good? What's wrong with that?*

"Noel. Wake up, Noel." Pat is standing over him in a fuzzy halo of lamplight. "You're talking in your sleep."

"What time is it?"

"Want me to bring you a blanket?"

"We need to talk, Pat."

"Yes, we do. But not now. I'm going back to bed."

"There's more I need to tell you."

"Can it wait until the morning?"

"No, it can't."

She is waiting, half turned to him at the door. She pulls up the collar of her robe, crosses her arms, and in that instant he realizes that what he must tell her is completely different than what he wants to say. Perhaps if the atmosphere were slightly different, without that "just get on with it, will you" attitude she also uses to snuff any erotic dimension in bed, he might have spoken differently. Now it is simply anger responding to indifference. Plus, he has seen her cell phone log and knows she is also keeping something from him.

"It's about Geneva," he says without looking up at her, and sits forward on the sofa with head bowed as if waiting to receive a blow. When at last he turns to face her, she is standing exactly as before, arms crossed, holding the collar of her robe closed at the neck. It is the first time they've faced each other this way in a long, long time, squared off as the two wholly separate lives they were the day they first met. "I'm going to tell you something you're not going to like. There are things I want to tell you and can't. This is something I don't need to tell you but can and should. I'm just trying to be honest with you, Pat. Please understand that, okay?"

Pat leans against the door frame, frowning, clutching her elbows.

"It was nothing. Really nothing. She was a prostitute. I met her in the hotel bar. It's legal in Switzerland. Totally legal. I don't feel guilty because it didn't mean anything. I wanted to tell you because I just want you to know."

She hasn't moved or changed expression. Finally, in a flat, emotionless tone, she says, "I need to be alone" and leaves the room.

The clock in the living room ticks more loudly in the silence that follows. Everything is suspended. He doesn't expect her to come back downstairs, but he also doesn't want to wait until morning to continue. Her reaction entails far more than just what she might say. He is looking for something beyond words. A slap in the face would be fine. A tremendous relief. Tomorrow will be too late. They will already be different people by then, too cooled down for slapping, reconciled to changed conditions and the sad reality of things.

He goes upstairs. "Pat?" he calls through the door.

"I want to be alone."

"I want to talk."

"I don't."

He opens the door. She is on her side, facing the wall, blanket pulled up over her shoulders. "There are a few more things I need to tell you," he says, standing in the doorway.

"I don't want to hear."

He steps into the room. "It's important. You need to understand."

"Stop it!" she shouts, throws off the blanket, stands up. "Just shut up, will you? I don't want to hear your fucking whore stories! I don't care, okay?" She stands there in her nightgown, trembling, then sits back on the bed. "You have no idea how little it matters!"

The charge draws him further into the room, but he feels like an intruder and stops after a few steps. "They're not whore stories," he starts to say.

"Be quiet!" she shouts and slaps the bed with the flat of her hand. Then in a thick voice, "Hannah, your daughter. Remember her? Or are you so wrapped up in yourself that you forgot?"

"Is something wrong?"

"No. Nothing wrong. She's just pregnant, and has decided not to keep the baby."

He returns downstairs to the sofa in the den. The neighbor's back-porch light casts rambling shadows on the ceiling. At some point, he wakes up from a dream—of fishing in septic waters, catching something amphibious, ugly, and large and afraid to touch or unhook it with bare hands, tugging and tugging on the line and, unable to free it, finally leaving the gasping thing to die in the murk with the bloody hook lodged in its throat.

Château Estavayer le Lac

46°51'05.14"N

6°50'56.17"E

The next day I set out to measure the distance to the château. A wooded footpath follows the base of a long ridge that runs for several kilometers along the shore of the lake. The satellite images of the area are remarkably detailed, but even the slickest three-dimensional GIS modeling can't convey the dramatic verticality of the forested slope towering overhead, the sense of being enclosed. I wear a Suunto X-Lander wristwatch. It's a magical instrument with built-in electronic compass, barometer, and altimeter. The only thing it lacks is a pedometer, but I was happy to count steps because a map measured out and drawn by hand yields a different order of location altogether.

It was a clear morning. Except for the birds chittering and singing in the canopy overhead, I was alone. I stopped frequently to take readings and sketch details. More than just a record of spatial relationships, each detail is a moment of emplacement, another bond formed with the landscape. There is something deeply satisfying in gathering them, like laying hands directly on the earth. It felt good to know precisely where I was.

By noon, I was back at La Corbière. The house felt deserted. In the dining room were the remains of somebody's breakfast—an empty coffee cup, a jam-stained knife and plate, an ashtray with a stubbed-out cigarette butt. A mild breeze blew through the open doors, and I could hear the strains of conversation under way on the veranda. I was about to step outside, but a sudden shyness held me back, and instead I went to the kitchen to scrounge up something to eat. It was large, institutional, with ceramic-tiled walls and long metal countertops. A woman was at the stove stirring a large pot.

"*Bonjour.*" The double doors swung shut behind me. I stood awkwardly for a moment, then asked, "*Puis-je obtenir quelque chose à manger?*"

"*Oui,*" the woman said, stepping back from the stove. "I'm Christine. What would you like?"

She showed me around the kitchen and invited me to help myself. "Bring your dishes right back, okay?" She tugged her hair around and wrapped it into a loose braid which she let hang over her shoulder. "Some people don't get it," she said, evidently referring to the dishes still in the dining room. "I'm not a fucking maid."

Her bluntness put me immediately at ease. I helped myself to an apple and a bowl of muesli with yogurt and ate it standing in the corner while she told me about her years in Berkeley.

"Are you an artist?"

She laughed. "No. I'm here to cook. It's my job. What brings you here?"

"I'm not really sure." I spooned up the last bite of muesli. "Maybe nothing."

She smiled. "You wouldn't be the first. How do you know about La Corbière?"

"I'm an old school friend of Werner. He's been inviting me to come and visit for years. The original plan was to work on a project about my father."

"You're writing a book?"

"I don't know what I'm doing. The plans I had kind of self-destructed in the last two days." I went over to the sink and washed my bowl and spoon, feeling somehow that I was confiding something all too familiar to her. "I'm lost. So I'm making a map."

"That's very practical." She laughed. "What of?"

"Of this place, right here."

I spent the afternoon reconstructing my notes on tracing paper. What emerged was crude and not useful in any practical sense, but it made me feel good. To be working with the most basic tools took me back to my earliest mapping experiences, the long weekends spent hiking and bicycling, meandering and measuring. A moped, my sixteenth-birthday present, which coincided with my parent's separation, considerably extended my range. My first large-scale project was done in a series of moped tours along the lower Rhein. By the time I graduated from high school, I'd mapped out a detailed network of small roads and footpaths that ran through the farming and industrial landscapes of Nord-Rhein Westphalia. From Düsseldorf through Rhein-Kreis Neuss all the way out to Viersen. In the '70s, postwar reconstruction was still under way in many places. To come across a partially restored church like something swept across my path filled me with a sense of belonging. If there was a certain falseness in feeling connected to an utterly foreign place, my imagination more than compensated with pleasant fantasies as I pedaled through it taking notes and making measurements: Roman garrisons, gothic churches, windmills, knights and peasants and burghers in floppy hats skating across frozen ponds in black woolen capes. As much as those early maps represented places I'd visited, they were also records of the prolix and reshuffled geography of my adolescence. Escape routes from a dreary home. All that mattered was the going to and the coming from; how to get from one place to the next. It was a permanent tourist perspective of views and sights and plaques, places to eat and sleep. There were no points of return and no memories. But I mapped on, taking in no more of a place than simply having been there.

At seven o'clock, I went downstairs for dinner. A large screen was set up at one end of the dining room. A shadow-puppet show was under way, with musical accompaniment by cello and clarinet. I tiptoed over to a candlelit buffet table, where a large tureen of vegetable soup, a platter of bread and cheese, and fresh fruit were set out. I helped myself and found a place at the table. The little Japanese girl from the day before was sitting on her mother's lap, absorbed in the performance in a language I didn't recognize. The puppets themselves were simple and charmingly natural and moved to an improvised Bartok-like folk dance. It ended in a flickering, shape-shifting crescendo with friendly shouts and happy applause from the audience. The puppeteers took their bows as silhouettes, then stepped from behind the screen: a plump, bald man in a full black leotard and a wiry, red-haired woman who seemed to have been cut from the same fabric as the fairy tale that had just been told.

The lights came on, and the meal continued. Introductions were made. There was Mariko, the little girl, and her Italian mother, Sonja. Next came her father, Masatoshi, and after that an elderly Russian gentlemen named Yuri. Farther down the table was a woman from Toulouse named Oceáne; two Germans, Marion and Dieter, whom I'd met; and Res, the Swiss director who ran the whole show. The puppeteers, Hannu and Riia, were from Finland. It was an easygoing, friendly atmosphere. The wine bottle was handed around, and I finished my soup listening to the polyglot being spoken. I didn't feel compelled to join the conversation, was happy, as a newcomer, to observe.

"Do you like being up in the tower?" Sonja asked.

"I do. The views are wonderful."

"We stayed up there the first time we came, when Mariko was a baby. Maybe a little too quiet for you now, isn't it?"

Mariko, slouching in her mother's lap, nodded drowsily.

"Have you spent a lot of time here?"

"We've been coming here for seven years. Masatoshi is making a film about the Mer de Glace, which is shrinking faster than anybody thought."

"He has been filming for seven years?"

"Every summer. When we started, nobody knew how quickly the melting would accelerate. It's moving very quickly, as much as one centimeter per hour in some places."

"Moving? Or shrinking?"

"Both. It's disappearing. He is documenting everything, new formations, crevasse activity."

The project seemed wildly ambitious and spectacular, even if her description sounded reasonable and down-to-earth. I've never thought of myself as an artist but understand and can appreciate the aesthetic dimension they seemed to be exploring. I have my maps and they have their film of a melting glacier, a moving terrain deforming and re-forming the landscape. I became excited and wanted to ask if they ever worked with cartographers but decided to wait until things were a little more familiar. I took in what I could of the gathered company, tried to pick out who was too grand to return their breakfast dishes to the kitchen. The room settled into a trembling yellow. Twilight fit the mood of the place. Parquet floors, a stone mantelpiece chiseled with a crest, a dusty chandelier. The lights on the veranda came on. Someone opened the doors. Hannu lit up a large postprandial spliff.

I helped myself to coffee from the dessert buffet and strolled onto the veranda. The sheep were grazing on the lawn, the entire flock. It was a soothing sight, and I said so by way of introducing myself to Oceáne and Marion, who were sitting on the steps talking. I felt immediately silly. Being charmed by the sheep only proved how out of place I was, how stuck in another wheel, like a child calling out from the backseat, "Look, Mommy, cows!" Certainly it wasn't the sheep that didn't belong. They might just as easily have been cows. But they were sheep. And it wasn't Washington, it was the canton of Fribourg, the Lac de Neuchâtel, and the measurements I'd taken that morning might just as well have represented the distance from cows to sheep as from La Corbière to Château Estavayer-le-Lac or from Blake's cottage to Dalat or Düsseldorf. The distances were not only intervals of space but also the sense I carried with me of permanent detachment. The significance of both lay in simply being there.

Something Blake said to me had popped into my thoughts as I

was working on my map that afternoon. "Just because your father never told you doesn't mean he didn't want you to know." It struck me as another empty Blake cleverness. Why hadn't he told me, then? Why had he kept it a secret? But why is always a question with any number of equally plausible answers. Taken as a whole, why only yielded what I already knew. It couldn't be plotted.

"Do you have a candle?" someone called from inside. Christine. "We're turning the lights out soon. I have a box in the kitchen if you need it."

The dining room was being cleared. Except for the puppeteers, who were setting up for another performance, everyone pitched in to clean up. I glanced around to see how I might help. The elderly Russian was the only one still sitting. He seemed amused by the proceedings, holding his cigarette at the side of his mouth, hand shaking with a slight tremor.

"Permis?" I asked, pointing to his empty plate.

"Oui, Oui." The man handed me his plate as if shaking himself free of an amusing but trivial thought.

I put it on the trolley cart, which I then wheeled into the kitchen.

"Why are the lights going off?" I asked Christine. Dieter came whistling though the door, carrying an armful of firewood, and continued into the dining room.

"For the next week, we will not turn on any electric lights in the house. Only candles." She began filling the sink with water.

"Some sort of environmental statement?"

"Indirectly, yes. Part of Hannu and Riia's shadow project. Not just playing with light and dark but how to appreciate the beauty of darkness and shadows." She rolled up her sleeves and began washing. "But we'll still have hot water, thank God." She grinned.

"The soup was delicious."

"Thank you."

"Are you going to cook in here without light?"

"I'm looking forward to it."

When the dishes were done, she gave me a box of candles and a book of matches. Back in the dining room, Hannu proclaimed *Semaine de l'Ombre,* Week of the Shadows, and started the show. My mind wandered during the performance, which, in spite of the ingenuity of the puppeteers, was far longer than necessary and this time in a didactic-sounding French that was difficult for me to follow. When Christine came in and took a seat across the room, I felt a slight stab of disappointment. Why hadn't she sat with me? I slipped out just before the finale and went upstairs, lighting the way with a candle.

With windows on all sides, the room felt bright in the moonlight. A few clouds drifted across the night sky. The red-tiled rooftop with its many ceramic chimney pots poking up in a network of planes and angles made the house seem sprawling and immense. I set the candle on the drawing table, reviewed the map, feeling drawn into another era. There was a chill in the air. I got into bed and pulled the blanket up under my chin. Reading was not easy by candlelight. I put the book away after a few pages and lay awake, wondering if it was more pleasant to think about shadows than actually to live in dimness. Filming a melting glacier was different from surveying and mapping its changes, too. Were profound and imaginative things taking place here? Or was it all just overly contrived, the fantasy of self-conscious artists? I began to feel foolish and empty again, not simply for finding myself stalled and without direction but also for being smitten by Christine. Anything a week of shadows might hold in store was going to be all tied up with my feelings toward her.

And I'd had enough of shadows.

East Potomac Park

38°42'8.62"N

77°8'26.72"W

Noel has been driving around with the sealed box in the back of the Navigator for a week. It isn't that he's forgotten, just that he has no use for what it contains anymore. The security inspection sticker and property pass taped on top give it a power that opening it would diffuse. Like a medicine bundle. He decides to leave it unopened, hermetic, a memory sealed within itself.

Father Neale is waiting for him at the East Potomac Park parking lot with his worn leather golf bag. "You're early," Noel says, getting out of the car.

"I strive always to be." The priest smiles. He is leaning casually against the trunk of his black Buick Skylark, taking the morning air. Noel had been surprised to learn he was a golfer. A week earlier he'd attended his first meeting at the parish, the Life Reflection Group. He'd gone hoping to take Father Neale aside and ask for a private meeting, didn't want to frame their talk doctrinally or fall into a discussion of the sacraments. Golf was the priest's idea. Noel seized on it.

Pat had been dressed for work and reading the morning paper when he'd come into the kitchen the morning after the clash. Her voice was thick with civility, and he could tell by the way she buried herself in the Metro section and gingerly sipped her coffee that they were a long way from resolving things. He was freshly showered and shaved and had put on the darkest, most formal suit in his wardrobe, the nearest thing he had to body armor for his meeting with the assistant deputy director.

"I'll call Hannah from work," he said, standing at the sink.

"She doesn't want you to know." Her tone was flat, matter-of-fact, which meant it was settled, there was nothing more to say.

"Then why did you tell me?" He leaned against the counter.

She put the paper down and turned to him with solitary coolness. "I could ask you the same thing."

He looked away rather than try to answer.

She returned to reading the paper. "I promised Hannah I wouldn't tell you. Wait until I talk to her before you say anything," she called to him as he was leaving.

"Or I could just go on pretending not to know," he wanted to call back, but stopped himself.

The assistant deputy director's assistant was waiting for Noel in the lobby of the main entrance. He sensed right away that things weren't quite right. They shook hands and made early-morning small talk as she escorted him up to the assistant deputy director's office. Less then ten minutes later he was being escorted by her again to his new office down the corridor. He'd been made "subject matter expert" and stuck into a special technologies program being run out of the newly established Defense Intelligence Operations Coordination

Center. "You're being kicked upstairs," the assistant deputy director had told him with a grin. "Congratulations."

As he was being shown his new quarters, he wondered what the hidden agenda was. It was hard not to notice all the things that had been left incomplete—the empty desk, the blank name plaque, the tack-filled walls, and all the details of administrative housekeeping that had been left for him to work out on his own. His staff consisted of just one person: himself. As for all the abruptness and mystery, no reasons were given. He was curious about Cowper. Was he involved? What was the Geneva junket all about? The assistant deputy director was as effusive as he was brief. He said he had personally recommended Noel to the deputy director, who had passed it up to the director, who had fast-tracked the new assignment as part of an agencywide initiative to recruit people with technical, analytical, and operational experience into a "matrix of cross-connected experts to keep up with state-of-the-practice, over-the-horizon technologies." Those were his exact words. At the very end of the meeting, he asked for a copy of Noel's report on the Geneva trip and suggested he think of it as a prelude to exactly the sort of network-extending the new position would involve. "Geography sensitivity is key. We want to know what's happening in other knowledge centers, the synergies we need to explore. Not just in Silicon Valley but in Bangalore and Romania and China and South Africa and Germany."

It was a work of genius. Noel appreciated the periphrastic beauty of bureaucratic jargon. The poetry. Here it was in praxis. He'd been returned to his natural abode, the place where aspirations and potential cancel each other and can be left alone to wilt quietly. The world is full of people just like him who live on the fringes of the group to which they belong. The genius of a large, inefficient bureaucracy is that it accommodates them all. In doing so, it secures and insulates, preserves and protects itself. It may not represent an ideal of social organization, but it is a real world, and the people who inhabit it can be seen at their desks every day all over Washington, spilling out of federal buildings and Metro stations, on jogging trails and bicycle paths and the inner and outer loops of the Beltway.

Or playing golf early on a Saturday morning, which is what Father Neale and Noel have come to East Potomac Park to do.

They carry their bags to the clubhouse and stand on the colonnaded steps, admiring the view down the ninth fairway of the dome-topped War College across the channel at Fort McNair and the DIAC building just across the Anacostia. A slight breeze blows from the southwest, and the dew on the grass glistens just brightly enough for Father Neale to speculate about the speed of the greens.

"This is a flood zone, Father. The greens are either swimming pools or hard as rock. If they don't get you, the swamps in the fairways will."

A trio of blue-and-white air force Hueys comes thundering up the Boundary Channel and passes directly overhead. Father Neale turns to watch as they bank and head out across the Potomac.

"Another feature of the course," Noel says dryly. "We're in the flight path between the Pentagon, the White House, and Bolling and Andrews Air Force Bases."

The priest takes this in, then shrugs. "Guess I'll have to be careful on my drives."

The joke suspends any immediate move toward the discussion Noel has planned. If the priest seems slightly displaced by the surroundings, at least he has taken notice of them. How could anyone not be thrilled to be out here with monuments poking up all around up like pieces on a chessboard? As they are teeing up, another set of choppers hurtles by in a great percussive whir. Father Neale ignores them, tugs on his white leather glove, and practices his swing with the formal absorption of a man serious about the game. He isn't wearing his collar, is dressed as regular as regular can be in a yellow polo shirt and khaki pants, wearing a red Nationals baseball cap from which his gray hair sticks out in tufts. Noel is amused. He has never played with a priest before, was brought up to regard them as somehow above the grit of sports.

Father Neale slices his drive down the left side of the fairway, watches it bounce into the rough, twisted at the waist, club hanging over his shoulder. He unwraps himself, tips his cap back, and plucks his tee from the ground.

"Nice shot, Father," Noel says, stepping up to the tee. His practice swings feel tight. He addresses the ball but checks his swing and steps away. He can't ambush the priest with questions out here. It is not Catholics for Free Choice or Canon Law or *latae sententiae* excommunication he wants to discuss. It's more than that. What he wants to know is how it's possible to believe in so much and understand nothing.

"Something wrong?"

Noel shakes his head and steps up to the tee again. He wishes he were a more likable person. Some people live behind walls, others spend their lives reaching out with good humor and good deeds and live in a state of permanent volunteerism. He doesn't live behind a wall because he doesn't have to. He's invisible. He's never had many friends. Pat is the one exception, but theirs isn't a relationship that began with overpowering attraction. They met in Madison, his senior year at University of Wisconsin. There was no big romance. They just liked each other. Maybe he felt comfortable precisely because there weren't any romantic illusions. After leaving Madison, they moved to Boston and started living together. Noel started grad school at MIT; Pat started the hospital work at Boston General that would become her career. They didn't ever plan where the relationship would go but realized they were more or less contented with each other. Then DARPA came calling, and they ended up in D.C., got married. A year later, Hannah was born. He began working at the Defense Mapping Agency halfway through Reagan's second term and has been through its incarnation as the National Imagery and Mapping Agency and now the National Geospatial Intelligence Agency, embedded since 9/11 as an image scientist at DIAC. Over the years, he's learned to keep very quiet. He's never felt isolated or estranged because of it. In many ways, he has always felt free, has been spared the jostling and striving and preening that most people in Washington claim to hate and find distasteful but engage in anyway. He never aspired to a career in military intelligence. Like his marriage to Pat, it just kind of happened. It wouldn't be fair to call him indifferent. He loves his wife. He also believes in the work he does. He's a technocrat. Utterly dispensable. It doesn't bother him. Nature itself is composed of a great many small, functioning parts. Redundancy is a necessary and vital part of it. His outlook on life is tempered by the nature of his work, which is harsh and messy and done from a distance. He doesn't make any moral claims for it and is disturbed by gratuitous violence and put off by gung-ho Hollywood warriors. He doesn't consider himself a hawk, either. The proudest moments of his career are the things he was spared having to do, things that can be avoided only by paying vigilant attention. He is a realist. The McDonald's hamburger has had more far-reaching consequences than the intercontinental ballistic missile.

He's not an especially interesting or outgoing person. That's enough to make him different from the otherwise "regular" guy he's always seen himself as. He wouldn't say he's a loner or antisocial. Except for golf and reading, he doesn't have any hobbies. He goes to church and is a Roman Catholic because that is the religion he was born into. It gives him a set of defaults to live by. He believes there are other defaults, and they are fine, but he doesn't think too much about them. He doesn't worry about Pat's agnosticism or regret that their daughter was brought up without religious instruction because he believes God doesn't pick and choose and all must all find their own ways to live in grace. He also believes that most people never do, and counts himself among them. The ritual of the mass reminds him to keep trying. He agrees with Saint Paul, who said, "Faith cometh by hearing."

All this runs through his head as they stroke and putt their way through the course. He hasn't rehearsed or prepared a speech but by the fourth hole realizes that if he begins talking, it is all going to come out sounding premeditated and prepared. In addition, Father Neale is having a bad day, slicing and topping his drives, missing easy putts. He isn't the soreheaded sort but doesn't hide the fact that he isn't exactly having fun, either. The atmosphere suddenly changes when, as they pull up to the fifth tee, a red fox dashes out onto the fairway, runs toward them, then darts back and disappears into the rough.

"Do you suppose it lives here?" Father Neale sits down on a

bench behind the tee. "In the middle of all this?" He removes his cap and wipes his brow. "Must be terrifying, balls raining down, people swarming around in carts. Think what it must do to them."

"I guess they've adapted. They wouldn't be here otherwise."

They sit quietly for a minute or so. Father Neale's thoughts are elsewhere. Noel never pegged him for the tenderhearted sort, but the animal has dislodged or reminded him of something. Noel has the feeling of being on a beach—the way children digging in the sand become quiet and draw into themselves. Suddenly, his questions— like questions about the fox—are just background to this quiet digging, an unnecessary interruption, like declaring a fine day with blue sky overhead.

The Washington Monument spikes into the sky directly ahead. Noel suggests that Father Neale hold his club a little lower and aim for the tip of the obelisk. The priest hits his best shot of the morning, a solid drive that lands in the center of the fairway. Noel coaches him on the next few shots, shows him how to adjust his stance, loosen his shoulders, make his head the still center of all movement. "Be silent inside, Father. That's the key." The priest cuts his eyes away and smiles strangely.

By the end of the ninth hole, Noel is glad not to have started a conversation that had no way of opening naturally or coming to any satisfying conclusion. Father Neale is eager for the tips and pointers. They start on the tenth tee very much in instructional mode. Noel points to the taller grass on the inside bend of the dogleg. "The ground there is soft and much wetter than on the other side of the fairway. Aim to the right."

"You missed your calling," Father Neale says.

"Actually, it's pretty much what I do all day."

"What's that?"

"Study features in the landscape."

The priest thinks for a moment. "Where do you work? I don't think I've ever asked."

Noel points with his club. "Right over there. The Defense Intelligence Agency. You can see the building clearly."

The priest takes it in, then shakes his head and says, "You must have a lot on your mind these days."

It is the opening Noel has been waiting for. Strangely, he's lost all desire to seize it. He doesn't know why and can only liken it to the reluctance someone who has been stranded for a long time might show to being rescued and taken away. One can become accustomed to even the most uncomfortable and inhospitable places—like those Japanese World War II soldiers lost for decades on remote Pacific atolls. To be led out, to join the happy crowd, is to become lost all over again.

Which is why, more than a week after telling him about Hannah, Pat has still not been able to admit to her daughter that she has done so.

They are both in a quandary, although not for the same reasons. "She's devastated, and the last thing she needs is to feel any pressure from us."

Noel drops another fifty-pound bag of mulch onto the cart. It is Saturday, and they both know exactly why, without plan or discussion, they've come to Home Depot together—something they never do. Gardening and outdoor chores are all part of his new exercise regimen. The diet is proving to be a bit more of a challenge. He hauls another bag from the stack and drops it onto the cart. "Pressure? I wouldn't know what to pressure her with, Pat. What do you think

I'm going to say? 'Don't do it, dear. You mustn't do it'?" He brushes the black crumbs from his hands. A knot tightens in his stomach. Towering metal shelves and orange hand trucks and people in shorts and flip-flops talking on cell phones, stacks and piles of big and bigger things lining aisles as far as the eye can see. He hates it all, every last bolt and brick and patch of it, up and down Route 50 and I-495, I-95, I-66, and into every carpeted, air-conditioned, and landscaped corner of greater metropolitan Washington.

Pat is too overwhelmed herself to let the matter drop. "She's scheduled the procedure but doesn't want me to come."

"Don't go, then." It comes out curt and cruel—which was exactly how he'd wanted it to come out. Pat was stunned. They are facing one another across two hundred pounds of shredded bark, one of those moments that can either veer into chaos or restore calm. He turns away and begins hauling another bag from the pile. Pat is suddenly at his side. "Don't. That's plenty for now. Come on, let's go."

They push the cart down the crowded aisle, maneuver to the cashier, swipe the credit card, sign, collect the receipt, shove the heaping bags across the parking lot in front of irritated drivers, iPods, iPhones, and flip-flops. He feels sunk in all of it, sunk into it side by side. All of a sudden, he sees the two of them the way the elderly often appear, lost together as one, barely in control, loaded down with matter. Then they are in the car, driving. Pat is sitting with her hands in her lap, overtly composed. The roomy front seats of the Lincoln Navigator both diminish and make them grand. Pat has taken to wearing a visor in the car, which she claims helps with the glare. The dowdiness used to irritate him. Now he not only accepts it but finds it sweet, the way he finds the little pouches of freckled flesh at her elbows (which she hates) sweet, or the way she bobs her head when she brushes her hair, or bends forward and dangles her breasts to slip off her bra.

"I'm going down to spend a few days with her afterward," she says calmly, as if returning to unfinished business.

"Am I supposed to know?"

Pat looks out the window. "Try and understand, Noel. I know it's painful. But try. You're her father."

"Yes, I am. And while we're on the subject. What about him? Where's the father in all this?"

Some atavistic maleness asserts itself. He feels a sudden solidarity with the excluded father, who, he has gathered from Pat, was too casual a fling to be informed, much less brought into the decision-making. It goes against all he's been taught about sanctity and respect for life. By the time they are back home, unloading the bags and hauling them, one by one, into the backyard, he begins to think he ought to be glad for the feminism that puts men squarely in the backseat of "choice," and he suddenly feels a twinge of disgust for the poor dumb schmuck who bedded his daughter (once? two times?) and will live out his life never knowing the consequences.

The afternoon passes in a frenzy of gardening and errands punctuated with brief exchanges that are reassuring and intimate only because they are so trivial. He likes how the wisteria has overtaken the rear fence and pushed its way through the wooden boards. Pat doesn't. The hedge along the driveway that he wants to take down? Leave it, she says, even if it blocks the walkway on that side of the house. The roof gutters badly need cleaning, which he does as Pat stands at the base of the ladder—completely unnecessarily—and then becomes irritated when some of the debris falls on her.

"Well, don't stand there!"

"How else am I going to hold the ladder?"

"Don't hold the ladder!"

"It isn't steady."

"It's steady enough."

"I'm not letting go so you can fall and break your neck."

When Steve and Margaret Kritsick drive by with a toot and a wave, Pat suggests having them over for drinks later on. Noel would rather not, but before he reaches the bottom rung of the ladder she is speed-dialing Margaret. He realizes she's merely trying to distract, following a sensible rule of married life, which is to avoid overstatements of ill-being and to be cautious and brief discussing issues that may veer in that direction. Minute detail is to be avoided. "Mindfucking," it's called. A curious term meant to express a general weariness with useless talk or meditation. And it can be done to death. He can't help suspecting that what the term really signals is something dried up within.

So the avoidance strategy continues with the invitation to the Kritsicks to dinner—which, Pat decides, will be simple and, given the fine weather, done outside on the grill. After he's cleaned the front and rear gutters, Pat goes to pick up what they'll need. Noel puts the ladder back in the garage, drags the bloated leaf bags down to the curb, then goes inside. After a moment of indecision, he picks up the telephone.

Hannah answers on the second ring, a cheerful "Hi, Dad."

"Hey, finally."

"I know. I'm sorry. Things've been really hectic. Finals. End of year. How was your trip?"

"I've been back over a week." There is a shuffle and some static on the other end of the line. "You there?"

"Stepping outside for a better signal. Can you hear me?"

"I can hear you just fine. Your mother and I have been worried about you."

"I know, Dad. I know. I'm sorry."

"Is everything all right?"

"Fine, Dad. Just crazy busy."

"Well, you had us both very worried."

"Everything's fine. Mom told you I'm moving into a new place, right?"

"Yes, I guess she did mention that." In fact, Pat hasn't said anything to him about moving at all. He realizes he is being probed. "Where is it you're moving?"

"A group house. Three med students and a nurse, close to campus."

"Are you coming home before the move?"

"Can't, Dad. I start work next week. Didn't Mom tell you?"

"I guess she did, yeah. What kind of job?"

"An assistant over at the Cell Biology Lab. Doing research on epithelial cell signaling."

"Epi-what?"

"Epithelial cell signaling. I'm totally psyched. Basically, we're working on a treatment for dry eye. You know what that is, don't you?"

When you can't cry, he is about to say, but resists the temptation. "It sounds like you'll be busy. Will we be seeing you at all this summer?"

"Depends. Mom's coming out for a visit and to help me move."

"She mentioned that. Can I do anything?"

In the brief pause that follows, an image flashes through his head of Pat and him as parents, changing diapers, warming bottles. "Well, actually, there is," she says. "I didn't want to ask." She pauses again, and it takes all his effort not to begin talking. "I'm going to need a security deposit for the new place."

"A security deposit?"

"I've got the first month's rent. And the people I'm sharing the house with said I could pay over the course of the month, when my paychecks start." There is another brief silence, as if she were suddenly distracted by something. A knock at the door? A tap on the shoulder?

"It's not a big deal. I can get by without it."

His heart begins to race as he realizes the veil is not going to be lifted. "How much do you need?"

"Twelve hundred dollars."

"For a security deposit?"

"First and last month's rent plus two hundred for cable and Internet. We've got broadband." When he doesn't answer right away, she says, "It's okay, Dad. I can get by without it."

He can't speak, is suddenly on the verge of choking up. It's the cheery tone of a hurt child, the stuff of bad matinees that goes right to the pit of the stomach no matter how transparent and kitschy. He wants to help but sees she is beyond any help he has to offer. All he can do is allow her to protect her dignity. Keep silent. And give her the money. "Where should I send the check?"

"Just give it to Mom. She'll be here next week."

"Who should I make the check out to?"

"Just make it out to me."

"Not the landlord?"

A pause signals her suspicion. "It's a group house, Dad. The landlord has nothing to do with it. The money goes into escrow."

"I see."

There isn't any point continuing, no way of offering or conditioning help without some form of admission or negation. It isn't
charity being offered. It's something else.

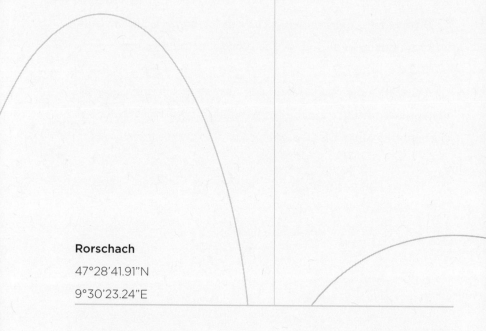

Coming into Washington, morning commuters are blinded by sunlight that backs up traffic on eastbound Interstate 66. The glare is especially intense between Ballston and Rosslyn, where the road suddenly narrows in a series of descending curves. High walls on either side seem to concentrate and focus the light. This "glare factor" will occasionally be mentioned in the morning traffic report on the radio. I always find that funny and smile at the thought of people strapped into their automobiles like crash-test dummies, blinded by the sun.

I've spent years driving into and out of Washington, D.C. But it wasn't until the CIA denied all my Freedom of Information Act requests—and the Agency Release Panel rejected my appeals—that I came to understand how visibility in this city rests on a peculiar paradox. Namely, that "transparence," the bureaucratic term of art for making the inner workings of the state visible, is the very attribute that renders objects *invisible*, i.e., permeable to light, vague and insubstantial. Even the language—"neither confirming nor denying the fact of the existence or nonexistence of requested records"—has entered the culture as an example of state obfuscation. The list of CIA exemptions to the Freedom of Information Act is extensive. My personal favorite is (b)(9), which "exempts from disclosure geological and geophysical information and data, including maps, concerning wells."

Wells? I couldn't help smiling at the thought as the Inter-City Express pulled out of the Zürich train station. It was early afternoon. I wondered if my abrupt departure from La Corbière had been noticed. On the outskirts of Zürich, the train began to gain speed. I took down my suitcase and decided to use the time to review more of the material I had brought with me. The months gathering it hadn't been wasted. In spite of the FOIA denials, I knew enough of my father's Vietnam experience. It had been personal, close up. *Last night one of the artillery batteries fired incorrectly and plowed into one of my favorite hamlets. Destroyed two "structures" and badly wounded one. Nobody likes this sort of thing and all hell is being handed out in the artillery. Sloppiness and bad coordination, I guess. I'll make it my business to go out and see the damage and ask what can be done to cut short whatever negative reactions this might have. Everyone is pissed off.*

I tried to imagine what a badly wounded "structure" was. The letters were filled with euphemisms and shaded references. I still couldn't connect anything with anything, was without a map or even the simplest set of directions. The only person I could talk to was my mother, whose retreat from the world I had always been critical of. I went over to see her when the final FOIA appeal was turned down, and of course, we started off immediately in the wrong direction. She'd been reading a book by an Irish writer named John McGahern, which I saw on the coffee table when I came in. As it happened, I'd read the book. That she was drawn to McGahern's depiction of contemporary rural Ireland, a world of people isolated by history, lifting their heads to observe but never taking part, made perfect sense. I picked up the book and leafed through the pages. "Why did you write 'Grandma Donahoe' here?" I asked, pointing to the margin.

"It reminded me of her, I suppose."

"Did Grandma Donahoe keep bees and make coffee from soaked dandelion roots, too?"

She lifted her eyes but didn't respond. I felt bad but couldn't help my reaction. The solipsistic personalization of everything she read always struck me as compensation for her willful detachment. If she would only face the world with a fraction of the intensity she directed to the margins of her books.

"Would you like to go to Ireland someday, Mom?"

"Why would I go to Ireland?"

"To visit. See it for yourself."

"Why would I want to do that? I have everything I need here."

"That's not the point."

"Oh? What's the point?"

I had to force myself not to get angry. "Well, to see the place you've always been so interested in, for one. You always talk about being Irish, and you've never set foot there."

She put aside her knitting and took off her glasses. "And go traipsing around like all the other Americans looking for their roots? I'm sorry, that's not for me."

"Why do you have to put it that way? You don't have to traipse around with anyone. Just go and have a look for yourself."

She put her glasses back on. "I don't feel the need. If I did go, I'd only be a stranger."

"At least you'd be seeing it with your own eyes."

"What would I see?"

"People. Places. Things!"

She smiled and picked up her knitting again. I knew the lofty, dismissive look. It made me angry. "Even going over there just to drink would be a break from doing it here all alone." I regretted my words immediately.

She eyed me calmly. "Do you really think so?"

"Yes, goddamn it, I do!"

"I'm not going to Ireland," she said.

I felt stupid for turning it into a fight. I went into the kitchen, poured myself a glass of water, and drank it standing at the sink. I wasn't above mentioning her alcoholism from time to time. But it was cruel. Feeling guilty, I returned to the living room and told her what I'd come to tell her about the rejected FOIA appeal.

She read the letter and handed it back. "You really think Dad was in the CIA?"

"Yes."

"It never occurred to me."

"Never?"

"Why would it?"

"You can't tell me you never suspected there was more to Dad's career than cocktail parties and inspection tours."

"What was there to be suspicious about? Foreign Service people are posted all over the world, and they certainly are not all with the CIA. We were no different."

"What about all the weird stories you've told me?"

"Such as?"

"Such as the one about being dragged out of the car by soldiers in Addis."

"That was scary, not weird. It happened right after a coup attempt. We were foreigners. It could have happened to anybody."

"But you said Dad disappeared right before the coup and only reappeared after it was all over. You weren't suspicious?"

"I was too scared to be suspicious."

"How did he explain himself?"

"He had to fly up to Asmara. He was only supposed to be gone for the day but got stranded there because of the coup."

"You believed him?"

"Of course I believed him. The whole country shut down for three days. The embassy called and said your dad was safe and told me not to leave the house. You were only two months old. Penina, the nurse we hired to help take care of you, was with me. We did what we were told. Stayed in the house and closed all the curtains and said rosaries and drank Campari. There was shooting in the streets. At one point the apartment building was strafed. It happened late at night, and we crawled under the bed, me and you and Penina. We were scared, but looking back, it was also kind of fun in a strange way. Don't ask me why, but I never really thought anything bad could happen to us."

"What about the soldiers?"

"That happened after Dad got back. Haile Selassie was back in the palace, and the police were rounding up people all over the place. We were driving back from a friend's house. A day or two after the coup ended. It was a weekend, I think. Some soldiers appeared in the road. They stopped us and pulled us out of the car and walked us down into a culvert. They made us sit down and put our hands on our heads. All I can remember is their guns and wanting to say the Hail Mary and not being able to. I couldn't remember the words!"

"What did they do?"

"They told Dad to hand over his watch. He didn't have it on, and they made him empty his pockets. He turned his pockets inside out, saying, 'American Embassy American Embassy.' They made us sit there with our hands on our heads. I don't know how long. Then suddenly, they just disappeared. Vanished. After a while Dad crawled out of the culvert and looked around. We got in the car and went home. We didn't speak the whole way. When we got to the house, he came around and opened the door for me, but I couldn't stand up. I was completely paralyzed. He had to lift me out of the car and carry me into the house."

The book she gave me that day—*The Emperor: Downfall of an Autocrat* by Ryszard Kapuściński—was thrown in among all the other reading material I had with me on the train. Why I hadn't bothered to look at it until that moment is difficult to say. I picked up the slightly yellowed paperback with the portrait of crevasse-browed, beribboned Haile Selassie on the cover and opened it to find the margins filled with my mother's neat, Palmer-method cursive.

The following day, at noon, the Emperor's eldest son and the heir to the throne, Asfa Wossen, read a proclamation on the radio in the name of the rebels. [we were hiding in the house] ... *The battle for Addis Ababa begins. Hundreds meet death in the streets.* [house strafed] ... *The airplane carrying the Emperor lands in Asmara.* [Dad was there Penina calls it Little Rome her brother lives there, a priest] ... *Once the shooting had died down, the army patrolled the quiet city that only now, long after the fact, was beginning to feel the horror and the shock.* [Bielak's house] ... *Every-one was waiting to see what the Emperor would do and declare next* [off to Bishoftu in the rain, once again].

I could hear my father's baritone. Anytime we started on a long car trip, he'd grip the steering wheel in both hands and sing the lines in his best mock Gilbert and Sullivan: *Oh, we're off to Bishoftu in the rain, once again.* The lake was a favorite weekend outing and forms part of the impression I have of my parents' time in Ethiopia. The dusty colonialism and imported antique splendor—Kaiser Wilhelm's monogrammed horse carriage, a well-aged fleet of Rolls Royces, Coptic Patriarchs under silk-tasseled umbrellas—had been molder-ing for a generation. During the coup, Haile Selassie was escorted by American advisers in white shirts and ties—not off to Bishoftu but, in secret, off to Liberia in a DC-6 to wait out the coup, then via Asmara back to Addis in time to see the body of Colonel Workneh hanging from a tree in front of Saint George Cathedral.

My mother's marginalia was not just a residue of private associa-tions but a fascinating parallel narrative. I didn't realize how intently I was following it until the woman on the train next to me began to chuckle. "I've never seen someone turn a book in so many different angles to read," she said.

"They're notes." I offered the book so she could see the neat, microscopic script for herself. She asked if I'd been to Ethiopia. I told her I had.

"Really? Me, too. I was also in Tanzania and Kenya," she said. "I didn't meet many Americans. Mostly it's Europeans you find travel-ing in those places."

I shrugged and admitted how little traveled and generally less cosmopolitan Americans are than Europeans. This put her on guard.

I felt bad for resorting to sarcasm, remembering how distasteful I always found my father's parlor game, playing the arrogant American rube. It bothered me that I had nothing more tangible from him than these bits and scraps. The image I keep in my mind is of him knocking the ash from his cigarette, gazing into a middle distance, as if looking beyond tedious clutter. He left nothing behind. No property, no money, no debts, no diaries, no journals. All I have are his letters from Vietnam, an old self-winding Seiko wristwatch with a black dial, and the tortoiseshell glasses he wore—so I know what his prescription was, and that he was very nearsighted. I also know that in recalling what he wanted forgotten, I am giving away all he ever kept. Is that a betrayal? I think of it more as a matter of saying goodbye. Not to deny him the forgetting but neither to let him slip into oblivion without forgiveness. It's forgive and forget, not forget and forgive.

But how to achieve either if what is to be forgiven will not be revealed in the first place?

In 1961, we were in Lagos; then we moved to Kaduna, where the Nigeria Defence Academy was being set up for the newly independent country. My parents never talked about what happened to them in Nigeria. There was a hasty, unplanned departure. In the documents I received from the State Department was a single letter sent back to Washington by my father: *There are excellent reasons for changing personnel rapidly in the Kaduna small-town situation. The British, who are very important to us, have very definite feelings about this.*

There is no further elaboration, and the only personal artifacts remaining from those years are a carved Yoruba head that my mother keeps on a side table in her apartment and some tattered editions of *Black Orpheus*, a literary journal out of Ibadan, compliments of the editor, Ulli Beier, the German founder. I had the magazines with me on the train, too. A newspaper clipping dropped out when I opened one of them, showing my very young, Buddy Holly–looking father with Edward R. Murrow, who was touring Nigeria as head of USIA. I slipped the brittle clipping back between the pages. It was a treasured object. I had always kept it where I'd first come across it, discolored by acidified newsprint and ink. I knew some of the story behind *Black Orpheus* and the Congress for Cultural Freedom, CIA funding of which had been exposed in 1967. The list of CCF publications was a long one. Most prominent was the magazine *Encounter*, founded and edited by Melvin Lasky, Stephen Spender, and Irving Kristol. It was one of dozens of magazines delivered to our many APO addresses. The picture in my head of those long-gone African years is not much more than a caricature: apartments furnished with the stuff of earnest graduate students discovering jazz, abstract expressionism, African art, and negritude, translating and transferring those symbols into the liberalism of the civil rights era. That was who my parents were and how I understood my father's career and his politics. Cold War liberalism seems a little naive today. Really, it was anything but. The enterprise was vast, hard-boiled, and ambitious, as much a bulwark against Soviet expansionism as a complete revamping of capitalism's image, smoothing the edges of what was going to become an even more dangerous, unfair world.

I watched out of the window as the train left Rorschach and sped along the Lake Constance shoreline. The sky was overcast. In the distance, a ferry moved across the choppy, slate-gray water. I felt as if I didn't belong there, an incongruous presence moving silently and at high speed through a pictured landscape. One of the pleasures in traveling alone is of being confirmed in one's nonbelonging. Even what I was carrying with me in my bags didn't belong. I took out another copy of *Black Orpheus* and leafed through the familiar pages. It conjured memories of televisionless rainy days staying home from school. My favorite story in it was by Gabriel Okara. I'd memorized the opening lines: "Some of the townsmen said Okolu's eyes were not right, his head was not correct. This, they said, was the result of his knowing too much book." To me, that was how African writers should sound. Conscious of their unique world and the impossibility of conveying it to outsiders. Okolu (which means voice) is looking for IT. In highly idiosyncratic English suffused with Okara's mother-tongue, Ijaw, the search for IT takes Okolu through a landscape both strange and familiar. We see palm trees, egrets, canoes being paddled in the hot sun by young girls with half-ripe breasts; we hear an old witch asking Okolu, "How or where do you think you will find IT, when everybody surface-water-things tell, when things have no more root? How do you expect to find IT when fear has locked up the insides of the low, and the insides of the high are filled up with nothing but yam?"

Again, the woman beside me took notice. "It must be very funny," she said, unwrapping a sandwich, half of which she offered.

"It is," I said, declining.

"Do you collect old magazines?" she asked.

"No," I said, momentarily puzzled. It hadn't occurred to me how odd it might appear. I showed her the passage that had made me laugh.

She finished chewing and wiped her fingers on her jeans before accepting the magazine from me. "Nothing but yam," she read, pronouncing it *yem*. "Are you an Africanist?" she wanted to know.

"No. But I lived there as a child."

"Your parents were missionaries?"

"I suppose in a way, yes."

"How in a way?"

"My father was in the Foreign Service," I said, switching to German. "We lived in many countries. Including here."

"So you speak German!" she said, also switching. "Where are you going?"

"München."

She handed the magazine back. "Are you on holiday?"

I had to think for a moment before answering, "I'm visiting family."

"You have family in München?"

"Yes. Well. Yes, I suppose I do." I didn't know what else to say. I'd developed a certain talent over the years for extending and contracting the boundaries of my private realm, as we all must, to fit changing situations. The larger constellations have always been more or less fixed, there was always a house to return to, and people in that house. I realized I had no idea what I was heading into. "It's a little complicated," I finally said.

"Families are always difficult." She used the German *schwierig*. I had the sense she'd chosen her words deliberately.

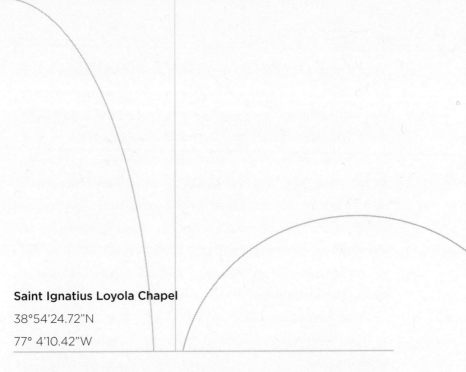

Saint Ignatius Loyola Chapel
38°54'24.72"N
77° 4'10.42"W

The box in the trunk of the Navigator has become a reminder of
everything Noel would like to say good-bye to and forget. It's taken
some effort, but his new office is beginning to function. Paper is being passed through it, his presence is now required at meetings. Topic
of the first meeting: *Achieving a global enterprise service delivery operating
model.* The jargon couldn't be more removed from the vocabulary he
is used to. It's pretty clear that he isn't the only newly tasked subject
matter expert around. The whole agency has been shaken from top
to bottom and the shifting tectonic plates shuffled together like an
enormous deck of cards, bringing strata into contact that previously
couldn't have been kept further apart. With him at the first meeting
were a retired army captain and mother of two who had lost an arm
to an IED outside Najaf and a twentysomething prodigy with a PhD
in chemistry who grew up in Islamabad and Fairlawn, New Jersey.
Since starting his new job, Noel has seen nothing of his former cell
colleagues. He looks for Cowper on his way in and out of the build-

ing, has rehearsed what he will say when and if their paths ever cross. All week there have been news reports out of Pakistan of drone operations. Yesterday a front-page story of another Predator attack in South Waziristan. Video of carnage all over the Internet.

An hour after he spoke with Hannah on the phone, the Kritsicks arrived riding brand-new bicycles. They coasted into the driveway wearing brightly colored helmets and shoes with clips. All the latest gear. "We've started bike commuting," Steve said, removing his helmet with a satisfied swagger. "Totally carbon-neutral. The commuter package. Panniers. Safety lights. Gel seat." He pushed a button and startled them with a loud blast. "Air horn." He laughed.

"Not exactly carbon-neutral," Noel said.

"Ever tried using a bell on M Street? Even a Metrobus driver'll hear this sucker."

"You pack all your work clothes?" Pat asked, pointing to the luggage cases.

"We have lockers and a changing room at the office."

"The full wardrobe," Margaret offered. "On Friday, it all goes to the cleaners. His laundry stays downtown. It's great."

Pat nodded admiringly. "We ought to think about doing that, too."

They rolled their bikes into the garage and went around to the back patio, where Pat had put out food and drinks. The Kritsicks' bike shoes clicked on the flagstones. The sun was setting, and the air was pungent with freshly spread mulch. Dark beds, emerald grass. Pat had gone to Costco and come back with twenty-ounce ribeyes, artichokes the size of grapefruits, mixed organic greens, a wedge of Stilton, bottles of cabernet sauvignon and pinot noir and a twenty-year-old port. Noel understood right away. It was a backhanded peace offering, protein- and alcohol-rich for full soporific effect. If it went pleasantly enough, maybe even an erotic finale, after which all would be disremembered and forgiven—mother-daughter conspiracies, hotel whores, marital fissures, and fault lines. The works.

Kritsick was his usual talkative self, complimenting the yard and describing the various bike routes he was exploring into downtown. Margaret and Pat were discussing the wisteria overhanging the fence. Noel's mind wandered, as it always did with Kritsick. Almost immediately, he became suspicious. Then alarmed. Had Pat said anything to them? It sickened him to think so. He sipped his bourbon (the rest were drinking wine), half listening to Kritsick, watching Pat talk to Margaret. Finally, he tossed back his drink and stood up. "Time for a refill. Can I get you anything?"

Kritsick looked into his largely untouched glass. "No, thanks. I'm fine."

"I'll be right back." He went inside, letting the screen door slam. The bourbon was on the kitchen counter. He hesitated, then called through the open window to Pat. She rolled her eyes and began to get up, but Kritsick was on his feet and clicking across the flagstones toward the kitchen. "Let me help," he said, bending down in the doorway to pull off his bicycle shoes. "Don't want to scratch the floor." Pat was right behind him. Kritsick hopped aside to let her through. There was nothing left but to give in to the whole cheery farce. Noel prepared the steaks while Kritsick, in his socks, set merrily about concocting a special dipping sauce for the artichokes. By the time he'd knocked off his third bourbon, Noel couldn't have cared less who knew what. He abandoned himself to the evening— ending it with fresh pears, scoops of Stilton, a generous glass of port.

He woke up on the sofa, vaguely recalling the Kritsicks pedaling off into the night with waves and thanks for "a really great evening" and a blast on the air horn.

Two days later, Pat left for Charlottesville. It was as if a weight had been lifted. A few hurried phone calls the night before had confirmed that, yes, Hannah had gone ahead with the "procedure"; yes, she was fine and didn't mind if Mom wanted to come visit; no, she still didn't want Dad to know.

"We've got to respect her wishes," Pat kept saying. "Things will be different when it's all over and she's had some time to recover and reflect."

He sipped his coffee, glanced at the kitchen clock. *Good Morning America* droned in the background—five must-knows about your 401(k). Pat had brought her overnight bag downstairs, was waiting to take some things out of the dryer. She let the comment slide, as he should have done, too. But he couldn't.

"Don't you find it just slightly, I mean just passing strange?"

"Find what strange?"

"She lied, Pat. It's one thing to keep quiet, to not say anything. But she told me she needed a security deposit. Not money for an abortion." As soon as he'd spoken, he knew that it was being entered into the list of conjugal utterances never to be forgotten.

Pat glared at him, shaking her head. "You are a Neanderthal, Noel. Really. I can't believe you. She's a grown woman. She has a right to privacy." She got up and marched down the basement steps to fetch her things from the dryer.

He flushed and grew hot. "And you're just going to pretend you never told me," he called after her. "That's not even Neanderthal, Pat. That's just plain fucking wrong!"

He was upstairs in the bathroom when she drove off. He heard the front door, then the car door slam, heard her drive away. It was not how he'd wanted things to go, but when he came downstairs, a sense of relief came over him. Yes, it was relief—and entirely unexpected. He went into the kitchen. The television was off, the breakfast dishes were still out. Toast crumbs, coffee cups, orange juice and milk; morning sun through the window. The sight of it drained away all his anger. He stood in the middle of the room. The house was quiet, and he was all alone.

For the past three days now, he has been trying to concoct alternative scenarios and outcomes. For Pat. For Hannah. For himself. It's a professional habit of mind, the image scientist looking for parallel orders of legibility, formulating plausible interpretations. Broadening connotations. Variations of what might also be. Was he getting back what he deserved? Even if it was silly to frame it like that, just thinking so was enough to give potency to the whole notion. Hannah's attitude was a reflection of his own lack of candor. What would that look like as a satellite image? With topographic, geographic, and moral overlays? Every day, as he drives through the main gate at Bolling, he finds himself at the center of a thousand potential relationships. The panel on the dashboard gives his exact location, sandwiched between the Anacostia Naval Station and the Naval Research Laboratory. Across the river is Fort McNair, the Army War College and National Defense University. On the hillside overlooking all this infrastructure is Saint Elizabeth's, now a dilapidated complex of gothic revival buildings. On his office wall is a framed 1861 Sachse & Co. lithograph postcard, *View from the Lunatic Asylum*. Ezra Pound spent twelve years there after being declared incompetent to stand trial on charges of treason. Today, a postcard view of this part of the city would have to include Pound looking down from the hillside asylum onto Curtis LeMay's house at Bolling—*The Poet and the Bomber General*—two madmen responding to the age. But even with irony and precision measurements, it's easy for Noel to forget where he is. He now has a reserved parking space, goes to work in a different part of the building in a capacity that still pinches like a new pair of shoes. Today, his schedule includes a meeting at the Pentagon on upcoming field tests being done in Sardinia under the auspices of NATO's Electronic Warfare Working Group. Trial Imperial Hammer. It's a welcome change from his last trip to the Pentagon with Cowper. Walking from the shuttle stop, he pauses to take in the view across the Potomac. It is a warm, muggy morning. A haze hangs over the river. The monuments on the other side only heighten the ant-like feel of the place, make him feel embedded in a vast, deposited experience.

He strides though the metal detector, gathers his x-rayed laptop and bag from the conveyer belt, and hurries to find the conference room. Up one floor, down Corridor 8 to C Ring, Bay 500. He grips the shoulder strap, presses the bag against his hip, and speeds along thinking of Tiger Woods's two eighteenth-hole birdies and sudden-death U.S. Open win against Rocco Mediate and of his last trip here with Cowper. The mishap meetings. He recalls his overheated concluding statement in the general counsel's office. It had drawn blank stares and a panicked, sidelong glance from Cowper. Rule number one—*Don't talk above your pay grade*. Was rule number two *Always talk above your pay grade*? He smiles, picks up the pace. Hell, if you want to piss with the big horses, you have to let them know you're up to it.

The corridors and ramps narrow his field of vision. He passes a group of pilots in flight fatigues. They are all slim, athletic, carrying identical laminated plastic folders. How can he not be thrilled? Or feel dowdy by comparison, prickling with sweat in his Jos. Banks suit and tie? A soft man doing a hard man's work? Or a hard man doing a soft man's work? The Pentagon is full of both. Noel can't help dividing the people he sees streaming down the crowded corridors into these two categories. It has never been clear to which one he belongs. How would Pat assign him? He can't say; and that is more troubling than either of the two options.

He arrives at the conference room in time to get a seat "at table," a good seat, and settles into it with a practiced air of preoccupation. Quiet greetings and murmured conversation run in the background. He clasps hands, fingers laced, focused and attentive, emitting wry confidence as light escapes through a crack. Hard charm only works when it seems inadvertent.

He has come prepared with a brief—"Interoperability and Situational Awareness: Tall Corn and the Taliban," based on after-action reports of patrols by Dutch NATO troops in Uruzgan, where the positions of Taliban fighters hiding in harvest-ready cornfields can be seen by high-altitude UAVs and coordinates delivered in real time. He came up with the subtitle riding over on the shuttle, penciled it onto the margin of his printout, where he has also written some talking points. But, by meeting's end, in spite of every effort, he has failed to get in a single word. He isn't the only frustrated one. Filing out of the conference room, he overhears a J2 colonel complaining about the NATO assistant secretary general, the distinguished speaker, who ran out the clock with a long-winded statement and a video presentation and then instructed them to pass their proposals to his adjutant on the way out. "Pompous fucker," the colonel declares. Noel makes sympathetic eye contact, then shoulders his computer and hurries off to catch the shuttle back to Bolling.

He considers stopping for a sandwich, then decides against it. A group of workmen is installing a new exhibit in a glass case at the end of the corridor. *Carrier Nimitz*. Just a few months ago, a Russian TU-95 Bear bomber buzzed the deck of the supercarrier, flew over it twice at under two thousand feet, and had to be escorted out of the airspace by F18 Hornets. Noel passes the display without slowing down. He feels pressed to leave every time he comes here. The place unsettles him. It's too big. He imagines FDR, cigarette holder clenched in his teeth, ordering it to be built out of sight of the monuments and the Mall. Put it over there in Hell's Bottom, Colonel Groves. That's what this stretch of riverfront was once called. Muddy marshland, a railroad yard, a dingy slum of tin and brick. Official groundbreaking date: September 11, 1941.

As he is waiting for the shuttle, Pat calls.

"Didn't think I'd get you." Her tone is slightly flat but not unfriendly.

"I'm at the Pentagon. How's Hannah?"

"She's fine. We're having a good time, considering."

"Did she get the check?"

"Yes, she did. And it was important. I know how it upsets you, Noel, but really. It was the right thing to do."

"Give her a security deposit?"

"Come on, Noel."

He steps aside to let a group of people pass by. A warm breeze blows across the lot, on it the smells of tar and car exhaust. He can see the airplanes stacked up beyond the Rosslyn skyline, coming downriver toward National, one by one. "When are you coming home?"

"I'm going to stay another day or two." She pauses. "I think being here is the right thing for now."

Noel looks down at his scuffed oxfords.

"To be honest, I'm enjoying the break, too," she says. "Things've been pretty lousy lately. I'm sure you'll agree."

He does agree, but not out loud. At the end of the platform, he turns and begins pacing back, hooking a finger under the shoulder strap to keep it from slipping. "Did you tell her I know?"

"No. We talked about it, and she's adamant. I don't think she's going to change her mind."

For the first time, the full meaning of it sinks in. Until now, he'd assumed he'd be told at some remove in time, when all were solidly and securely recovered. It would be presented as something to accept and get beyond, a minor feature of family geography to be passed over, preferably overlooked entirely. It wouldn't matter.

"Are you still there?"

"I'm here."

"Have you been getting any exercise?" she asks, changing the subject.

"Not really, no."

"Why don't you try walking with me? You might like it."

He'd like to give her a flat-out no but instead says, "Maybe."

"Listen, Noel. I just wanted to let you know I'm staying another day or two. We'll talk when I get home."

The air conditioning on the shuttle is turned up high. He holds his computer case on his lap, closes his eyes as the bus maneuvers through the lots, pulls directly onto I-395. He knows his precise location as they cross the Fourteenth Street Bridge, where he is in relation to all the monuments, the city grid, traffic patterns, the federal bureaucracy, budget processes, election cycles, wars in Afghanistan, Iraq, GWOT—all the big structures. It's reassuring to know his place, not a man of destiny but a cog—a cog with teeth and gears. He fits just fine. It's ordinary life he can't connect to. Getting dressed and coming downstairs, backing out of his driveway, waiting in traffic on Route 50, going to the post office, getting coffee. Being let in on Hannah's secret. It's always been his job to work with privileged information. Like seeing fighters in a cornfield from high above. But what good is knowing something when there is nothing to be done about it? When knowing is not a function of clear seeing but only clouds and muddles things?

The trip back to Bolling takes nearly an hour because of an accident. The long ride has everybody in a bad mood. He files off the bus with a muttered thank-you to the driver. It's already midafternoon. He needs to get off a memo before he can quit for the day. It feels odd to be working alone, outside the cell, free to come and go. The wind is blowing in gusts off the river. Storm clouds are massing. It often happens that the rain he sees falling up in Northwest never makes it down to the low-lying plains of Southeast—except as runoff. He once bet Cowper that more rain fell on the National Cathedral than on the National Mall. It was true, a meteorological fact. The NOAA data showed two inches more of average annual precipitation in Northwest than in Southeast. It was also hotter down here in Anacostia—three degrees hotter—and average wind speeds were two mph higher. Hotter, drier, windier. There are plenty of other inequalities, too. But high fences and highways keep them out of view. The slice of Washington, D.C., known as Ward 8 may as well be another planet.

Back at his desk, he has trouble arranging his thoughts. Everything is a distraction. A buzzing light fixture. The whirring hard disk on his computer. SIPERNET, NIPRNET, Internet windows and tabs he keeps open or minimized on screen: another missile strike in Pakistan, USAFCENT daily Airpower Summary, the Delta II launch at Vandenberg carrying the third Cosmo Sky-Med earth observation satellite, Diabetes Awareness Day, his e-mail in-box. Everything he must keep keeping up with. Lately, he's been wondering how long he can continue. But even if he quit tomorrow, would it really be possible to step back and say, okay, go on, but without me? Blast into speed-walking, power-steering, air-conditioned, motion-picture old age?

At 17:45 he is squeezing the Navigator into a tight parking space on N Street in Georgetown. He finally manages on the third try, but not without touching off the alarm of a blue Porsche just behind him. He gets out to inspect. The alarm wails away, then stutters abruptly and falls silent. Nothing broken, just a little scraped paint. He glances about, waiting for the owner of the angry automobile to materialize, thinking it must be a man, and a man still young enough to overprize his car, whereas Noel feels old enough not to prize anything or give a damn about his own or anybody else's dents and scratches. He looks at his watch. It's late. If he runs, he might still make it in time for communion. A few more seconds pass. Then, feeling absolved and within his rights, he crosses the street and walks briskly away.

Father Neale is just giving the dismissal—*ite, Missa est*—as Noel enters and stands at the back of the chapel. Except for an elderly couple seated near the front, the pews are empty. Noel is about to turn and leave, but the priest beckons to him from the altar. *Me?* Father Neale nods. Noel walks up the aisle and follows him into the sacristy.

There is something unsettling about watching a priest remove his vestments. Noel hasn't been in a sacristy since his altar-boy days. He remembers the walk-in Diebold safe with combination lock where the gold chalices and wine were kept. Father Neale chats amiably as he removes and carefully stores away his vestments. A leaky roof, drafty windows that need reglazing, unreliable roofers. He genuflects, holding on to the edge of the vestment table with both hands, then turns to Noel and asks, "So. What can I do for you?"

Is it that obvious? Has he come for something? Mass is all he'd had in mind, but, well, here he is, a little tired, nobody waiting for him at home. The priest stands, hands clasped in front, as if waiting for Noel to catch up. "Well, Father." Noel shifts, looks down at his feet. "Have you ever considered giving everything up?" Immediately, he feels foolish and begins to qualify. "Well, I don't mean everything. Just the things you've always taken for granted."

"Such as?"

"You know, the little things," he deadpans, attempting bathos. "Career. Family."

The priest looks at his watch. "Well, since it's just the little stuff, why don't you come to the rectory and have a drink?"

A short time later, after a brief introduction to the housekeeper, a cheerful Nicaraguan woman whom Father Neale, in fluent Spanish, introduced as the *señora de casas*, they are sitting in an old-fashioned Georgetown drawing room with curtained windows and a fireplace. A television is set into an open cabinet in the bookcase, which also features a built-in sink and generously stocked bar. Hanging over the mantel is an old portrait of Bishop John Carroll, founder of Georgetown University. On another wall is a photograph of the pope. A crucifix hangs over the door. Noel shifts uncomfortably. In spite of the scotch Father Neale has offered him, he can't help feeling invited in off the street.

"Renunciation is serious business," Father Neale says at last. "Not a word to be tossed out lightly."

Noel is unsure how to respond.

"And family, you say?" The priest's tone rises, perhaps involuntarily. "What so terrible has happened that you would want to renounce your family?" He comes forward in his chair, elbows on his knees, holding his glass in both hands.

Noel cuts his eyes away, looks into the empty fireplace. "Maybe I exaggerated at little, Father."

"Maybe? A little?"

"I didn't say 'renounce.' You said that. I said 'give up.'"

"Is that different?"

"I don't know."

The priest leans back and sips his drink, eyes fixed directly ahead. Noel is unsure he wants to explain, much less try to defend himself. A few moments pass. "What is it you are trying to tell me?"

"I don't know."

"Have you discussed it with your family?"

"Discussed what?"

"How you feel. What you're thinking."

Noel likes the priest's directness, feels suddenly more at ease. "I guess that's part of the problem."

"Have you talked to anyone?"

Noel shakes his head.

"Not even your wife?"

"We speak. But we can't really talk."

"Why can't you?"

"It's complicated. My situation. I take the blame for it."

"Your situation?"

"You're good, Father. Straight to the chase." He tosses back his drink and holds out the empty glass. "Pour me another, and I'll tell you."

There's no fire in the fireplace, and that's too bad because a fire would be the perfect thing to look at. Instead, Noel's eyes move around the room, resting here and there. The half-drawn curtains, the tree branches swaying just outside the window, the portrait of the old bishop (friend of Benjamin Franklin), the television set with satellite hookup, the tassels of the worn but vibrant Persian carpet, the metal Christ on the wooden crucifix, Benedictus PP. XVI. Father Neale listens, slumped in his chair, fingers pressed into his cheek. Noel stops frequently to back up, and back up again in search of contexts and prior causes. It's the first time he's tried to anatomize, give an account of himself. Tensions, unfolding, meshing and collapsing, ready to blow sky high. More drama than he'd realized. He warms to it, then begins to glow. At one point, Father Neale is called to the telephone. "Hold it right there," he tells Noel. "I'll be right back."

Noel helps himself to another scotch and goes to look out the window while the priest takes the call. When a man passing by on the sidewalk glances up at the window, Noel imagines what he must look like from outside, in silhouette. Not from a distance, but standing right there with his drink, another who-I-am, a wholly other person, whose story is being told to the priest. Scotch has opened him up. But it isn't alcohol talking, and he isn't deluded or confused by the two lives he is presenting. He isn't trying to be exotic, either, with big ideas showered down from great heights. Or to indulge in grandiose conceits and dilemmas. He is perfectly ordinary, rational, well intentioned, a man who goes to work every day and dislikes talking about himself too much or hearing others talk about him. He is skeptical but clings to what he's been taught. And this he can do only as a complex personality attuned to a dizzying spectrum of contradictions and paradoxes, a good guy/bad guy sipping scotch in the rectory, talking about oaths and secrets, infrared grubs and dead schoolchildren on the other side of the world.

Father Neale returns, grim-faced, and closes the door with a firm push. He goes to the bar and refills his glass as well. "It's been a very busy day. Lots of drama."

"I'm not helping any, I guess."

The priest returns to his chair, brushing off Noel's remark with a sip of his drink.

"I can come back another time, if you'd prefer."

"No. Please stay. What you've been telling me is very pertinent."

"Pertinent? To what?"

"Well, not that it's the same by any stretch. But I'm part of a company, too. Referred to as such, as you may know. Over the years, well, let's just say we have a long history of arousing strong aversions."

Noel is about to interrupt, but Father Neale stops him. "I'm not drawing comparisons. The DIA is no Society of Jesus." Both men smile. "But I can speak to what you've said about fealty and dislocation and incoherence. I've often asked myself if the order I belong to is the same order I joined nearly forty years ago, or if it is I who have changed. It's not an easy question to ask or to answer. Of course, you can say that both have changed. Or that everything changes. But what, exactly, does that mean? Even now—I'm about to turn seventy—the confusion is painful. I joined the order in the 1960s, under the Arrupe Generalate. It was an exciting time. I wasn't radical like the Berrigans, but I was politically engaged, part of the antiwar movement. Mainly, I was inspired by Father Arrupe's humanism and his message of social activism. Also, of course, by the big thinkers. Teillard, Karl Rahner, John Courtney Murray. They were my heroes. I wanted nothing more than to follow their example." He stops talking and glances toward the door, as if expecting it to open.

"What happened?"

"It's a long story. Father Arrupe was a visionary and found himself at odds with the higher authorities." He shakes his head, sips his drink. "1981 was a terrible year. The Holy Father was shot in May. In August that same year, Father Arrupe suffered a stroke and never recovered. I was working in a rural community in Nicaragua at the time. A terrible struggle ensued—not just over what positions priests could fill in the Sandinista government but whether priests would be allowed to serve in political positions at all. What the mission of the Church was. It touched everybody. The whole order was consumed by it. They really were very difficult, terrible times."

"When did you leave Nicaragua?"

"Almost immediately after Father Arrupe's stroke. I was appointed to this parish and have been here ever since."

It's hard to imagine the gray-haired, soft-spoken priest as a liberation theologian. Iran-Contra was just spilling over when Noel and Pat came to Washington. He wonders if Father Neale is just reminiscing or if he is sharing his history because he sees a parallel, in spite of what he claims. Discernment, hierarchy, moral and political order and disorder. "So, the company changed—and changed you."

Father Neale smiles and shrugs. "Well. I guess you could say that. Although I prefer the term 'grace' and believe I was guided by faith and the Holy Spirit."

"Do you have any regrets?"

"I wouldn't ask for anything different—except maybe to improve my golf swing." He laughs.

"Golf isn't a very Marxist game."

"And I was never very much of a Marxist. Christian socialist, if you want to put a label on it."

"What were you doing in Nicaragua?"

"Setting up a literacy program for rural youth."

"Do you miss that kind of work?"

"I do," the priest says, looking directly at Noel. "But my work is also right here."

"So when they told you to stop what you were doing and come here—into the belly of the beast, so to speak—you felt comfortable with that? You didn't object?" Noel flushes, realizing he is asking the priest to answer the very question he is struggling with himself.

The priest's brow furrows. He glances at Noel dubiously, lets a few moments pass. "We all have to find a structure we're comfortable in," he says at last. "You are questioning yours. From what you've told me, you have good grounds for doing so. The Church is a structure I am comfortable in. Yes, there have been periods of doubt. But in the end I decided that—for me, at least—it's a structure that gives coherence to the world. I am willing to accept the terms it lays down in order to function within it. This is not blind obedience, just a necessary framework that gives meaning to my days."

It's the standard program, which somewhat irritates Noel. As if all he needs is to sign on, have faith, and, presto, the proper direction of his entire being will be guaranteed. "Well, Father. My work is also right here. I'm a creature of structure, and structures, too. But I do have regrets. And I doubt very much that the word 'meaning' applies, since ninety percent of the daily things I deal with are meaningless and would be better solved by just doing nothing." He settles back in his chair, can't think of anything else to say. He has parsed enough information over the years to know the value of a simple declaration— even if carelessly considered or just plain wrong.

"Do you think talking to your family might help?"

Noel shrugs. "It isn't a question of opening up, Father. I could have done that a long time ago. It has more to do with what you called grace. I barely recognize myself anymore—or anyone around me, for that matter."

A lawyerly expression comes over the priest. He sits up as if to rebut. Noel, winding up inside and feeling a sudden rush of pressure, stops him. "I'm not exaggerating, Father. None of us is who we think we are. Not you. Not me. We're all murderers! Every one of us." His deflation is almost immediate. He can feel the air leaving him. It isn't that he thinks what he has said is wrong, or that he has overstated, gone too far. Quite the opposite. It's the thrilling shock of world disparagement, the plain and horrible truth, like calling a tiger beautiful.

Father Neale comes forward in his chair. He puts his half-finished scotch on the table and hangs his head, hands folded between his knees. Seconds tick by. Is he praying? Footsteps sound in the hall beyond the closed doors. Noel gets up and walks over to the window. His earliest impressions of Georgetown are of tree-shadowed sidewalks, brick orange at night, the sheen of old trolley tracks laid down in cobblestone, high society, officialdom, and discerning Jesuits behind high, ivy-covered walls. He'd wanted Hannah to go to college here, as much for the trolley tracks as for what the priest has just called structure. She wouldn't apply. Too close to home, she said. She wanted out of the house and out of D.C. Most of all, like her mother, she didn't want any part of his Catholicism. She was with her mother all the way. Smart, secular, backed by volunteer spirit—Bread for the City, Toys for Tots, AIDS walks—more vital, undecayed, and in control than his soul-sick devotion. Midnight mass on Christmas and Easter were the two concessions. They joined him for the music and spectacle. Oddly, he liked it that way, felt deeper for going it alone.

"I can't agree with what you've said," Father Neale says at last. "Yes, the dynamism of sin is undeniable. But it doesn't follow that since all are touched by it, all are, as you say, murderers. That sounds to my ears like someone trying to rationalize a bad conscience." The priest picks up his drink, swirls and finishes the rest.

"My daughter has just had an abortion," Noel says, still looking out the window. "What should I do?"

"Ask Christ's forgiveness. And forgive her."

"I'm not supposed to know about it."

"Then you must also ask her forgiveness."

"For what?"

The priest stands up and joins Noel at the window. A taxicab has pulled up. The two watch as the driver helps an elderly man to the front steps of the rectory. "Mr. Weissmiller," Father Neale says, glancing at his watch. "On time as always." He puts a hand on Noel's shoulder. "Would you like to try a retreat? We can guide you in the full Spiritual Exercises. A full Nineteenth Annotation Retreat, which we can work around your daily schedule if you can't do the closed thirty days."

The door opens. A priest whom Noel has seen at mass but never spoken to pokes his head into the room. Father Neale preempts him. "Yes. I know. I'll be right there," he says. He leads Noel to the front door, where the younger priest is helping the elderly Mr. Weissmiller off with his coat. Noel shakes hands all around, loopy and flushed from the whiskey. He steps outside and turns to Father Neale. "Thanks for the drink, Father." The priest waves, about to close the door. "Wait. What am I supposed to ask her forgiveness for?"

"For telling me," Father Neale says and steps back inside.

The hotel was a short walk from the train station. I chose it for the name: Jedermann. The desk clerk, who wore his hair neatly pulled back into a ponytail, smiled indulgently when I mentioned this, confirming me as a typical guest, an everyman. I'd never been to Munich and had come with nothing more than the letter Blake had given me. Google supplied me with a telephone number, directions, and precise distance from the hotel as well as directions by tram and U Bahn. It also supplied a link to a web site for Omnia Optik, where a Bettina Lüneburger was listed as the owner. The site was professionally designed, with artfully lighted photographs of satisfied customers, fashionable eyewear, and an attractive, dark-haired woman in her early thirties. I studied the face for a minute, then jotted down the address and put away the computer.

The photograph was unsettling, much more than I wanted to know. I unpacked my bags, put my field kit with half-completed map of La Corbière in the closet, arranged and organized my things. At one point I reached for the telephone, but I couldn't bring myself to make the call. I've taught myself to savor these solitary hotel moments when you see yourself with absolute clarity, as you actually exist: all alone. But everything felt different this time. Not alone but pent up, on the verge of waking from a dream. I took out my camera and photographed myself in front of the mirror. To depict myself on the verge of another variation. The me before. No such photograph of Bettina would ever be possible. There would be no interval like this for her, no moment of interpolation. For her, there would only be before and after. Nothing in between. It didn't seem fair that I should have all the power of surprise on my side. But there was nothing I could do about it.

What would he—Dad—have made of this? Had it ever occurred to him that it might someday come to pass? All the vagueness in our relationship precipitated out of these two questions like a fog. Could the pains he'd taken to conceal himself be transformed into a kind of bond? The fabric of something new? If the concealed truth was like an aching muscle, would relief come with revelation? Not to him, of course. Maybe not even to us. But to the distortion caused by falsity; not simply a need for order but to let flow what had been diverted and blocked?

I arranged my things on the writing desk, lined the books up on the windowsill. The room felt like a college dorm, efficient, modern, with a view into a rear courtyard. I stacked files and folders in piles on the floor. I had only a few photographs of him—and two were old newspaper clippings. There was nothing from the Düsseldorf years except a catalog for The Hudson and the Rhein and a complimentary issue of *Encounter* magazine containing a review of the exhibit and a note from Mel Lasky: *Nice to see you, Pete*. I have a vague memory of Lasky at a cocktail party at our house. He looked like Lenin, bald on top, with a sharply trimmed goatee. I was introduced to him and to an elderly German man he was talking with who, my father later told me, had lost his arm on the Russian Front.

A detail? How to fill it all in? I was still wondering as I prepared to set out the next morning. I studied the map again and memorized the route I wanted to take: Bayerstrasse east to Goethestrasse south one block to Schwanthalerstrasse east to Schillerstrasse north one block to Adolph-Kolpingstrasse east one block, cross Sonnenstrasse to Herzogspitalstrasse east one block to Altheimer Eck to Färbergraben to Rosenstrasse up to Marienplatz around Petersplatz to Viktualienmarkt cross Frauenstrasse south on Reichenbachstrasse to Buttermelcherstrasse to Klenzestrasse to Aventinstrasse.

It was a bright spring morning. The desk clerk told me I could take the tram directly to Reichenbachplatz and was delighted by my decision to walk. *"So ein schöner Tag!"* she chirped and pointed me in the direction of Marienplatz. I couldn't help noticing her resemblance to the ponytailed man who'd checked me in. "Is he your brother?" She smiled and shook her head. "Everybody asks that. We're cousins."

It seemed the perfect foreshadowing. I started off at a brisk clip, refreshed by the morning air and the noise of traffic in the street. Before I knew it, I was standing in Marienplatz, watching the famous Rathaus clock chime the hour with all the other tourists. I began to feel nervous, unsure what to do. I took the envelope from my jacket pocket. Blake's address had been scratched out, the stamp and postmark torn from the corner. I didn't like seeing that, removed the letter and put it in another pocket. It suddenly seemed necessary to keep them separate.

Marienplatz was all primary colors mixed with browns and grays and forest greens, shopping bags, leather briefcases, elderly couples shuffling, chic shoppers, office workers, ears plugged with telephones and music. An organ grinder in Lederhosen was setting up on the corner of Rosental, undeterred by the repair crew in orange overalls who were preparing to begin work on a section of pavement. On a billboard behind them was a huge poster of spindle-legged Karl Valentin, the comic and silent-film star, with trademark putty nose and enormous pointed shoes, bent over the handlebars of a tiny tricycle. The glass doors of Kaufhof slid open, releasing gusts of warm air, a jackhammer erupted across the street. I lingered for a few minutes, taking it all in; wanting it all to cohere, to feel attached and fully present, to feel as dropped down in raw belonging as the workers and the organ grinder, Karl Valentin, the Rathaus clock. But I had no place there, just very complicated and dubious reasons for coming. When Karl Valentin reappeared, this time as a fountain statue in the Viktualienmarkt, I couldn't help feeling taunted by local spirit. I later discovered a museum dedicated to him tucked up in a tower of the Isartor. The spot is appropriately inscribed: *Anno 1333½ wurde der Karl Valentin 549 Jahre spatter unweit der Istatorplatzes, an Stelle einer Tochter hervorragender Eltern, geboren*—Not far from Isartorplatz, 549 years after the year 1333½, Karl Valentin was born in place of a daughter, to excellent parents.

I made two circuits of the Viktualienmarkt, browsed among the vegetable stands, the gourmet food stalls, and bought a pretzel, which I shared with some pigeons at the Karl Valentin statue, partaking, as it always is with statues (and pigeons, too) of the power of being in place. Unable to decide whether to ring her doorbell at home or look for her at the shop, I let the clock decide for me and was standing across the street from Omnia Optik when it opened for business.

I'm not sure how long I stood there, but it was long enough to feel conspicuous. Instead of crossing the street directly, I walked to the end of the block and crossed at the intersection. The shop front was covered by a bright orange awning emblazoned with the store's logo: a simply sketched eye with long lashes. "Omnia Optik" was printed in small type underneath. My heart thumped as I examined the display in the window. I couldn't bring myself to look inside and focused instead on the whimsical window display—a colorfully decorated female figurine, tall and gaunt and angular, emerging Venus-like from piles of broken bottles and jars and stained glass scattered among twisted and bent eyeglass frames. I lingered, speculating on the lyricism of the display. It was private; there was no doubt in my mind about that. It was private, and it contained clues. There was also no doubt in my mind that, since I had broken into a nervous sweat, felt a pit in my stomach, I was too shaky to go inside. I glanced into the shop and saw two women. One was seated, looking at a computer screen, the other was standing just behind her, looking over her shoulder.

I turned and walked away, feeling cowardly. I couldn't simply waltz into her shop, the easygoing American with ruthless business to transact. I walked to Gärtnerplatz and sat down at an outdoor café called Interview. The day was warming up. The flower beds in the circle were bursting with tulips. I ordered a coffee and sat facing the morning sun. It was a cozy spot, surrounded by orange- and red-painted buildings with the neoclassical facade of the Gärtnerplatz Theater wedged in between, the perfect contrast to my grand confusion. The air was crisp and clear. I would have preferred a little cloudiness and a storm but had to make do with spilled coffee mopped from the table and the front of my pants with a wad of paper napkins. I ordered a second cup and lingered over it for the better part of an hour, dividing my attention between the *Süddeutsche Zeitung* I'd taken from the hotel and the comings and goings around Gärtnerplatz, until I grew too disgusted with myself to stay. I shouldered my day pack and marched back to Omnia Optik.

There was nobody at the desk. *"Guten Morgen,"* came a woman's voice from the back room. She appeared a moment later and, smiling, said she would be out to help me in just a few minutes. That first glimpse is how she will always appear to me, fixed the way an image in a dream is fixed at the moment of waking. I knew right away it was she. There was no doubt, and that was more important than the resemblance she bore, like physical traces shaken loose, to the father only I had known. My heart was pounding when she reappeared. I pretended to be browsing and flushed bright red when I turned to her. The tips of my ears were hot. She took this as nervous shyness and apologized for startling me. "Do you have an appointment?"

"No," I said in English, then, flustered, switched to German. "I would like. I need, I think I need, new glasses." My accent seemed to explain the awkwardness.

"Do you have your old ones with you?"

I took out the drugstore readers I've always used. She seemed amused, gave them a cursory appraisal, and handed them back. "These are just magnifiers. If you like, I can give you a proper prescription."

I didn't know what to do and put the glasses away. The other woman emerged from the back to ask a question, and I was given more time to consider. They conferred by the desk. I listened to every word that passed between them, the tone as well. Bettina was clearly the boss, but there was friendship in play, too. I returned to the display and stole glances as I tried on frames in front of the mirror. The hair color was mine, minus seventeen years. Even the thickness, the waviness. She wore it parted off center. Her eyes were a wonderful, translucent, grayish blue with slightly arching brows that must have come from her mother. But her nose and the shape of her mouth—even her teeth, the inwardly inclined uppers—were all familiar. I have them, too.

"So," she said and stepped out from behind the desk. I put on the frames I was holding and turned to her. "Very nice," she said. I put on another pair. She smiled and nodded approval, but I saw not the slightest flicker of recognition. When I tried on a third pair, and it was clear there would be none, I couldn't help feeling disappointed. It was silly, of course. Even if I had struck her as somehow familiar-looking she had no way of recognizing me. It was only herself she could have recognized.

She set aside the frames and suggested we start with the eye exam. I hadn't anticipated any of this and felt completely unprepared. We sat at the desk, where she took down my basic information. Name, address, date of birth, medical history. No allergies, diabetes, hypertension, major illnesses, medications, or surgery. She ran down the checklist. I watched intently as she entered the information. She finished, gave me the forms to sign, then stood up and gestured to the examination chair.

It all felt completely, totally wrong. On the desk in front of me was a small dispenser with her business card. I took one. "You're Bettina Lüneburg?" I asked.

"Yes," she said, putting out her hand with an at-your-service smile. I hauled myself up, conscious of our age difference in a way I hadn't been initially. We shook hands, a single pump and release, a now-we've-got-that-out-of-the-way gesture. There was brightness and a light in her eyes that I couldn't bring myself to disturb. Happiness, I hoped it was. I reached underneath the chair for my day pack, stooping slowly and deliberately, as an old man does. It was too late now to spring any surprises. Changing track would be devious; make it seem I'd manipulated her and come with an agenda. Which I hadn't. Or that I wanted something. Which I didn't. Given everything I knew, and our difference in years, to present myself by surprise seemed to verge on assault. Maybe not open trenchcoat lechery—we were siblings, after all—but in the realm of something dark, taboo, and too close for comfort.

I followed her to the examination chair and sat down. Each step of the exam deepened my sense of unwholesome loitering. I submitted quietly, brow to brow, eye to eye, to stabs of light and puffs of air and a test that depended on flipping lenses—this or this—and narrowing choices until, at last, she found the precise correction. "Your eyes are healthy," she pronounced when it was over. "Your vision is normal for distance. Perfect, except for a slight ocular variation in each eye—totally normal for your age. You only need glasses for reading."

She rolled over to her instrument table and jotted some notes onto a form. Even the way she held her pen! Thumb and three fingertips!

"Can I use one of the frames I chose?" I asked.

"Of course." She smiled. "No problem." The telephone rang, and she excused herself to answer. I remained in the exam chair, which was set by the front window of the shop. A delivery truck was parked outside. I watched the driver unload crates filled with bottles and listened as she scheduled an appointment—and found out she was going on a ten-day vacation to Spain.

"Where in Spain are you going?" I asked when she put down the phone.

"Ibiza."

"I couldn't help overhearing," I said, getting up from the chair.

"I go every year. Have you been?"

I shook my head and choked awkwardly when I asked, "Is it nice?"

"It's wonderful. I love it there."

I went back to browsing the eyewear display. There was a knot in my stomach, something wrong in the whole situation, an absence of sympathetic magic to steer and make everything turn out grandly. The moment should have been bursting with it, and yet it was precisely the opposite. There was no magic at all, just an everydayness, acute and real and evocative of nothing beyond each of us simply being ourselves. Suddenly, the letter in my pocket, which I'd imagined producing in a flourish of proof like a fairy-tale slipper, seemed a sinister thing, not lost and returned but dredged up.

I decided on a pair of frames and brought them to the counter.

"Very nice," she said and launched into a description of all the various lens options available to me. She took out a laminated plaque with graphic illustrations of each type and explained the advantages and disadvantages of each. I paid close attention, more to her manner of delivery than to the substance, and so had to ask her to back up and repeat, blaming it all on my poor German.

"But your German is excellent," she said and went over everything a second time. We settled on a progressive lens optimized for intermediate distance and reading. "Perfect for the office." She clipped some sort of metal device to the frames I'd selected, instructed me to stand in front of a video camera mounted in the corner of the room. "Look directly into the camera," she said.

"What is it for?"

"To determine the position of the pupils." She went to her computer, typed in some commands. "That's good," she said. "All finished."

"I've never seen such a thing," I said, handing back the contraption. My face was staring out from the computer screen, pupils marked in the center with a green cross.

"It's called Visu-point, a new technology," she said proudly, putting the frames and all paperwork into a plastic tray. "They'll be ready on Monday. I won't be here, but Gabi will do the final fit. She's very good." She stood up and offered her hand.

"That's it?" I asked, hesitating. She seemed to shimmer in the halogen shop lights. We were nearly the same height, both small-boned, narrow-hipped, had the same slightly nervous energy. As if on cue, the door chime sounded and a customer entered. She shook my hand with the same little pump and release and said, "I think you'll find them a big improvement."

I stood in front of her, unable to answer, not knowing what to say. She sensed my discomfort and asked, "Is there something else?"

"Yes," I blurted, but with the customer lurking in the background and Gabi grinding away in the back room, I couldn't continue. She

stepped back, curious, waiting for me to come out with it, but everything dissolved into a puddle of impossibilities. I let out a nervous
laugh. "I'm sorry. It slipped my mind. I completely forgot what I was
just going to say." I shook my head and laughed again. "Really. It was
right on the tip of my tongue. I'm sorry."

"Oh, don't worry." She smiled, waving away the apology. "It happens to me all the time, too."

Fort Belvoir Golf Course
38°42'34.92"N
77° 8'38.02"W

Noel often loses his train of thought, yet is never more certain of what he wants than when he acts impulsively. Being alone helps. He doesn't need to explain himself and can pace around the house, stare out the window, lie down on the couch, rummage in the fridge. He finds himself doing odd projects at odd hours. Today, he came home early and began clearing out the garage. Last night, after his talk at the rectory with Father Neale, he found himself out in the backyard pulling weeds with a scotch in his hands. A nightcap. He knew it was crazy, out there in the dark, but he was drunk and it felt so right. He even hoped someone—a neighbor, or Steve Kritsick, would come back there and find him doing it. He looks at the clock and the GPS on the dashboard. It's just after two o'clock. He's stone-cold sober. He rolls down the window, lets in a blast of night air. There is virtually no traffic on I-66. Route 29 past Gainesville will be even emptier. Easy driving. He'll be in Charlottesville by four.

Running into Cowper that morning rattled him. The man

seemed changed. Noel had just pulled into his new parking space when he saw Cowper coming down the walk, hunched up, wearing a bright red windbreaker. Noel had never seen him dressed that way before. He always wore a coat and tie. Noel watched as he passed, then got out and called to him. "Geoff!"

Cowper stopped and turned. He stood there for a moment, as if not quite sure who had called to him. He didn't come forward but waited for Noel to approach him.

"I was wondering when I'd run into you. You coming or going?"

"Going," Cowper said, keeping his hands in his pockets. "How about you?"

"Coming."

"Life treating you well?"

"It's all right." There was an awkward silence as each decided how much to invest in the encounter. "How are things with you?" Noel asked.

"Just got back from Kabul. Grim fucking place." Cowper glanced away and started talking about moving his boat to a marina near Saint Michaels. Noel cut him off. "So what the fuck happened, Geoff? Were you in on it?"

Cowper cut his eyes back and looked directly at Noel. "Well, now that you put it that way, I guess I was, yeah."

"Why?"

"It wasn't just me, Noel."

"You could have said something to me first, at least discussed. What was the problem, Geoff?"

"You know what the problem was."

Noel's face reddened. "No, Geoff. I don't think I do. I thought things were going fine."

"Well, you were wrong."

"How was I wrong?"

"Look, Noel. Don't take it personally."

"Don't take it personally? You fucking knife me in the back and tell me not to take it personally? The least you can do is tell me to my face what the problem was."

"I'm afraid I can't discuss it with you. You know that."

"It was the after-action report, right?"

"I can't discuss."

"Don't give me that crap, man."

"Look, Noel, your job is maps, all right? Beginning, middle, and end. Not criticism. Not second-guessing. Just maps." He turned on his heel and walked away. "You ought to thank me for getting you bumped up a step," he called over his shoulder.

"Whose idea was that little junket?" Noel called back, but Cowper ignored him and kept walking.

It was a busy morning with back-to-back meetings and a conference call to clarify an item that had been misreported in the Joint Chiefs' morning briefing. The encounter with Cowper had begun to fade into the background when, just before noon, CNN began running reports about a Special Forces cross-border ground assault in Pakistan, quoting an anonymous intelligence source. A closer look at the CNN story and what was being reported by Reuters left little doubt. Noel got up and paced his little office, feeling worse for knowing he was right than for the convoluted regret over the encounter in the parking lot. He pecked over the details—of Cowper bunched up under a black cloud, silver hair sticking out in tufts from underneath his cap.

He scanned the news again for updates, then gathered his things and, claiming a last-minute dentist appointment, left for the day. He couldn't have said where exactly he was going or what exactly he would do when he got there. As he drove through the main gate at Bolling and got on 295 in the direction of the Wilson Bridge, he wasn't conscious of anything beyond a queer feeling of unrest, of needing to get straight things that had gotten out of kilter. In the approach to the newly opened span over the Potomac, the whole network of ramps leading onto the bridge had been shifted, the flow of traffic rearranged. It brought to mind what Father Neale had said about change and being changed. The priest had claimed his reorientation was an act of grace. He denied it was blind obedience; but the outcome, nevertheless, was the same conformity. Something Noel understood. The inert permanence of earthly institutions, particularly ancient and powerful ones, could seem divine. It was easy to be confused, especially if the comfort being sought was to be freed from doubt.

On the bridge, he glanced upriver. A cloudless afternoon. Sunlight flashed off the water. In the foreground, the three rust-stained radar orbs of the Naval Research Lab contrasted with the marbled whiteness of the Capitol dome in the distance. Beyond that on the ridgeline, the gray silhouette of the National Cathedral, the vertically ventilated white box that is the Russian Embassy, and the enormous radio and TV towers rising from Chevy Chase and Silver Spring. It was a nineteenth-century view—minus the orbs and towers. No industrial waterfront, or skyline. More Currier and Ives than *National Geographic*. He could imagine coming up the river on a sailing ship, seeing the city rise out of the lithographed landscape in all its superimposed and unfinished actuality.

Traffic snarled on the Alexandria side. He made an attempt at a detour by getting on Route 1 South, which seemed to be flowing. After going a short distance, he pulled into the parking lot of a shuttered and abandoned Colony Court Motel to reorient himself and collect his thoughts. When a young Hispanic man in backward cap and work boots approached the window, he realized it was a pickup spot for day labor and pulled away without rolling down the window. Unnecessarily uncivil, but such was the feel of the whole area.

He drove for a while, dividing his attention between the map on his dash and the suburban landscape unrolling beneath him. It wasn't until he was in Fort Hunt, meandering up and down unfamiliar streets, that he realized where he'd been headed all along. He pulled up across the street from Cowper's house, a split-level ranch with red shutters and boxwood growing under the windows along the front and side. He waited a few minutes before getting out. He'd been there twice before. What little he knew about Cowper he'd gleaned during those two visits. Besides sailing and baseball and keeping fit, there were interests in jazz and military history. The living room bookcase featured a First Folio Society edition of Napoleon's diaries and a complete set of Patrick O'Brian's Aubrey Maturin novels.

Ann answered the door, stepping outside with a finger to her lips as if talking to a child. "He's sleeping," she said. "Came home and went straight to bed. Is there something you want me to tell him?" She knew perfectly well that Noel didn't believe her yet persisted with all the friendly gleam. "How are you doing?"

"Me? I'm pissed off. You can tell that to Geoff for me."

The smile vanished. She shook her head. "Were you just in Kabul, too?"

"Not on the ground, no," he said with hermetic irony.

She accepted it, brow furrowed. "Well, Geoff came home completely worn out. Just terrible. I've never seen him so exhausted."

She watched from the doorstep as he returned to the car and went back inside as he drove away. He got as far as the end of the block, then, in a sudden flare of self-disgust, slammed on the brakes and reversed back up the street. He pressed the doorbell with his thumb and held it. Ann looked through the spyhole before opening the door. "Wake him up," he said. She was startled, and when he saw her hesitate, he said it again. "Wake him up."

Cowper appeared before he'd finished. Ann immediately vanished inside the house. "I told her to say I was sleeping," he said and pushed the door wide open. "Come on in."

Noel remained on the front step. Cowper's face was completely neutral. Noel's pulse began to race. Neither confirm nor deny. "Look. I've been carrying as much on my shoulders as you and everyone else. You say my job isn't to criticize. Well, that's right. But when you step in shit, you don't just keep walking around as if you don't notice anything. My write-ups never threatened your career, Geoff. Or my second-guessing. Don't worry, you'll get your level-six DISES one day. And when you do, don't pretend you got there all on your own, but with the help of a lot of us whose job it was not to criticize."

It was all Noel had to say. He was trembling when he finished. He turned to leave and knew without looking back that Cowper had gone inside and closed the door. As he drove off, he knew nothing would follow from this airing—if their exchange could even be called that. No whistles would be blown, reputations or careers damaged. There weren't any whistles, in the first place; reputation was irrelevant and careers nearly over. It was all part of the ebb and flow, the degeneration and regeneration of organizational substance. Pressure doesn't rise to the top; it gets blown out sideways from the middle, where the tiers collapse on top of one another but leave the main structure standing. Recently, a young targeting analyst who had been covering Iraq had gone to work for Human Rights Watch, where he'd gotten a nice big platform from which to air his conscience. Now he goes to conferences, appears on talk shows, writes books. It would probably surprise him to know how many of his former colleagues support what he is doing. Everybody would go out and talk if they could, especially those whose work is most densely cloaked and protected. It doesn't take a thirty-year career to yearn for clear skies and the resolution of all inner doubts and conflicts. What does take thirty years to understand is how ego-bound all secret-keeping is, that the only difference between keeping and breaking is who will suffer most from the truth. Secrets don't keep, they putrefy.

He drove around aimlessly for a time and ended up at the Fort Belvoir golf course. He sat on the clubhouse patio and had a beer, taking in the view of the rolling landscape and the Donovan and Natalie Cole tunes piping through the loudspeakers tucked up under the clubhouse eaves. A ladies' foursome sat down at the table next to him, officers' wives. He listened as they chatted about drawing classes at the arts and crafts center and an article in *The Eagle* reporting $100 million in Belvoir commissary sales—the highest figure in commissary history, topping even Pearl Harbor and San Diego. He always feels like an interloper, intruding on a parallel middle America nestled into an unsuspecting landscape. The base is a blander emulation of the suburban sprawl surrounding it, a culture firmly embedded in the everyday of day care and drive-in banking, fast food and daytime television. He always wonders, passing through these citadels, if they think modestly of themselves or if, like him, they are conscious of the immensity of their presence. Or is it only the young recruits with their flags and decals and tattoos? For sheer variety, nothing compares to the plantation-sized installations scattered around the region, the forts, bases, and air stations: Belvoir, Meyers, Mead, Bolling, Andrews, Patuxent. The decommissioned SM-1 Nuclear Plant right next to the golf course, surrounded by barricades and fences topped with barbed wire, is the most conspicuous sign of this world apart. How many people know there is an idle full-scale nuclear reactor just a few miles from downtown Washington, D.C.?

He finished his beer and tried calling Pat but got no answer and hung up without leaving a message. They'd spoken just twice since she had left. He felt shut out and didn't know how to take it, if he should be offended and hurt or grateful to her for shielding him. He knew what he thought and Pat and Hannah knew what he thought and nobody needed to be reminded. Still, it seemed unfair to have it held against him. If he brought the same certitude to fighting intolerance and inequality and hunger and AIDS, he'd be a hero to them. But an elegant orthodoxy wasn't possible anymore. The country was too squared off in unfriendly directions. Certain insights could only be held privately. All they could do was learn to live in the aftermath of their mutual disappointments.

He lowers the window. A blast of night air to keep from getting drowsy. Route 29 between Washington and Charlottesville is named the Twenty-ninth Infantry Division Memorial Highway but is also posted with signs calling it the Seminole Trail and the James Madison Highway. An old road once overhung with mature oak and maple and elm and lined with old stone walls and fences. Civil War commemorative plaques are the last vestiges of that epoch. The rising and falling highway and the humid night air conjure up the earlier times. He hangs his arm out the window, feeling a nostalgic connection, as if his sleek black Navigator were a rattling pickup and his chinos and Eddie Bauer polo shirt, jeans and a grimy old V-neck. He misses the whitewashed gun shacks and roadside fruit stands. But at seventy mph, any connection to the vanished landscape is purely sentimental. At that speed, he has no right to be bothered by the disappearance of anything.

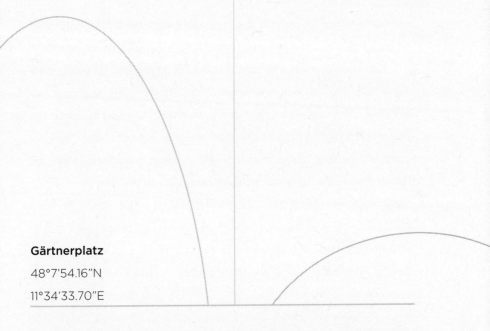

Gärtnerplatz
48°7'54.16"N
11°34'33.70"E

I took the tram back to the hotel and escaped from the midday city bustle by hiding out in my room. It was more than a failure of nerve. I'd miscalculated badly. Rather than just drop all pretense and go directly to the point, I'd run away. It was more than evasion. It was like drowning within sight of land. Giving up. I don't think there is a better word for it than the good old German *angst*. Initially, I suppose it was simply fear of being seen. I don't just mean me, but Bettina as well. It wasn't until I was back in my hotel room that I realized what I was about to give up, what I would have forced her into giving up as well: that precious tranquility that comes with being alone, and being left alone, and not in someone else's world but in your *own*. The ease and freedom of being able to walk around, talk out loud to yourself without the bother of appearances, of being seen. And to be within your rights when you hear a stranger coming up the stairs and, anticipating the knock on the door, remain perfectly still and pretend no one's home and wait for the unwelcome stranger to go away.

The glimpse I'd had of her, and her life, rattled me. It had been a mistake not to call first, to introduce myself over the telephone and give her the chance to decide for herself if she wanted to meet me. At least she might have had time to prepare. We could have met on neutral ground, appraised each other with skeptical curiosity and either passed naturally into delighted amazement or cooled down right away into polite, neutral regard. Maybe it was the latter that had seemed more likely to me in the shop. Perhaps I'd intuited it, unconsciously, and run away rather than risk indifference or outright rejection. I whittled away at these and other variations like a lovesick teenager until there was nothing left but bits and pieces. Annoyed for having wasted the entire afternoon in my hotel room, I decided to go back and start over again.

"She left," Gabi told me. "Is something wrong?"

"Will she be back later?"

Gabi looked at the clock on the wall and shook her head. "She's getting ready for her trip." She took a business card from the dispenser and jotted a number on the back. "You can call her mobile if it's urgent."

I thanked her and hurried out. Unsure all over again, I went to see if she was at home. Her building was in a rear courtyard, access to which was through a narrow alley. I'd walked by twice without noticing. It was an old, ivy-covered brick building, set between a cabinetmaker's workshop and a dance studio. The front door and first-story windows were secured with iron bars that looked as if they hadn't been touched or painted for half a century. There were three separate doorbells. The name on the topmost was B. Lüneburger.

I rang several times, but there was no answer. I didn't know whether to leave a note or try the number Gabi had given me.

I ended up back at Gärtnerplatz, where the cafés were now bustling. The place felt more intimate for being crowded, more vivid and colorful in the evening twilight. As I was about to sit down at the café Interview again, I saw her sitting alone at the café adjacent. Instead of going directly over, I left Interview and approached from the other direction, stopping as if by surprise at the table where she was sitting.

"Hello," I said.

She looked up. There was a slight pause. "Oh. Hi," she said in English.

"May I sit down?"

With a quick glance past me, she said, "Of course," and gestured to an empty chair. The tables were packed closely together. I took the seat directly across from her. Wanting to seem casual and not too intrusive, I turned the chair to one side before sitting down. She had a cappuccino, which was what I ordered right away, feeling touristy, uncertainly joined in. The seconds ticked by. She seemed amused by my unexpected appearance. "Are you enjoying your visit?" she asked.

"Very much. This is a nice part of the city."

As I said this, we were joined by someone she'd evidently been waiting for. He appeared out of nowhere, bent, and gave her a kiss on the cheek. It all happened so fast. I scooted aside to make room, but he took no notice and sat down without so much as a glance at me.

She introduced me. "He's my patient—from Washington," she said. The man turned to me. "I'm Thomas," he said in English.

We shook hands. "I'm sorry. I didn't realize you were meeting somebody."

Thomas called the waiter over and ordered a glass of wine. He looked to be about Bettina's age, was tall and prematurely bald with a small gold hoop in one ear and some sort of Chinese character tattooed on the side of his neck. "So, how is life in Washington?" he asked in a casual tone meant only to suggest but not actually open a conversation.

I took the hint. "All right, I suppose." I answered vaguely. "Have you been there?"

He shook his head dismissively.

His arrogance annoyed me, and I decided to dig in. "What about you?" I asked Bettina.

She shook her head. "I grew up in the east," she said. "Washington was another world."

"It was another world if you grew up in the west, too," Thomas said.

The acid tone was my license to stay, I decided. "Where in the east?" I asked Bettina.

"Berlin."

"I lived in Düsseldorf for a time." I searched her face for a sign, a flicker, then added, "Back in the 1970s."

"Where you learned German," Thomas offered. "It's quite good," he said, taking out a pack of cigarettes and placing them on the table.

I thanked him for the compliment and turned back to Bettina. "When did you come to Munich?" I asked.

"Nearly eight years ago. For *Meisterschule*. Then I worked two years in a special clinic for contact lenses before I started the business."

"When did you open your shop?"

"Omnia will be three years old in September."

I felt a charge at this mention of a date. She must have sent the letter just as she was starting up her business. It was as close to an opening as I could have hoped for. "What was it like growing up in East Berlin?"

She lifted her cup, sipped, and put it down before answering. "It was a long time ago. I don't think about it much." She looked at Thomas as if inviting him to cut in. But he was thumbing a message into his phone and not paying attention to our conversation. I leaned forward, feeling a rush of possible openings and an equal pressure to close down and draw in. With Blake's spotty story blinking in the back of my brain, I wanted to know more and also knew that there was nothing more to know. Facts and details are just facts and details, disturbances of space and time that can as well be imagined as admitted. More important was what *she* would care to know and if it was *my* right to tell her.

I noticed that my right leg was bouncing. Thomas, who'd finished his texting, noticed, too. To him I was just some strange American tourist taking up space at their table, which he made plain by saying to Bettina, "I'll call and tell them we're on the way."

"Final arrangements for our trip," she said. There was a measure of apology in her explanation—and maybe also a change of subject. Clearly, there was not going to be any bonding between Thomas and me, or any lingering when he got off the phone.

"Ibiza?"

She nodded.

As Thomas talked, his eyes rested on me as if holding me in place. It made me uncomfortable—which, I suppose, was what he wanted. For an instant, I wondered if maybe he noticed a resemblance. My imagination raced with the various ways I might respond when he put his phone away and remarked, "You know, the two of you could really be brother and sister." But the fantasy ended even before Thomas's conversation was over, and Bettina, returning to small talk, said, "I hope you like your new glasses. Don't worry, Gabi will take good care of you."

I fingered the letter in my pocket, was about to take it out but stopped short when Thomas finished his call and said, "It's set. We can go pick up the keys."

"Really?"

Thomas nodded.

Bettina thrilled to the news and clapped her hands. She turned to me and explained. "The house we are renting. It's a famous old villa. Belonged to Elizabeth Bergner, the old movie star from the 1920s. We weren't sure we could get it."

"Anything for a price," Thomas said with dour pomp that eased some of the antagonistic feeling.

"Sounds nice," I offered.

"It's wonderful. Totally private. Up on a hillside surrounded by lemon and olive trees. And the view!"

"You've been there?"

"We saw it on a walk last year. Tucked away at the end of a little road. Thomas tracked down the owners. It took nearly a year. They've never rented it out before, but Thomas was able to convince them."

"A crazy family," Thomas offered and called for the check. "I won't believe it until I walk in the door myself."

I watched and waited as he paid the waiter. It was like having a rope pass through my hands. Her spacious world. I was seeing it in glimpses and could only slither in, disrupt and destroy. She was happy,

had her own full life and didn't need me to complete or fill in anything for her. She had her own story, was moving along on her own
track. What could I offer but a bizarre detour that might only wreck
whatever peace she may have made with her mother and her past?
The dark recess to which I belonged—the parts she knew and the
parts she didn't—were places she was happy to have left behind. She
had every right to.

They stood up together. Bettina smiled and put out her hand.
Her blue-gray eyes were like an opposite shoreline. I knew she was
startled by my firm clasp, and the way I held her gaze made her uncomfortable. Typical overdone American sincerity. All I could say to
her was "Thank you," and when she replied, "No. Thank you. I hope
you like your new glasses," I suddenly remembered how my father
used to call me "Stromboli." I don't know why or what it meant to
him, but it was always a friendly, cheerful, "How ya doin', Stromboli?" when I came in from playing outside or turned up at the side
of his bed to wake him on Saturday mornings, which was always a
favorite thing to do. I don't know why I remembered it just then
(she had her Ibiza, I had my Stromboli?); but it caused me to tear up
as I watched them thread their way between the crowded tables.
They crossed the street and walked through the circle with its blooming tulip beds. She took his arm, a cinematic gesture that was not at
all the ending I had envisioned or hoped for but the only one that
could match the happy forgetting I wished for her and for myself,
the forgetting that must always be accomplished before reflection
can begin.

I left the café a short time later and passed by Omnia Optik,
which was closed and the window display brightly lit, then by her
place on Aventinstrasse—although I didn't enter but only glanced

down the alley at the old, ivy-covered building. I was glad she lived there. It's the sort of place I would have chosen, too: centrally located but off the beaten track, a little musty and past its prime. For the briefest moment, I considered sliding the letter under the door, then immediately regretted the impulse, took it out of my pocket, tore it up, and put the shredded bits into the nearest trash container. That gesture also had a cinematic quality of which I was self-conscious, but it seemed the right thing to do, like tucking a bouquet of fresh flowers into the crook of Karl Valentin's arm in the Viktualienmarkt, as I noticed someone had done when I passed by a few minutes later; then standing in Marienplatz with the other tourists to gawk at the Rathaus clock chiming the hour; keeping track of my location and my changing place in the interior map I carry with me, an interim report on the progress of becoming.

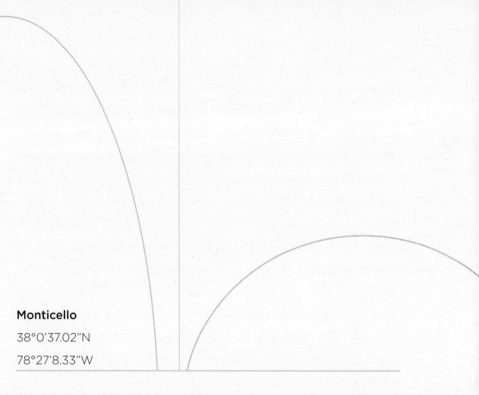

Monticello

38°0′37.02″N

78°27′8.33″W

Noel notes his coordinates, both GPS and internal, as he arrives in Charlottesville. He almost hadn't come, might as easily have gone home, straight to bed. He'd returned to the office late in the afternoon, still unable to get over Cowper. There was enough guile stored up there for three careers. All Noel could hope for was not to run into him again.

If nothing had called him back to the office, he felt called there nevertheless. His report was nearly finished. He was at that voilà stage of completion where he knows the product exceeds all specifications and the image in his head of the singular authority who has called for the work is replaced by a recession of anonymous eyes that will consume, condense, and regurgitate it in altered form until it vanishes in the bureaucratic mists. What troubled him wasn't the assignment itself. Rampant Lion was an eminently worthy GEOINT enterprise. What troubled him was some new video footage that flashed across his screen as he was finishing the report, of corpses being dragged from a mud-walled compound. A wedding, the wire services were already reporting. He knew exactly what had happened, all the precision handiwork down to the last detail. He went through the database and cued up footage of other strikes, the whole panoply of fused multispectral views and shuddering flashes of light, including the last one he and Cowper had been called upon to explain. The images spiraled into an ever blacker vortex of justifications, aftermaths, and repercussions until, finally, he couldn't look anymore.

The rest unfolded automatically. He e-mailed his first-level supervisor, emptied his desk, packed his things. When he drove out the front gate, it was well after midnight.

It is still dark, another hour at least until daybreak. He ignores the directions on the Navigator's dashboard, follows University Avenue to the center of campus, and parks in front of Booker House. He gets out to stretch his legs, walks up the hill to the domed Rotunda. The last time he walked here was to drop Hannah off at the start of her freshman year. He climbs the Rotunda stairs and walks around to the Academical Village and the Lawn. The place is deserted. The long brick walkways beneath the colonnades are quiet, with stacks of firewood and charcoal grills left out on the stoops, posters and notices tacked to the students' doors, pizza boxes, empty bottles bagged and ready for the dumpster. There is no nostalgia for college life this time, just a feeling of incompleteness. He imagines Jefferson surveying, staking out the ground, planning these buildings, and wishes there were some symmetry, a way to hook up and connect—even a simple alibi for wandering in the wee hours under the colonnades of the old university, a private citizen.

FREDERICK REUSS

He makes a complete circuit of the Lawn and returns to the Rotunda as the sky is beginning to lighten. He still isn't sure what, exactly, he has come for, other than just to show up. Maybe that's enough. From the top steps, he can see the blinking lights on the radio towers that stud the mountaintop next to Monticello. It's as close a view as can be had from this vantage point and reminds him of the list he once memorized as a student, of instruments used by Meriwether Lewis on his covert reconnaissance of the trans-Mississippi West. That was the most important covert mapping operation in U.S. history. Official cover—"a literary pursuit"—suggested by Jefferson himself in a letter to Congress: "to prevent the obstructions which interested individuals might otherwise previously prepare in its way."

Noel still knows the list of tools by heart.

1 Hadley's Quadrant

1 Mariner's Compas & 2 pole chain

1 Sett of plotting instruments

3 Thermometers

1 Cheap portable Microscope

1 Pocket Compass

1 brass Scale one foot in length

6 Magnetic needles in small straight silver or brass cases opening on the side with hinges.

1 Instrument for measuring made of tape with feet & inches mark'd on it, . . .

2 Hydrometers

1 Theodolite

1 Sett of planespheres

2 Artificial Horizons

1 Patent log

6 papers of Ink powder

4 Metal Pens brass or silver

1 Set of Small Slates & pencils

2 Creyons

Sealing wax one bundle

1 Miller's edition of Lineus in 2 Vol:

Books

Maps

Charts

Blank Vocabularies

Writing paper

1 Pair large brass money scales with two setts of weights.

They are all things he has used, and all have personal associations: of long walks through open countryside, bicycle tours, open traverses of Canadian tundra, an old professor who talked about a fourth dimension of cartography that extended deep into the self and who called a map an existential project, a one-to-one encounter between a person and a terrain. The associations have been buried under decades of technological advancement, applications and operations he could never have anticipated. Now the old tools are among the only instruments he has for putting things back together. Places, people, memories, a head full of things he's left fluttering around to be regathered, plotted, and joined up again.

He returns to the car and sits for a time as daylight breaks. Mist hangs in the air and condenses on the windshield. He starts the engine and plugs Hannah's address into the GPS on the dashboard. The

FREDERICK REUSS

place is only blocks away, close enough to walk, but he drives over anyway. Pat's car is parked out front. He drives past it, turns around at the end of the block, and parks two houses down.

By seven thirty he is too drowsy to keep up the vigil and is about to get out and ring the doorbell when Hannah suddenly appears. Jolted, he sits up, then sinks back down in his seat, watches as she locks the door, skips down the front steps, checking her bag as she goes. He feels a twinge of shame, a flutter in his stomach. She pauses for a moment, then turns and starts walking.

He gets out and follows, knowing how thuggish it would be to pull up alongside in the car. Passing in front of the house, he turns and tucks his head in case Pat is watching from the window. Something tells him she isn't. He jogs to catch up, calls to her as she crosses onto the next block. "Hannah!"

"Dad?" she stammers, flaps her arms in a gesture of helpless surprise, and allows herself to be gathered in his arms, limply, without resistance. He holds her closely for a moment and for only a moment, which is the time it takes to make further explanation unnecessary. It passes quickly, without tears, just a little moistening and reddening of the nose. It's a relief to know there is feeling still between them. More importantly, that she can face him squarely and look him in the eye.

"Does Mom know you're here?"

"No."

She takes this in with a dubious look.

"Let's walk," he says and offers his arm.

There is an initial reluctance, but it fades quickly. Apart from some joggers and a garbage truck, they have the street entirely to themselves. The silence hangs between them, then gradually begins to deepen. She grips his arm, leads him down a series of empty side streets and bare campus walkways. He notices, as if for the first time, what a tall woman she has become. Her stride nearly matches his. And how self-contained she seems, piping and ready at the start of the day, her long hair still damp from a morning shower. Their pace is quick but not hurried, the silence intimate and reassuring, not solemn or forced or uncomfortable at all. He feels a sudden surge of pride to see that she is not disturbed or discomfited by silences, can face and take them in as well as hold her own.

At last they arrive at the building where she works, a modern colonial, brick-and-glass cluster behind the Hospital and Health System complex. The sun is up, orange light breaking over the rooftops. People glide in from all directions on foot and on bicycles with packs and bags slung on their backs. A shuttle bus idles, the driver chatting through the open doors to someone standing on the curb.

"Want to come in and see the lab?"

He shakes his head. "I think I'll pass."

"It's not much to look at, really. Just a lab." Her eyes begin to well up, and she looks away. He puts an arm across her shoulder and draws her to his side, his thoughts shot through with too much to say and no need for saying any of it.

"Can we have dinner together tonight?"

"You and me?"

"And Mom. You pick the place."

Her hesitation is swept away quickly enough, but he can't help notice the child struggling to contain her wants. She draws away, cuts her eyes to the building's entrance, then shakes her head. "No."

"No what?"

"No. I don't want to go out to dinner."

"We don't have to go out," he begins, but she cuts him off.

"I want to be left alone, Dad." She looks squarely at him. "You and Mom ..." She stops. "You and Mom." She tries to continue but chokes. This is as far as she gets. *What about us?* he wants to ask, but his surprise is too heavy with disappointment. Hannah steps back again, runs a hand over her head, looking at him with those lovely blue-green eyes.

"Of course," he begins, recalling what he'd said to Pat, what he'd known all along, feeling all at once vindicated and woefully misunderstood. She wanted to be left alone. He'd known it and had said so and would like to tell her right now, wants her to know, yes, that he knew it all along. Even said so to Mom. *I knew it*, he wants to say. But he can't. The very fact that he is standing there is a contradiction. And Pat, who is likely just getting up from the sofa she's been sleeping on these last few days, tugging on her bathrobe, the two of them having zoomed here out of deepest feeling and need and with nothing, nothing but the best intentions. "If that's what you want," he says and can't believe how it comes out with fullest, self-pitying parental pathos, automatic and unintentional but as inescapable as a solid object rising up between them, the freshest, sturdiest new barrier between what they will see, what they will say, what they will know of one another from here on. Hannah is the first to acknowledge it. She steps forward, amazes him with the speediness of the hug, the purposeful turn. And strides off. He can remember himself so well in her shoes and can still smell her freshly washed hair as, unsmiling, she turns and waves to him before pushing though the door into the building behind someone carrying a bicycle wheel.

A short while later, the radio towers on top of Carter Mountain absorb his attention. He drives down Monticello Avenue, riding his brakes, ignoring the flashing dot on the dashboard that marks his location. They spoil something, the antennae, as does the arterial network of new highways and bypasses that have erupted all across this Virginia landscape. But change is the true measure of all important relationships, and if his cartographer's instinct is to look for permanent features, enduring in old attitudes is a sure sign of collapse among feeling beings. He presses more firmly on the brakes, craning to keep the towers in view. The driver following leans angrily on his horn, swerves and passes in a rage. Noel ignores him, coasts to the bottom of the hill, then turns left and follows the road up to Monticello.

Pat's car was gone by the time he'd walked back to Hannah's house. He rang the bell and waited on the front stoop for a time, thinking maybe she'd just stepped out briefly. After a while, he returned to the Navigator, wondered if he should try calling her. But he couldn't do it; he didn't want to. She was on her way home; he was certain of it. Hannah had asked Pat to leave, too. He was certain. That it pleased him was more consolation than he would ever admit. Maybe it hadn't been as abrupt. Maybe they'd talked things over first, found common ground, come to some womanly understanding. But something told him it hadn't happened that way. He could see Pat clenching the steering wheel and hear the light rock playing on the radio in her car. He knew that when he came through the front door later that day, she would greet him with the mildest cheer (which he would reciprocate) and wait until he'd changed out of his work clothes and come back downstairs before telling him, with an initial sham detachment that would quickly dissolve, all that had happened. He would assume his role, too. And that was as it should be. All of it was. Although he wasn't quite sure of the order in which he would begin to tell her everything that needed telling, or what connections he would make and what linkages they might discover together as the conversation he was hoping for deepened, became truthful and elemental.

He crosses the stone bridge and follows the newly paved road into the parking lot, already crammed with school buses and tour groups. The brand-new visitors' center is crowded, too. Noel studies the wall maps and reads through a stack of brochures before buying his ticket, which is handed to him by a folksy, gray-goateed volunteer who recommends the Spring Wildflower Walk and who might have just retired from government work himself, continuing the legacy of the place as a retreat from public duty.

Before setting out on the trail to the mansion, Noel returns to the car and puts on his windbreaker. After some initial indecision, he takes his three iron and a souvenir ball marked with the DIA insignia, which he bought in the DIAC gift shop years ago and has never used. With maps, binoculars, and, compliments of the gentleman volunteer, a brochure guide to local wildflowers, he starts up the trail to the mansion, using his three iron as a walking stick.

The trees are just budding. Chartreuse light filters through the canopy. On either side of the gravel path, the forest floor erupts with new growth. Noel takes his time, lets the school group pull farther ahead, stopping at the gravesite to look through the tall fence at the buried Jefferson generations. He is usually impatient at tourist sites, critical of contrived significance. But tombs are different. They are true places; the truest, maybe. He can't help feeling a thrill of connection to the buried president as he stands there, freshly resigned from duties the founding father could never have imagined. Jefferson had fought his own war on terror, which had produced the very first

U.S. naval hero, Stephen Decatur, who had dispatched the Barbary Pirates in hand-to-hand combat aboard the captured *Philadelphia* in the Bay of Tripoli. In building "our little navy," Jefferson had gone for small gunboats over big frigates to keep "these smaller powers disposed to quarrel with us" in order. Would Jefferson have liked the Predator? Or the Reaper or the Global Hawk? And GBU-12s and 38s dropped by air force B-1B Lancers and A-10 Thunderbolt IIs on places called Musa Qaleh, Nangalam, and Ghazni? And what about those little infrared grubs, the dead schoolchildren? Would he call that tyranny? Lethal power delivered from afar. He certainly knew the difference between being hard and being hardened.

It is less than a quarter mile from the grave to the house and just two miles to the birthplace in Shadwell, a one-to-one relationship as impossible for Noel to conceive in life as it is for a mapmaker to draw. There is a grand modesty in the proximity of those three points: birthplace, hearth, grave. He takes out his map showing local elevations. The house sits at the highest point: eight hundred sixty-seven feet above sea level. He follows the gravel walkway called Mulberry Row along the southeastern side of the mansion, passes by the excavated foundations of several buildings. This entire side of the hilltop is terraced and serves now as a museum of vegetable varietals and a small, well-tended vineyard evoking Jefferson the horticulturalist and connoisseur of the good life. A brick pavilion is the only manorhouse feature on the tilled ground, and the excavated foundations of the slave quarters just beyond are the only evidence on the landscape of the people and the secrets that were kept here.

He leaves the gravel path and walks down among the beds of newly turned earth. At the end of the planted rows, the terrace drops off steeply, supported by a stone wall. The view is glorious. Gleams of sun and puffs of cloud cast dappled shadows across the valley floor and up and down the Blue Ridge. The map names all the old farms at the foot of the hill: Slate Field, Franklin's Field. At the far end of the garden, a groundskeeper in overalls pushes a wheelbarrow heaped with dung. Noel glances over his shoulder toward the mansion, where the tours are just beginning, and tries to think of a proper salutation, some words to convey the portion of the story he will keep to himself and the portion he will leave me to tell.

It is the portion that has fallen to me, what I am given to pass along, that preoccupies me back here in Washington, where, at three o'clock in the afternoon, sitting at my desk, looking out the window, I am still struggling to find the relevant order among all the parts and pieces. What to put here, what there. Most important, what to leave out entirely, those things we must keep to ourselves. There are ways of illuminating them obliquely, by refraction, bouncing light. Paradoxically, a fuller view often emerges by concealment, the way character is revealed in the shading of a face. I had the first inkling of it in Munich and the second when I returned home and went to see my mother. When she asked if I'd found what I was looking for, the only answer I could give was yes and no, thinking of you, Bettina, and of Monticello and Sally Hemings and the secrets forced upon generations of children and wondering what possible good could come from learning of another secret patrimony story involving my father, your mother, and my own concealments. A thing revealed only adds another mystery. There is a world we inhabit and a world that inhabits us, and both largely pass us by without our ever knowing. How is it that we can know so little of ourselves and of the world, yet have so much to answer for? Secrets, and those who keep them, must always be pardoned when truth comes to light. For me, it's still an open question whether we are relieved of anything when we come to know the truth about ourselves. Is it always a relief to find out who we really are?

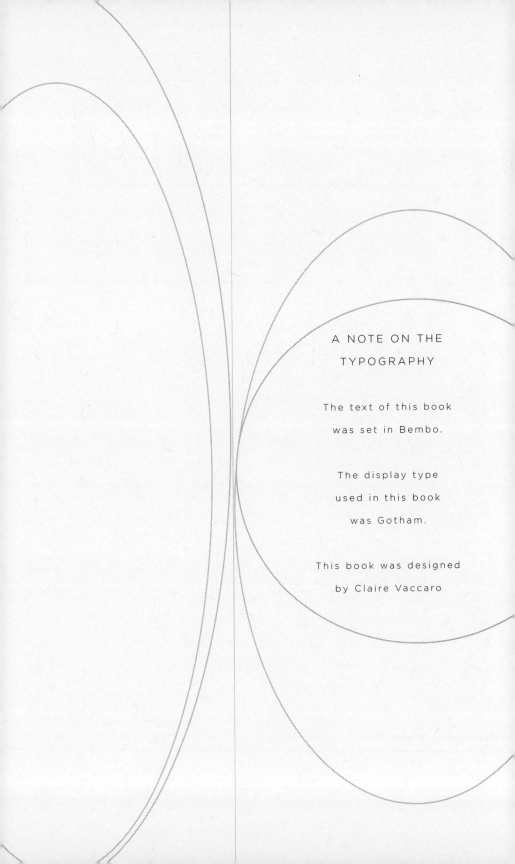

A NOTE ON THE
TYPOGRAPHY

The text of this book
was set in Bembo.

The display type
used in this book
was Gotham.

This book was designed
by Claire Vaccaro